HOWL

THE BLACK MOUNTAIN PACK BOOK 2

LANA SKY

Howl

Howl By Lana Sky

Copyright © 2022 by Lana Sky
All rights reserved.

No part of this publication may be reproduced, distributed, or transmitted in any form or by any means, including photocopying, recording, or other electronic or mechanical methods, without the prior written permission of the author.

This is a work of fiction. Names, characters, businesses, places, events and incidents are either the products of the author's imagination or used in a fictitious manner. Any resemblance to actual persons, living or dead, or actual events is purely coincidental.

Cover Design and Interior Formatting by Charity Chimni
Editing by Charity Chimni

ACKNOWLEDGMENTS

Thanks so much to everyone who supported this draft along the way, including the many beta readers who provided encouragement! Please keep in mind that this story includes dark, graphic, and explicit content matter that may not be suitable for readers under the age of 18—or for readers who are uncomfortable with the following subject matter: age-gap relationships, explicit sex, and graphic depictions of violence.

There was an old saying, "better to be safe than sorry." Whoever coined it had obviously never spent a week with William McGoven.

The man was anything but safe—and Loren found a strange peace in his wild nature. As far as the men in her life were concerned, he was a welcome anomaly. Violent and brutish, Fred Connors, her supposed father, had been ruthlessly predictable.

William McGoven, on the other hand, was an enigma. Frustratingly so. He single-handedly made decisions for her, only to claim, in the next breath, that she wasn't his responsibility. He could be moody and unreadable, and so damn closed-off she could count his few facial expressions on her fingers.

She should have resented him and how confidently he'd inserted himself into her life—but anger wasn't the feeling spreading through her chest whenever she saw him. Just confusion. Despite his gruffness, he was always there when she needed him the most.

And he hadn't held that fact over her head. Nor did he ever ask for anything in return, other than her trust. All in all, he made for the perfect hero after the hell her life had become.

Until he kissed her. Not a chaste peck, either, but a wild assault she could feel the aftermath of days later.

No one could blame her if she claimed he'd taken advantage. But when she went over her own emotions, things weren't so simple.

He kissed her, and there hadn't been anything "weak" and "meek" about her reaction. Even now, a part of her demanded…something. Craved it from him alone. The actual name for it eluded her, but the more she tried to puzzle out an answer…

Her throat went dry. The thin material of her shirt irritated the skin beneath. It felt…too tight. Especially when she recalled the feel of his lips on hers.

Get a grip, Loren. You need to forget, a part of her insisted. Obviously, he'd gotten carried away. Adrenaline could make people do crazy things—like kiss traumatized teenage girls on impulse, apparently.

But what's your excuse? she wondered. Looking back, she hadn't been confused or conflicted. Definitely not *sorry,* either. Being with him had felt *right*—and that was the scary part.

"I think you might be wearing a hole through the marble —" She flinched as a hand came down to gingerly grab the cloth she'd been scrubbing the countertop with. "I'll just put this over here," Micha added, tossing the rag in the sink before she could protest.

They were in McGoven's narrow kitchen. Wearing a mud-stained pair of sweatpants, Micha looked like he'd just come from outside and was in desperate need of a shower. Instead of rushing to change, he leaned against the fridge and crossed his arms. Despite the casual stance, his green eyes were unusually sharp, devoid of their playful gleam.

"You've been scrubbing the same spot for an hour." He nodded to her wet, pruned fingers. "Wanna talk about it?"

Loren turned away, feeling her cheeks flame. He was right. While she couldn't comment on the amount of time that had passed, she wouldn't have been surprised if it had been more than an hour.

"Ignoring your problems isn't healthy," Micha playfully scolded. "You can talk to me, you know."

With a sigh of defeat, Loren shrugged. True to his word, Micha didn't look judgmental—merely exhausted. Mulling over the complexities of a kiss with him wasn't very appealing, though. "Talk about what?"

"Everything."

That word wasn't vast enough to encompass the various dilemmas weighing on her mind, impromptu kiss aside. She still needed to reconcile what it meant to be lupine, not to mention her father's death, and the question of her paternity. Add to that what happened with Naomi—according to Bill, she was home resting, but it was only a matter of time before she would return. Then what?

Loren couldn't stop dwelling on the possibilities—and, so far, her usual method of distraction hadn't worked. It was only mid-afternoon, and she'd cleaned the kitchen twice. Done the dishes and mopped up the mud stains by the front door. Wiping down the counters had been a last-ditch diversion.

It hadn't worked. While she barely knew Micha, she was afraid she might explode if she didn't talk to *someone*.

Meeting his stare, she blurted out the first question to come to mind. "What do you know about him?" A pointed glance toward the window, in the direction of the trees, conveyed just who she referred to.

"Bill?" Micha wrinkled his nose. "That depends on what *you* know," he muttered under his breath. "But, back where I'm from—the pack, I mean—he's considered something of a legend."

"A legend?" Loren had a hard time picturing it. Sure, McGoven was brave, and maybe a little larger-than-life at times, but he seemed way too closed-up to inspire any legendary tales. In fact, when he wasn't sprouting black fur, he seemed boringly normal.

"Are you kidding?" Micha's eyes widened, and his usual exuberance returned in full. "Yeah. He's a *legend*. The young pup plucked from the crowd by the Alpha himself and groomed to lead. That's almost unheard of. Even more insane was what happened in the end. The guy had everything and just walked away from it all… I never met him in person before a few days ago, though. Just heard the rumors."

His cheerful grin fell flat. Going off his expression, those rumors weren't all positive. Loren felt a twitch of apprehension run down her spine—quickly followed by a stronger sense of greed. She needed to know.

"What kind of rumors?" As she spoke, her gaze returned to the window, once again hunting for a head of dark hair among the endless green. In a few more hours, it would be exactly a full day that he'd been gone. Presumably, he was patrolling for danger, though Loren suspected his real motivation was far more trivial—he was avoiding her.

"Just…stuff," Micha said, deliberately skirting the question. "Maybe, you should ask him?"

Ask him. Loren would have scoffed if she weren't so tired. Last night, she'd had the longest conversation with the man since meeting him, and she felt more clueless than before.

And even more confused.

"I wouldn't be asking you if I could ask him," she admitted in a small voice.

Her imploring stare seemed to tip Micha over the edge.

"Okay, I'll cave." He inched closer and cocked his head conspiratorially toward hers. "Rumor has it that he was set to take over when the old Alpha, Lukas, died—not Lukka, the guy's own son. Then there was an attack by hunters on the outskirts of the property. McGoven wasn't fast enough to respond, and as a result, his own mate was…" He grimaced and drew a finger across his throat. "McGoven stepped down after that and left the pack altogether. I'm not sure what exactly he did to become a rogue, but he's been on the outside ever since. I don't know if he could return to Black Mountain, even if he wanted to."

Mate. He said that word with the same reverence as another term Loren heard in reference to McGoven. A wife. Emma.

"He left behind a lot to move all the way out here," Micha added. "I don't think I can name anyone else who would willingly walk away from the position of leader in exchange for…this."

"Why are you here?" she asked, curious. "You haven't gone back to the pack either. Does that make you a rogue, too?"

Micha blinked as if the idea hadn't crossed his mind. "I don't know. Though, I will admit that it seems pretty interesting here so far. Things in the pack can be so boring. Safe, ya know. We don't have nightly ambushes, that's for damn sure."

In response to her blank expression, he flashed a sheepish grin. "Not funny?"

Loren shook her head, thinking of McGoven out pacing the fields. "Not funny."

"Well, I'll tell you what *is* funny," Micha began. He stood back and ran a hand through his thick hair while his eyes flashed wickedly. "You're right. I'm kind of a rogue myself. I never thought about it until now, I guess." Grinning, he puffed out his chest and placed his hands on his hips like a caricature of Superman. "I don't really belong to a pack either. Lukka hasn't accepted me fully yet, meaning I'm more or less a free agent."

"Why not?" Loren asked.

Given how McGoven stressed the importance of *her* joining a pack, she couldn't understand how Micha could be so nonchalant about not belonging to one.

His cheerful grin slipped. "It takes a while to integrate as an outsider. I came in on kind of a trial basis. I don't have a ranking yet—a place in the hierarchy. I'm more or less at the beck and call of everyone else."

He hid it well, but the sadness in his voice was evident. Loren recalled what little of his past he revealed during their ill-fated trip to Black Mountain. "You said that your dad was an Alpha?"

Micha nodded. "I'm a transplant. From Virginia, born and raised. My sister and I belonged to our father's pack, but he died."

His tortured expression gave her the feeling that he had fonder memories of his father than she did of Fred

Connors. Considering how hazy her memories were, that wasn't much of a stretch.

"I'm sorry—"

"Don't be," he said tightly. "It's *life*. He ran the pack fairly. There's nothing to be ashamed of. Let's just say that after his death, the transition didn't go so smoothly. When he died, I got pushed out, but I was too young to put up much of a fight—" He made a "so what" gesture with his hands.

"My sister and I got separated. I came north, she stayed south—didn't want to leave our dad's territory—and I've been kind of bouncing around since then."

The whole time he spoke, he kept his smile, but as the minutes wore on, Loren figured it was more out of habit than anything else. His pain was obvious.

"I'm sorry," she repeated. As cruel as her life had been, she had no idea what that felt like—having a family member out there, lost.

"Don't be. Violet can take care of herself—" He chuckled. "I know I should probably say something along the lines of —*you remind me of her*—but you don't. You're the complete opposite. She's loud and bossy, and she would *never* in a million years let someone—"

He broke off abruptly and changed tack. "She's a firecracker, and you're not."

"So, what am I then?" Loren fully expected him to drop some lame, cheesy line to make her feel better.

"You're different," he said finally. He inclined his head, casting her a searching glance. "More like a brushfire, I think. Slow to start, but in the end just as bright as a firecracker." He winked, and Loren couldn't help the smile that tugged at the corner of her mouth.

"Ah! A smile!" He reached out to trail the length of her chin with the flat of his thumb. "I didn't think you had one in ya—"

Don't let him touch you like that! The thought tore through her mind, like a slap. She flinched, jerking on the balls of her feet.

"You okay?"

"F-Fine," she stammered. Inside, she felt anything *but* fine. Her heart was pounding, and her skin prickled where he touched her. But not in a good way. Not good at all.

"Maybe you should get some sleep? I know you didn't get much last night." Micha pursed his lips into a sheepish frown. "I heard you tossing and turning. It sounded like one hell of a nightmare."

A prickling heat crept over Loren's cheeks. "It's n-nothing," she stammered, turning to face the sink.

"You want to talk about it?" Micha asked. "I get bad dreams sometimes, myself."

Again, it was a tempting offer—only there was nothing to talk about. The nightmare had been the same one plaguing her since she first woke up in McGoven's house. It was hard to describe—endless darkness and a feeling of ruthless pursuit, though she never saw the culprit's face.

Her mind was probably just processing the residual shock of her father's death. That night was still hazy. Supposedly, he'd been killed by debtors, but…

Loren couldn't shake a shadowy whisper at the back of her mind that warned the explanation was a big fat lie.

"Hey! Earth to Loren." She glanced over to find Micha jerking his head toward the stairs. "I mean it. Go sleep. You've been up all morning. I heard you get up well before dawn. You must be exhausted. A nap won't kill you. I'll keep watch. And if you were worried about the…uh, mess from the other night, I took care of it while you were cleaning in here." His sheepish grin conveyed a sense of pride despite the grisly topic.

"Thanks." Loren took a step and hesitated. "I really should do the dishes…" Or maybe the chore was just another excuse to stay awake. At least until McGoven came back. Before she could finish the statement, a yawn ripped from her chest, and she found herself stumbling into the foyer anyway.

Rather than head up to that big empty bed, she entered the living room. She collapsed onto the armchair across from the couch—which repulsed her, even cleaned of Naomi's blood. As her eyes drifted shut, a part of her stubbornly remained alert.

Waiting for him to return.

*S*he was running. Her chest heaved as if her heart might explode from it, but she couldn't stop. Not ever.

He was coming, and there would be no escape…

The sensation of the world shifting beneath her jolted Loren awake, but one realization kept any fear at bay. Heat. Pleasant warmth engulfed her, radiating from the body of someone strong enough to hold her suspended in their arms. Those two details alone narrowed down the potential list of suspects, not that she had the energy to be alarmed.

"You two can get some sleep," someone called. "I'll keep watch." The chirpy voice sounded far enough away that she knew Micha couldn't be the owner of the heartbeat surging beneath her cheek. Intrigued, Loren stirred sleepily, peeling one eye open.

She couldn't see much—just a corner of the living room drenched in shadow.

"It will only be for an hour or so," a man replied in a voice rumbling through her skin. "Then, I'll go out again."

"Do you really think they'll come back?"

"Don't know. Eislanders are unpredictable. If they do return, I'll be ready."

"Me too! I'll shout if I see anything,"

"Fine," the speaker holding her replied. "But...I don't really have to threaten that if you go running off to the pack, it will be the last thing you ever do, do I?"

"Nope!" Loren could picture Micha emphatically shaking his head. "But murderous insinuation noted, regardless."

McGoven didn't reply—because who else's voice could affect her so viscerally? Instead, he just made a sound of agreement in the back of his throat. Then, heavy footsteps echoed in tandem as she turned—or rather, the person *holding* her turned—and headed for the stairs.

It seemed to take forever for her eyes to adjust to the faint, gray daylight creeping in through the windows. She could smell musk, sweat, and pine—a scent that seemed more familiar than her own these days.

Finally, the person holding her set her down, so gently that she barely felt the impact of her body hitting a familiar mattress. With a sigh, they dragged the top sheet over her, tucking it in, and Loren went still, squeezing her eyes shut. If the past was any indicator, he would leave next, probably to go camp out on the couch.

Suddenly, the mattress squealed beneath the weight of a heavier, muscular body that settled in, right beside her. Before she could adjust, an arm went around her waist, dragging her closer. While her heart raced in alarm, the halfhearted embrace seemed more comforting than anything else. The same way a dog might curl up against another for warmth.

Warily, she opened her eyes again, twisting around to face him directly.

He wasn't asleep. *Caught,* was the expression that flickered through those gray eyes.

"You're awake." He sounded so exhausted she had to resist the urge to yawn just looking at him. "Good. It's about time we talked."

2

He watched her from beneath that curtain of damp black hair but made no other move. He might not have been able to. Coming face to face with him drove in just how long he'd spent outside. Mud streaked him from head to toe. Beneath his usual scent, he reeked of sweat and musk—though Loren found herself breathing in the primal scent, anyway. It meant he was really here. She wasn't dreaming.

"Go back to sleep," he told her, moving to get up. "I'll sleep on the couch—"

"No." She beat him to it, lurching upright first. "If anyone needs the sleep, you do. I'll go downstairs."

She tugged the sheets from her legs and scrambled to the edge of the bed. The second her feet hit the floor, he was already dragging her back by the wrist. In one smooth motion, he maneuvered her onto her side, with her back facing him.

"If I left," he began, applying just enough pressure to keep her pinned, "would you stay?"

Loren didn't have to think it over. "This is *your* bed—"

"Thought so," he said, cutting her off. He held her down for so long her arm started to go numb. Then…with another sigh, he released her.

"Fine." The mattress groaned beneath his weight, and Loren turned, expecting to find him slipping through the door. Instead, he faced her with his head resting on the pillow. One eye was fully open while the other drifted shut.

"I don't have the energy to compel you," he said. Compel? It was a strange word. Did he mean order her? That made sense—he looked barely capable of carrying on a conversation without passing out.

"Though," he added, "I doubt that you would listen anyway."

Something in his tone made a part of her flare in agreement —*Damn right.*

He raised an eyebrow, appearing to read her mind. "Well, then, it seems we're at an impasse."

He lifted his arm and made a "do as you wish" motion with his hand. Then he closed his other eye—but Loren wasn't fooled. His posture was way too tense.

When she laid down with her back to him, she half-expected him to crash through the mattress like a lead weight. For a few seconds, he went silent, presumably asleep.

"You could have slept here last night," he said finally, dropping the charade. "You didn't have to stay downstairs."

She lifted one shoulder in a shrug. "I wanted to wait up. In case…"

"In case what?"

"In case those men came back."

He exhaled heavily. A heartbeat later, his voice dripped directly into her ear—he'd shuffled even closer. "You know that I would never let anyone hurt you. Don't you?"

The heat in his tone threw her off. Made her shudder, even as one question burned through her mind. *Why?*

The way he protected her seemed more than just out of duty. *More* than him being a concerned citizen aiming to get his good deed in for the day.

You don't track a stranger for five hours for the hell of it, she thought. Not only that… But, no one would kill for someone else on a whim.

He went silent for so long Loren figured he might have fallen asleep for real. But, no—his heartbeat pulsed so loudly she could hear it.

Thump…thump…thump.

"I'll make you a deal," he said, proving her right. "Give me three days. Three days with no questions. Three days where you *listen* to me—" He sighed again, so deeply that the warmth was like a blowtorch against her shoulder. "And then I'll tell you everything."

"There's more." It wasn't really a question.

There were a million subjects she wanted to ask about. Lycans. Questioned paternity. Having her entire world turned upside down, on its head. When stated plainly, it almost seemed doubtful he could adequately answer them all.

"There's more," he admitted. "But if you trust me, and give me those three days… There won't be anything else that I haven't told you. I promise you that much."

His grim tone didn't make it sound like such a prize—*I'll tell you—but it's bad, and you won't like it.* Still, it was better than nothing.

"Three days." She mulled it over, wondering what else she had to lose. "Okay. But you can't order me to leave—especially not there."

"Black Mountain," he surmised, naming the location he'd unceremoniously tried to have her shipped off to.

"Yes," she said. "You can't ship me away. Not now."

"Deal." His voice was softer, barely a whisper. "But, for three days, *you* trust me. No questions asked."

Haven't I already been doing that? Before she could voice the thought out loud, he was asleep—she knew without having to turn around. His breathing changed, tickling the back of her throat in a slow, steady rhythm. Something told her that it was the first time he'd drifted off in days.

If only it could be so easy for her.

3

She was running. Panting. Falling. With every stumble, he was gaining. Soon, there would be no escape.

He'd silence her forever…

Loren's eyes flew open. As harsh daylight stabbed at her vision, she groaned, more exhausted than when she first laid down. Blindly, she reached for another pillow—only, she felt *heat* instead of fabric. Panicked, she lurched upright, gaping at the figure lying beside her.

He looked tense even while asleep. There were some hints of softness, though. His jaw was more relaxed, and, for once, those black curls freely fell over his forehead, rather than be ruthlessly slicked back. That alone transformed him.

He looked so much younger, not that he seemed very old in the first place. Older than *her*, definitely—mid-twenties, maybe? Thirty at most. It was so hard to tell when he rarely deviated from a frown. In fact, Loren wondered—if she

21

reached out right now and touched him—would he feel like stone, hard and cold to the touch?

Fingers shaking, she did. The pad of her thumb brushed the corner of his jaw, so gently that it barely counted as "touching" at all. Even so, she sucked in a breath. He was…soft. His skin had a gentle amount of give to it. Like silk.

In response, he made a wordless sound and turned, rolling onto his side—but his arm flew out, catching her across the waist. Loren froze. Her heart pounded as she waited for him to wake up, but he never did. If anything, he just shifted closer, burying his face into the pillow.

The touch reminded her of a little kid reaching out to snuggle a toy bear. But something told her that—though maybe not for a while—he was used to sharing this bed with something other than a toy. A woman—Emma.

Someone he didn't have to be guilted into sleeping beside.

At the sobering thought, she shifted, gingerly easing herself out of reach. Her feet hit the cold floor with a shudder, and she took off, tiptoeing into the hallway.

Downstairs was silent. Micha was gone, most likely out patrolling. Fortunately, she found plenty with which to distract herself—a pile of dirty clothes waited by the door, and someone had tracked mud across the foyer.

With a sigh of relief, Loren went searching for a mop. While living in Fred Connors' house, she'd fallen into the same defensive routine. As long as she cooked and cleaned, she didn't have to think, or listen to the little voice at the back of her head screaming at her to run.

Lost in the rhythm, she moped the entire first floor. The clothes, she tossed into an empty hamper she found inside what seemed to be a small laundry room near the back of the house. Afterward, she drifted into the kitchen, desperate for a new distraction.

On impulse, she snatched the carton of eggs from the fridge. Just as she started to crack one, a knock rattled the front door. Several more followed, increasingly incessant. *Tap, tap!*

She froze. Was it Micha? Or someone else…coming back to finish what they'd started two nights ago? But why come knocking on the front door?

Besides, a quick glance out the window didn't reveal anything out of the ordinary. Naomi's pink car was still in the driveway, stuck in the same spot it had been since the night of the storm. There were no hordes of murderous men, or wolves, prowling hungrily on the front lawn.

And if they had come…Micha was still out there. Wouldn't he have warned them?

Heart pounding, Loren turned away from the sink and moved cautiously for the door. She opened it mid-rap, and came face to face with someone who, in another life, *could* have been Naomi Tanner.

She was pale, her face devoid of expensive makeup. Her highlighted blond hair was pulled back into a bun, and a gray tracksuit and mud-stained sneakers replaced her designer clothing and heels. If Loren had to guess, the girl had walked all the way here from New Walsh.

"Is...*he* here?" she asked, in a voice that wasn't laced with bitchy undertones.

Loren blinked. "W-who?"

Naomi fidgeted with the collar of her jacket while eyeing the floor. "*Him.*"

"He's sleeping," Loren blurted. But that was beside the point. She knew damn well that Naomi wasn't here bearing gifts of good fortune.

There was a scratch on her left cheek, opposite the scabbed-over marks Loren's nails had left. Beneath her tracksuit jacket, she wore a gray top with a high turtleneck to cover her throat.

The strangest change of all was in her *eyes*. That hazy green seemed brighter, greener, than before. They had the same, odd glow to them that Micha's did, or McGoven's for that matter.

"Well, can I come in and wait until he wakes up then?" Naomi's voice lost that tired edge, regaining the snappiness Loren was used to.

"Yes..." Warily, she stood back and allowed the blond inside. Before closing the door, she scanned the fields for Micha, but caught sight of no one, wolf or otherwise.

She shouldn't have felt so disappointed, but the lack of anyone else meant she had no choice but to face Naomi alone. The girl in question lingered awkwardly in the foyer. For a long time, they didn't speak.

"Are you one too?" Naomi asked suddenly. Her eyes darted around the room—anywhere but Loren's face.

"One of what?" It wouldn't score her any points to play dumb, but Loren couldn't resist the urge. Why make it easy? She wanted to hear her say it. Admit out loud that her happy teenage dream was over, and the real world had intruded.

Violently.

"A lycan." The blond peeked over her shoulder as if expecting McGoven to burst from the shadows. "Are you a lycan, too?"

Loren frowned. "Wolf" or "thing" she would have expected —but Lycan was *his* word.

"Yes," she said tightly. "I am."

Naomi bit her bottom lip. "He said you were. He said...that —" She broke off with a dry swallow, wringing her hands. When she glanced up again, those green eyes held an emotion that Loren figured the girl had never experienced in her life—fear. "So, can you?"

"Can I what?" Loren snapped. She felt guilty even before Naomi flinched back as if stung.

Why was she so defensive? Prickly? She had begged McGoven to turn Naomi, but now…

The sight of the girl irritated her. Or maybe it was just the knowledge that Naomi knew everything she did? Maybe even more. *Three-day rules don't seem to apply to her,* the shadowy part of her murmured.

"S-shift," the blond said weakly. "Can you shift too? He said I should ask you for advice on—"

A rush of emotion welled up in Loren so quickly, she rushed into the kitchen before she did something stupid— like scream. Approaching the counter, she grabbed a fresh egg with a vengeance, cracking it hard on the edge of a frying pan.

Despite the clamor, she still heard Naomi creep in after her.

"Well, *can* you?"

Crack! Went the sound of the butter sizzling in the heat, as Loren added a dollop to the pan and began to whisk the mixture with a fork. She was ruthless, scraping until the eggs resembled something more "whipped" than scrambled.

She made two more batches, utilizing the entire carton before starting on toast. As she reached for the loaf of bread on the counter, a pink-manicured hand snatched it away.

"I didn't ask for this!" Naomi's eyes were slits, her face mere inches from hers. "I'm not even sure what 'this' is! So don't you dare stick up your nose at me and act like this is my fault. You were always such a stuck-up little bitch, walking around with your nose in the air like you're too good for any of us."

Loren stumbled back. Not because she was intimidated by the tall blond but… Because her eyes darted automatically to the knife drawer, itching to grab something sharp.

Screw that, a part of her purred. *I don't need a weapon.*

"I'm going to wait in there," Naomi announced before flouncing into the living room. "The air's too bitchy in here. Pun intended."

Loren watched her go. Though, if she were being honest, she regretted wasting a whole carton of eggs more than snapping at the blond. At least until Micha stumbled through the back door an hour later and ate a majority of the food in one sitting, assuaging her guilt. His only reason for stopping was a grumbled realization that he should leave some for McGoven.

Then, he pulled up to the center island, spread his lanky body out over two stools, with his feet resting on one, and just watched her. Whatever he saw in her expression made him decide another talk was in order. "I saw you know who came back. How ya holding up?"

Loren darted for his plate before he had a chance to bring it to the sink himself.

"I'm fine," she lied, reaching for a washrag. "I just feel like… Like everyone is keeping something from me."

Shock nearly made her drop the plate on the floor. *Where the hell had that come from?*

She glanced back at Micha, but he just raised an eyebrow. "Like what?"

She didn't know the answer to that. "Something *big*," she settled on. Maybe why she couldn't "shift" like everyone else? Or why she couldn't remember a single thing about her father's murder?

Or why every single time she was around McGoven, a part of her wanted to…

Bite him? Kiss him? More? Hell, she didn't know.

She wasn't used to dealing with such a volatile range of emotions. Up until now, she had always excelled at keeping them locked up tight—but these days, it seemed as if everything was pouring out all at once. And she couldn't stop it.

"I just don't feel like myself anymore," she added half-heartedly.

In some ways, that was a good thing. Loren Connors wasn't the same meek little girl from a week ago. This new iteration wanted to punch something. Kick. Stomp her feet and screech for someone to tell her the truth.

Unfortunately for her, Naomi's presence was a lit match meeting dry tinder.

Three days, she tried to tell herself. He promised her that much. But since when did anyone keep their promises?

"Um." Micha cleared his throat. "I kind of meant…how are you holding up, with *that*?" He jerked his head toward the living room, where Naomi still sat, seething, on the couch. "New bloods can be a little prickly. It's their emotions, you know. They're all out of whack. Try not to take it personally. Their weird vibes can throw everything off. Especially if…" He flashed a sheepish grin. "There is already some unresolved tension going on."

Loren sighed and shook her head. *Don't even go there.* Naomi's presence irritated the hell out of her—only she didn't know why. Whenever she caught sight of that blond head peeking over the back of the couch, something in her *growled*.

"I need some air," she said finally, setting the plate down in the sink.

She slipped through the back door before Micha could react. In one long stride, she crossed the porch and headed straight toward the west field.

Her teeth chattered. The bitter cold made her instantly regret not grabbing her jacket and shoes. Ironically, the chill seemed to help her finally regain enough clarity to think— only it wasn't all happy, pretty thoughts.

She was frowning by the time she made it into the barn. Like always, Bunny, Esther, and Xavier greeted her the second she stumbled inside. They didn't seem too worse for wear, despite everything that had happened around them these past few days.

With a sigh, Loren worked the latch on the nearest stall, intending to slip inside and disappear, like she used to when seeking an escape from her father.

Before she could even get the door open, a shadow fell across the floor. The horses grunted their alarm, nearly drowning out the deep voice that echoed throughout the wide space.

"You okay?"

She looked back, unsurprised by the figure standing in the doorway, hands carefully at his sides. He had showered, swapping out the mud-stained clothing for a clean pair of jeans and a sweater. Her belly flipped at the sight. He didn't require fangs and fur to seem intimidating.

"I…I thought you were sleeping," she stammered.

Despite the freshened appearance, he still looked exhausted. His hair was a rumpled mess, and he yawned, even as he shifted to reveal something he held in one hand.

"It's kind of hard to sleep amid tension," he explained.

Loren flushed crimson. Obviously, he had heard everything that happened between her and Naomi. He didn't seem to hold a grudge, though.

"Here." He extended his arm, offering what she realized was another windbreaker, in black this time. "It might snow."

"Can you tell?" she wondered out loud. When she glanced through the doorway, the sky was the usual dreary shade of gray.

He shrugged and took a small step closer. "It's a combination of moisture in the air and the temperature. You'll be able to pick up on it eventually."

Loren doubted that. She couldn't smell anything but pine. Still, she took the windbreaker and slipped it on without comment. He wasn't wearing a jacket himself, though—not that the cold seemed to affect him. Standing there on bare feet, he didn't even have the decency to shiver.

"Come here—" He surprised her by jerking his head toward the front of the barn, but his voice lacked the urgency of an order. "I…I want to show you something."

Loren inched closer, but he only pointed to the tack supply hanging on the nearby shelves.

"Look under the crate over there."

She did and found something that made her gasp—a black riding helmet. Ignoring his effect on the horses, the helmet was way too small for someone of his size anyway. When she tried it on at his urging, it fit her well enough.

"Grab that saddle over there, the one in the middle—yeah." He nodded when she hefted the leather seat. "Put it on the rack. Now grab the tack and bridle…like that."

When she set everything aside like he told her, he inclined his head toward Esther's stall.

"Bring her out—clip on the lead. Be gentle…good."

He talked her through saddling the horse. Told her how to secure the straps and make sure they weren't too tight. Then when she finished, he turned and headed for the paddock. A wave of his hand was her only indication to follow.

Confused, she led Esther out after him and into the enclosed field.

It was small, with a patch of dirt in the center just big enough to ride circles in. The sight almost reminded her of the pony ride course at the fair, where ten dollars bought you a few laps.

"I know you can *mount* a horse," McGoven began, watching her from across the gate—far enough away that Esther didn't seem to be affected by his scent. "But let's see if you can start off in something a little steadier than a full gallop."

4

There was a time for primal instinct. For hunting and fighting and embracing the thrill of battle.

Unfortunately, a good leader also made time for politics—even if it meant parlaying with the leader of a greedy band of rivals hellbent on taking more than their fair share. Luckily for Eric Lannister, he wasn't Alpha and therefore not responsible for the nitty-gritty of said actions.

He merely had to stand and watch. Though, sometimes, he found it more infuriating than if he had to hammer out peace agreements himself.

"You are the one who advocated for action," Lukka Grehmaine snarled. With his arms crossed, blue eyes narrowed, he resembled a scowling pup more than a leader. "Yet you give McGoven even more time to surrender. How much longer are you going to cower to a rogue and his aggression?"

Eric knew he couldn't keep his disgust from showing.

Loreck, on the other hand, excelled at diplomacy almost as well as physical prowess. He sat behind the ornately carved desk in the central room of the main lodge. This wooden structure in the heart of their territory served as the root of all commerce and guidance for those in the Eislander pack.

From Lukka's haughty grimace, he wasn't impressed.

"You forget that presumably, I am the one with an actionable grievance against McGoven, not you," Loreck pointed out, his tone level. "Considering that you refused to accept the mated female initially, she was never integrated into your pack. Therefore, you have no claim over any crimes committed against her. I will lead an assault on McGoven when I decide to."

"Then you might be too late," Lukka countered. "He might kill again while you hesitate."

Eric couldn't silence a growl and surged forward, leaving his position in the corner of the room. One look from Loreck stopped him in his tracks.

"McGoven is the least of the concerns plaguing my pack," Loreck continued, addressing the upstart before him. "For instance… I am far more concerned about the increasing rate of perfusion between my border and yours. Our hunting lands are being depleted at a rate we have never experienced. It's almost as if the mouths our resources feed has doubled within the past year."

Eric had to give Lukka some shred of credit—the bastard didn't flinch, even while being presented with his own transgressions.

"It sounds like stray humans," he said dismissively. "Your pack has a history of tension with the nearby towns from what I hear."

"I doubt a few hundred farmers and laypeople could encroach onto my territory so stealthily," Loreck said coldly. "Your point stands. McGoven will be dealt with. In the meantime… I suggest you watch your borders carefully, pup. I won't tolerate an outright invasion for long."

Lukka said nothing before leaving, his entourage in tow.

Eric watched him go, more irritated than he figured he had the right to be. Even so, the unease persisted, nagging like an itch he couldn't scratch.

Something was off amid this entire mess with the Black Mountain wolves and their wayward rogue.

And he longed to get to the bottom of it.

5

Fuck, she made him reckless.

The Eislanders were at his throat. Lukka didn't seem to give a shit. He was still convinced Kyle had abandoned Loren in enemy territory on purpose—a capital offense. Not to mention that he had two young females and an unaffiliated rogue crashing on his property.

And yet, here he was…giving riding lessons. The strange part? Even as the cons mounted, he didn't feel remotely inclined to do anything else. This was a long time coming.

He'd bought that damn helmet at a thrift shop a few months back. *Not for her,* he told himself then. He had always thought about selling or renting out those horses— anything to get them exercise. It only made sense that he should toss in some supplies for the new owners…

But a helmet in *her* size, exactly? Bought only a few days after he first noticed her on his property?

Besides, he had been telling himself that lie about selling the horses for years and never acted on it. It was time to admit that those animals were stuck with him, whether they liked it or not, and that he had picked out the stupid helmet with only *her* in mind.

Seeing her finally wear it, he couldn't really bring himself to regret it. He had suspected she would love to ride, but witnessing that joy for himself was…

Indescribable. She couldn't hide her excitement. For once, her mouth wasn't wrinkled with worry, but flat in an expression of calm that made something in him ache to see her smile. Her body wasn't tense with anticipation or fear, but loose and languid as she easily adjusted to the rhythm of the saddle.

It was dangerous, letting her near those animals, considering what she was, but a part of him had to admit that they didn't seem to sense the predator lurking within her.

Oh, but *he* could.

The scent of her unease had jolted him out of a deep, dreamless sleep. Anger gave a dark edge to her already strange aroma—an animalistic, primal flavor that had a part of him humming in appreciation, even as his body throbbed with a need he couldn't ignore.

It was instinct—a male called by the strength of a female.

When she finally came into her own, she would be…

Not his. The thought had him gritting his teeth in irritation —but tough shit. He had already made up his mind. The night of the attack was the final straw. Seeing her in danger shattered any resolve he had left.

He couldn't protect her here for long. After sleeping on it, he'd made his choice. The best course of action was to train her to hold her own. Teach her as much of their ways as he could in three days. Then he would break the bond and deal with whatever fallout came after. It was better than the alternative, if not ideal—Loren needed the safety of a pack. She needed a *real* Alpha to tame the wolf she would become —not to mention, protect her, should the Eislanders return. Once her safety was no longer an issue, Bill was more than willing to face his judgment.

On his terms.

He felt his eyes narrow as he watched Loren circle the paddock. She had a willowy ease in the saddle that was almost unnatural. He had never seen anything like it. Like her…

The difference from the frightened, bruised girl he'd found huddled at the edge of his property was stark. She was stronger than she thought she was. Strong enough to handle the truth.

And strong enough to withstand the shattering of the mating bond—even if he wasn't. It affected him in ways he couldn't ignore. Made him do things…like curl up beside her merely because some greedy part of him craved her heat, her warmth.

Her scent.

He still had that damn dress she had been wearing that night in the woods. That nightgown. It was locked in his truck, hoarded like some pirate's treasure under the passenger seat. At the back of his mind, he knew it was creepy. Wrong. Sick. But that didn't help the urge to keep a part of her—any piece he could…even if it happened to be mud-stained, torn, and covered in blood.

She's mine; the possessive thought raced through his entire body like a pulse as he watched her circle the paddock for the hundredth time.

He tried to rationalize her youth, her innocence—all those delicate little details that humans liked to harp over. The beast in him just scoffed. "Rules" or "facts" or what was socially proper didn't matter to a lycan. They relied on instinct—fate.

And *fate* claimed that she was *his* the moment she unknowingly slipped onto his property. *His* the second he found her, traumatized and scared in the woods, desperate to take her own life. *His* when she marked him, sinking her teeth into his flesh, in a primal form of possession.

That kiss—despite how he might spin it—hadn't been a damn mistake. For that one, brief moment, he had *finally* been in control. The lycan instinct had broken free of its leash and claimed what it wanted. And her reaction had been unanticipated…

Don't go there, he told himself as she trotted past.

She was too busy concentrating on keeping her balance that she didn't see how he flinched, as her scent hit him like a punch in the gut. He leaned forward anyway, gripping the wooden fencing until his knuckles ached.

It wouldn't do him any good to wonder what she might feel for him, if anything at all. Her emotions were warped by the bond. Twisted. Besides, she wouldn't be here for much longer.

Like a grim herald of what was to come, he heard the distant sounds of gravel crunching under tires. His body tensed as he turned toward the main road, and a list of potential intruders marched through his mind. Lukka? The Eislanders? Someone else who wanted him dead? There were plenty of enemies to choose from these days.

When the black car zoomed into the driveway, he assumed it was the first of the three options. Thankfully, the slender figure exiting the driver's side was *not* Lukka.

"This is a surprise," he called while crossing the field in her direction. From the corner of his eye, he saw Loren remain mounted in her saddle.

"So nice to see you're still alive," Sonia called, slamming the door behind her.

Uh-oh. Her cheeks were flushed, blue eyes flashing as she marched toward him. In all the years they'd known each other, Bill had rarely seen her so angry. Despite the petite mortal frame, she was *all* wolf. And she was pissed.

"Do you have any idea how worried I've been?"

Smack! The flat of her hand connected hard with the side of his face, but Bill was already turning to confront another threat.

"Loren, no!"

Quicker than he knew how, she had dismounted, already bolting from the paddock. The second his shout reached her, she faltered, staring down at her hands as if she had no idea why they were balled into fists.

"Do you have any idea what you've done?" Oblivious to the sight, Sonia was still shouting in his ear. "Do you have any idea what will happen to you? BILL, ANSWER ME!"

A shadow flickered in his peripheral vision.

"Sonia—" Desperately, he scanned his surroundings for a way out—and found one.

Micha had scrambled out onto the porch, and Bill jerked his head in Loren's direction.

"Get her inside."

The kid lurched into action, bounding across the yard to intercept Loren before she could reach the road. In the distance, the abandoned horse shrieked and darted into a corner.

Bill just hoped that the animal wouldn't try to jump the fence, but he couldn't worry about it now. With a heavy sigh, he turned to Sonia, who glared at him, tears streaking down her cheeks.

"Ignoring repeated direct calls? Do you know how worried I've been? How hard it's been to talk Lukka out of sending an entire unit out to you?" she demanded, a hitch in her throat. "What happened? Why on earth would you attack an Eislander?"

Bill sighed. "It's a long story, but we can start with the fact that while I *did* kill—" He raised his hand as Sonia began to speak. "It wasn't an Eislander, that's for damn sure. I'm surprised Lukka sent you here to berate me for that. Considering that all this happened because he sent a minion to do his dirty work. What does he want now?"

"You got your wish," Sonia said coldly. "Loren's been accepted. I'm here to bring her back."

Bill figured he should have been relieved. Thankful? As it was, he only felt apathy. The events of the past few days had cemented the cold truth that his old life was far behind him.

"About that… I changed my mind."

Sonia blinked, raising an eyebrow. "What do you—"

"Loren's not going anywhere. *Yet*," he added through clenched teeth. "I owe a duty not just to her."

Sonia raised an eyebrow. "What do you mean?"

He took a breath. It was one thing to decide on a plan in his head, another entirely to voice it out loud. The second the words left his mouth, there would be no going back. "I'm going to petition Lukka to release me from all pack ties.

Then I'm done. I'll head north, far beyond the territory. I'll push into Canada, even. He'll face no threat from me."

Sonia hid her shock, if any, well. Her only response was another question, "And Loren?"

Here came the tricky part, far more complicated than forsaking his entire life on a whim. "I'll break the bond and let her decide. After I teach her what she'll need to know to survive on her own. If she chooses to go to Lukka of her own accord, then so be it. But I won't force her."

He didn't even see the second slap coming.

"Have you lost your mind? Even I know that whatever is between you and Lukka goes beyond your standing as a rogue. He will never let you go. But you know that, don't you?" Horror dawned over her features, and Bill felt a pang of guilt. "Don't tell me… If he doesn't agree to sever ties completely, then… The only course of action would be to challenge him. Are you insane?"

It sounded so grim when put like that. "I plan to make him an offer he can't refuse," Bill said, eyeing the ground at his feet. "Win or lose, he can remain Alpha, but I get my freedom—no matter the cost."

"I know you can be stubborn, Bill, but I never thought of you as reckless! Do you even remember the terms that a challenge dictates? You need to face him first. Do you really think he'll risk meeting with you one on one? I'm sure you realized what I did—he sent Kyle for a reason."

"*Now* you admit that," he grumbled. "As for your insinuation, I may have been gone for a while, but I remember our customs well enough, thank you."

"Oh, do you? Then you won't mind if I refresh your memory," Sonia countered. "You meet him one on one. You issue the challenge—and he gets a full day to prepare. Let's not forget the witness, either—"

"I haven't," Bill snapped. Admittedly, his knowledge of pack law had gotten a little rusty. There were so many damn variables involved in issuing a rightful challenge.

"Do you think Lukka will honor that?" Sonia asked. "And who will serve as your witness? You know he would never allow me to do so, even if I wanted to—"

"Soni…" He looked up to find her watching him with an expression he couldn't decipher. "You've made your point."

But she wasn't done with him.

"Let's say it does come down to a challenge, and you win," she added. "To hell with the rest of us, right?"

"What I do shouldn't matter. Besides, I thought Lukka was a *good* leader?" He couldn't help the anger in his voice. "You sang his praises last time."

"Don't give me that! I knew that all it would take was the slightest hint of trouble for you to intervene. Despite all your talk, and your resentment toward us—"

"Not toward the pack," he clarified. "Never toward you."

Sonia flinched. "Well, I didn't tell you the whole truth. A part of me thinks I shouldn't. But before you take on Lukka you should have the whole picture."

"Tell me."

"It's a long story," she said tiredly. "He'll be waiting for me to call in. I'm meant to convince you to bring her back. I'll send word that it will take the rest of the day at least. Then we can talk. About everything."

"Before you head inside, there is something else you should know," Bill admitted. Gruffly, he reiterated the story of the Eislanders and Naomi's newfound status as a made.

Had he tried to predict Sonia's reaction beforehand, he wouldn't have come close.

She just sighed, utterly deflated. "Well, that kind of diminishes the chances that Lukka will just let you walk away," she said, but despair wasn't the emotion coloring her voice. No, Bill recognized that hard note, alright. "Good. Maybe that means I can convince you to seize this opportunity as more than a chance to run."

"I don't like the sound of that." Bill groaned. "Sonia… Don't tell me that you want to convince me to challenge Lukka for more than my freedom."

Sonia shrugged. "I'm going to try."

6

*L*oren said nothing as Micha all but dragged her into the house. Once inside, she headed straight for the bay window in the living room and…

Watched.

They were still by the car, yards from the house. Sonia was shouting, waving her arms through the air, while McGoven just stood there. They were practically toe-to-toe. Only a foot separated them but…when Sonia deflated, arms falling to her sides, he didn't hesitate to engulf her in his arms, holding her close.

No! A rage so intense it burned shot through Loren. She dug her nails into her palms just to keep from shouting. Screaming. It was the same impulse she felt when the woman had slapped him.

A need to fight. Defend. She couldn't recall ever *wanting* to get off the horse, but the next second, she'd been on the ground ready to—

What? she wondered helplessly. Hit her? *Attack* someone she didn't even know, just because the woman had the nerve to touch a grown man she had no hold over?

Yes, something inside of her growled, completely unashamed at the fact. *Mine—*

"Who is that?"

The sound of Naomi's voice was like pouring grease onto a smoldering fire. Utilizing her last shred of self-control, Loren moved as far from her as she could and bit her bottom lip so hard she tasted blood, just to keep from saying something nasty in return.

"That's Sonia Carlisle," Micha replied with admiration in his tone. "Her father was well-respected in the pack when he was alive, and she is a liaison for Lukka. That's probably why she's here—sending word from the pack. I wonder if they know about—" He seemed to stop himself from mentioning the attack or any of its relevant aftermath. "Actually, I think she grew up with McGoven. She's probably just here to see him. Rumor is, they're pretty close."

Only the relationship between them didn't seem so "close" now. Sonia broke away from his embrace, shouting, while McGoven frowned, replying to her intermittently with a nod or a shrug.

From his nonchalance, one might assume they were talking about something as trivial as the weather. But Sonia looked…

Terrified. Those blue eyes were wide, pleading with a desperation Loren could feel, even from inside the house. Whatever they were arguing about, it wasn't good. But that didn't give Sonia an excuse to lean against him, pressing her face into his shoulder.

"She his girlfriend or something?—"

The fact that Naomi spoke from halfway across the room was the only reason she didn't end up on the floor as Loren spun around. There wasn't a single thought in her head. Just the impulse to *hit* something.

"Hey! Whoa! Easy!" Micha darted in between them, quick as lightning. With both hands on her shoulders, he held her back. "Just take it easy."

His tone snapped something inside her. Heart pounding, she realized her nails were drawn—ready to do a whole lot more than scratch a pretty face this time. She wanted to kill.

The irrational anger surged through her veins unabated. She couldn't think. Couldn't breathe. The only logical thought she had left in her head was the knowledge that she was acting *insane.*

"What the hell?" Naomi had retreated to the corner of the living room, her eyes narrowed to slits.

Smart girl, something in Loren murmured darkly, relishing the fear in those green eyes.

"What the hell is your problem?"

Loren wanted to know the answer to that as well—what the hell *was* her problem? Why couldn't she even see straight? And why did the thought of Sonia, out there alone with McGoven, make her want to…

"I need air." She broke away from Micha, turned on her heel, and raced through the kitchen.

She wanted to run outside, fade beneath the trees, and hide until the strange emotions disappeared.

She barely made it past the foyer.

Slam! From the back of her mind, she knew that someone had barged through the front door, rushing straight in her direction. Before she could turn, a solid force dragged her back, spinning her around to pin her body against the side of the staircase.

Familiarity kept her from resisting. She just inhaled, breathing in pine. Just like that, all the anger…

Evaporated.

Though the newfound clarity might have had something to do with the man pressed against her so tightly she couldn't feel anything else?

He didn't say a word. He didn't have to.

He just stood there, with his hands braced against the wall on either side of her head. He wasn't close enough to completely block her in—not that she would move anyway.

"I leave you alone for five damn minutes…" His mouth was dangerously near her throat. Loren blinked as she remembered that he had been outside, yards from the house only a few seconds earlier.

He didn't look angry, though. That silver gaze just held her stare, as indecipherable as ever.

"Then, m-maybe you shouldn't leave me alone?" She didn't even have the strength left to feel embarrassed. A part of her relished challenging him, even in such a small way.

Until he eased back, enough for her to see Micha and Naomi watching from the living room.

Suddenly, that rebellious inner voice went silent in the face of shame. She turned to the stairs, desperate to hide.

"Wait—" His tone called her back before she could take a step. "We should talk. Get your shoes." He turned for the door, pausing only to swipe his keys from the hook, and grab a gray jacket and his boots. "I'll be out in the truck."

He wasn't asking.

She sighed, spotting her boots in the corner near the door. Aware of Micha and Naomi, she didn't even pause to put them on before slipping through the door after him.

She felt a hint of relief that Sonia wasn't anywhere in sight. Not in the field, not in that black car…and *not* in the passenger's seat of McGoven's truck.

Though why should I care if she were? she wondered. By the time she made it across the driveway, bare feet crunching over gravel, she hadn't come up with an answer. With a sense of dread, she opened the passenger-side door and climbed in, keeping her gaze lowered as she slipped her boots on one at a time.

McGoven drove without uttering a word and true to his prediction, fragile snowflakes began to speckle the windshield. Loren watched them fall as a tiny, apprehensive part of her wanted to ask where they were going. She kept her mouth shut, but she wasn't surprised when he parked in front of a crumbling, two-story ranch house at the end of a deserted block a moment later.

"Are you ready for this?" With a heavy sigh, he watched her from the driver's seat. Flurries drifted down from overhead, coating the hood of the truck. Eventually, he seemed to take her silence as an answer. "That's okay. I can—"

"I'm ready." Loren unsnapped her seatbelt, trying to ignore the fact that her fingers shook. Or the tiny little voice at the back of her mind screaming that she *wasn't* ready at all.

And that she never would be…

Still, it wasn't like she could turn tail and run now. It had been her idea to come here, after all.

"I'm ready," she repeated, slamming the door of the truck behind her—but she didn't know if she were speaking more to him…or herself.

"Okay." Face expressionless, McGoven led the way up the narrow concrete path, where a single ribbon of yellow caution tape dangled from the knob of the front door.

Besides the splash of color, the place looked as dreary and cold as it had a week ago.

After fishing a set of keys from his pocket, McGoven unlocked the front door and looked back. "Are you coming?"

Loren realized that she was still on the curb. For once, something else held her attention other than him. The house looked the same. Empty, neglected, and cold. Had she really lived here?

"Loren?"

She could see him there, waving to get her attention. Out of habit, she lurched into motion. Then stopped. Every single time she tried to take a step, something held her back. A memory? The last thing she remembered was climbing up the stairs to go to bed...

"Loren—"

"I..."

She shook her head, turning on her heel, and...

Ran. The snow came down harder as she darted around the side of the house, into the backyard, as she skirted the porch, where the screen door swung on its hinges. If she were trying to get away, heading straight in the direction of *his* house wouldn't help her any. Before stepping on the path that cut through the woods, she turned, bracing herself against the trunk of a thick oak tree instead.

I can't do this. Whether it meant that she was weak, stupid, spineless—whatever. She couldn't step foot inside that house.

"Loren."

She wasn't exactly surprised when McGoven appeared, moving slowly as if expecting her to bolt at any minute.

"I'm sorry," she blurted. "I shouldn't have had you bring me all the way out here. I—"

"It's alright." He didn't even have to raise his voice for it to carry across the yard. "You're not ready yet."

Yet. At least he seemed optimistic. She wasn't. That house was like a dungeon, full of dark memories. Why unlock that gate?

"It's okay. I'll take you back."

"No." She shook her head. After spending the day cooped up with Naomi, Micha, and her confusing emotions, it felt good to be out in the open. Alone…

With him. She tried shaking her head to clear the thought, but it was still there clinging to the inside of her skull. *He belongs here,* a part of her insisted in a dark murmur. *With me. He's mine—*

"Do you want to wait in the truck?" He was closer now.

She could smell him. *More* than smell him—taste him, right there on the tip of her tongue. It was a scent that seemed way more natural than cologne and muskier than that crisp pine. Something sweet and wild and dangerous, all at the same time.

"No," she whispered, turning around to face him. "I…"

She trailed off as her eyes caught the jagged line of flesh right below his throat, partially hidden beneath the collar of his shirt. It looked grisly, more like the result of an animal attack.

But she knew the real cause—her. Horrified, she reached out. "I'm so sorry. I didn't mean—"

At her touch, he jerked out of reach, eyes flashing a shade so dark it was damn near black. *"Don't!"* The corner of his mouth twitched as if he wanted to say something else, but held himself back. Abruptly, he whirled on his heel, marching away. "I'll be in the truck."

"Wait…" In the end, Loren didn't really know what made her follow him—just a step. But he froze anyway.

Are you crazy? some rational part of her railed angrily at the back of her mind. She moved toward him regardless, cautiously slipping around that bulk to block his path.

She couldn't help it. Some sick, morbid curiosity infected her brain. Without hesitation, she fingered the fabric of his shirt, exposing the wound fully. It looked even worse up close. She could make out every individual tooth mark, etched into his flesh.

"It's nothing," he grunted, pulling back.

Liar, a part of her whispered. *It's everything…*

She let her hand fall, but she couldn't turn away. Because, even as she stared at the impression of her own teeth, cut into someone else's skin… She didn't feel one ounce of shame. Or guilt.

Mine.

The thought shocked her, and she took a hasty step back—but her foot never even touched the ground.

He moved so fast. His arm hooked around her waist, yanking her so close she had to brace her hands against his chest just to keep standing. Horror flashed in his gaze.

But he didn't pull away. Not even as her hands spread out tentatively over the hard, pure muscle of his chest.

What are you doing, Loren? the logical part of her demanded. *This is bad…*

But, it didn't *feel* bad. In fact, pressed against him, bathed in his heat, she felt better than ever. Warm, and so dizzy—like she could just give up right now and never even hit the ground.

Just float.

"I'm sorry," she repeated. She could only stare down at her fingers, pale against his tan skin. "I shouldn't have done that."

"Don't—"

"Does it hurt?" Without thinking, she let her fingers travel a fraction lower, amazed at the way he felt. Like stone, so damn solid. He barely seemed to breathe or move at all, even as delicate snowflakes melted against his skin…

At least, until he growled. The low sound broke from his throat, raising the hairs on the back of her neck.

She recoiled. Her hands had inched lower than she meant to, catching the two dark pink peaks that centered his pecks.

Uh-oh. Like a good girl who rarely interacted with the opposite sex, Loren knew that she should have turned and left him right then and there.

Hell, it seemed to be his way of handling things.

But she couldn't.

Mine. The thought was a fly buzzing around the inside of her skull, demanding acknowledgment. *Mine, mine, mine.*

"Loren…" As if from far away, she saw his hands gingerly encircle the fragile bones of her wrist—but he didn't brush her off. He just held her for so long that she finally forced herself to glance up at him through her lashes.

His eyes were *glowing*, as bright as moonlight. He looked confused. Torn. She could feel his hands twitching as if he wanted to let her go, but something deep inside wouldn't let him.

Loren figured it was the same, dark impulse that had her leaning up, pressing her mouth firmly against his.

7

Their lips met, and for that brief expanse of time, her entire world centered around *him* and nothing else.

Not the wind moving through the trees or the falling snow. Not his age. Not their situation, or the voices screaming at the back of her head that he was a grown man, and she was…

Stupid.

It didn't matter. Bold, her tongue slipped out, running along the seam of his, aiming to slip inside and—

"Stop!" He ripped his mouth from hers, shoving her back. "Loren, no. We can't."

Her heart sank as every argument against her attraction returned in full force. "I'm sor—"

He put a finger to her lips. "Will you *stop* saying that?" It was a plea, someone begging for torture to end. "You never have to apologize to me."

He just stared down at his outstretched finger, as if wondering why it was still there. She felt the pressure shift, slowly moving down from her mouth to cup her chin.

"If anyone should be sorry, it's me," he added, almost in a whisper.

She held her breath, feeling his hand move easily down her throat as if he'd memorized the slender curve.

"You have no idea—" Those fingers glided swiftly down her collarbone. "No idea…"

Yes, a part of her agreed whole-heartedly. He *should be sorry.* Sorry for stopping her. For holding her back. Especially because—despite all his insistence on stopping—he wasn't exactly slapping her on the wrist for being a naughty girl and dragging her back to the truck.

After eighteen years, Loren knew anger. She had spent months living in fear of that very emotion, glinting in her father's dark eyes.

She knew regret and pain.

And, in him, she didn't see a damn bit of either one.

Instead, he looked…

Hungry. His gaze centered on the column of her throat with an expression he couldn't hide. Like he wanted to bite. Tear. Lick. Mark her flesh the same way she'd marked him.

And she *wanted* him to.

The potential consequences didn't even cross her mind as she reached up, lacing a hand around the back of his head before he could stop her, dragging him down.

"Stop." He resisted, fighting to pull away. "Loren—"

No!

Impulsively, she seized his bottom lip between her teeth before he could, and tugged.

A sound like the roar of a jet engine broke from the back of his throat. He wrenched her closer, palming her waist, pressing her against his chest.

"Stop," she heard him whisper again—even as he brushed his lips over hers—but, considering how the next second his tongue plunged deep, it was kind of a moot point.

His mouth slanted against hers, but as his hands fanned out over her lower back, Loren sensed his true aim—not a kiss, but submission. He demanded it with every brush of his lips, and she couldn't find the strength to match his pace.

So, without an ounce of guilt, she bit down. Hard. The flavor of copper exploded over her tongue. Blood? His— and she relished the taste, greedily seeking out every single drop. Disgust didn't even cross her mind.

This felt right. Natural. The salty tang melded with the overall musk of him, creating a more visceral picture of who William McGoven was at his core. Someone dangerous. Virile. Wild.

A part of her recognized his strength and only wanted to prove her own in return. The bite wasn't a challenge but a warning. *Nobody will ever make me submit,* that shadowy voice at the back of her mind whispered—but he didn't have to.

She was already his. Body, mind, and soul. And he was hers.

He stiffened beneath the brutal assault, groaning in shock. She looked up to witness alarm flit through those silver eyes, right before a dark determination replaced it.

So you wanna play? That look warned her. *Let's play.*

The next second she was on the ground. He moved so quickly that her mind barely processed the motion of his leg sweeping out to rob her balance. Impossibly fast, he had her flat on top of a pile of damp leaves. Dead leaves. They smelled like rust, tangling in her hair the same way his fingers did. He fisted both hands within the thick strands to keep her pinned, uncaring as the weight of his body knocked the air from her lungs. His smell swamped her. She could feel his heart pounding in a steady rhythm that confounded her shock.

It wasn't the unsteady beat of someone experiencing regret or fear, or doubt. Nope. It was the steady thrum of a predator—one who knew *exactly* what it wanted. Her.

A blur of motion robbed her senses. All she knew was that her windbreaker was gone, tossed somewhere along the back of the house. She should have been freezing, but a raw heat displaced any chill. His mouth. Recklessly, he skimmed over her bare collar bone, finding her mouth again before he abruptly pulled back.

"No." Loren panted. "Don't—"

A deep, throaty growl ripped from his throat, silencing her instantly. Apparently, he wasn't the type to submit to anyone else, either.

That point, and more was proven as that silver gaze bore down on the tender skin of her throat. He moved slowly. So damn slowly, she felt about ready to scream when his lips finally feathered over a distended vein.

Her heart stopped beating. She stopped breathing. Every single nerve in her body seemed to hinge on the feel of the two warm lips spreading against her flesh, catching the thrum of her pulse.

Teeth next. Gingerly, he seized a bit of flesh, applying just enough pressure to sting. She gasped, throwing her head back to bare more of her throat to him.

But then he froze, wavering between the desire to pull back or…

Give in.

And, damn it, she was tired of him holding back. *Claim me.* The thought was so fierce Loren wondered if she'd said it out loud. Those silver eyes flashed as if she had, darkening to a shade identical to the sky overhead.

He needed to claim. Bite. Mark. Tear.

"Please." She slid her hand along the back of his neck, applying just enough pressure to let him know what she wanted. To make him…

Relent.

Suddenly, he surged, kissing her with the same ferocity she'd bitten him with. Her lips stung. Burned. It hurt. It felt… incredible. Adrenaline mixed with agony, feeding a giddy sense of triumph that she had pushed him to this. Driven him to this state.

Unhinged.

"Fuck." He hissed the curse against her open mouth, rearing back on his knees. Before disappointment could even settle in, his hands came down to settle over her hips. Higher, raking up the material of her shirt with every inch traveled, until…

Her chest became bared to him, heaving with the tumult of emotions washing through her. Excitement. Alarm. Some fear. The logical voice in her brain warned that he could see her bruises—the ones left by Fred Connors that had yet to heal.

Before she could think to shield herself, he noticed them. Heavy-lidded, his eyes skimmed over each and every one before settling over her face. His jaw tightened as another sound rumbled from his chest. Not quite a growl. More like an acknowledgment. *I see the damage done to you. You will explain.*

She nodded, feeling her entire body heat. It pooled in familiar places that only ever seemed sensitive around him. Her nipples she could feel hardening while exposed to the air. Inside her belly. Between her legs.

That ache was the most pressing. She had a sudden urge to rub her thighs together just to ease it. The second she tried to, he cocked his head, and she stilled. It was a warning. *Don't.*

Cautiously, one of his hands bridged the space between them, ghosting up her knee. As the contact registered, closing her legs became the furthest thing from her mind. She needed to spread them. Let him in. Let him…

"Bill!" The shout came from a distance, but sounded eerily familiar. A woman?

Loren froze. McGoven, however, was already on his feet, grabbing her wrist.

He barely managed to haul her upright before a breathless Sonia appeared through the gap in the trees. Judging from her frantic breathing, she'd run all the way here.

"Bill! Are you alright? I heard…" She trailed off, apparently realizing that McGoven—even as he swiped blood from his lip—wasn't exactly in mortal peril. "Growling," she finished awkwardly.

"It's fine, Sonia," McGoven grunted. "Go back. You too—" He didn't even look in Loren's direction. "I need to scout the perimeter."

Sonia frowned. "Bill, wait. We still need to talk—"

"Later." He darted into the woods without ever looking back.

"We'll talk tonight, then," Sonia called after him.

When the woman finally turned to her, Loren expected a barrage of questions. *What were you two doing out here? Why was he bleeding? Why is your jacket crumpled on the ground near the porch?*

But she didn't. Loren couldn't help feeling that Sonia knew damn well what she'd just interrupted. And she didn't like it.

"It's cold," she said softly, turning back along the path. "Let's get back."

Loren followed, but she couldn't stop herself from scanning the woods with every step, searching…

8

There weren't many things that Eric would classify as reaching a level of requiring discretion from even his own Alpha. The short of it was, he didn't trust Lukka. Not a fucking inch.

Loreck, being the leader of a pack bordering the bastard, needed to rely on a delicate balance of diplomacy and healthy skepticism. Eric, however, had no such limitations. He couldn't get the words of the rogue from his head. Or the girl…

Her presence made no sense, but he was beginning to suspect that some things about her weren't a coincidence. Her age. Her eye color. Her knack for demanding submission from wolves twice her size.

It was one thing to speculate. On the other hand, probing gossip was a step too far—and yet, Eric found himself leaving the pack borders under the guise of patrolling the perimeter anyway. An hour's drive, the town of Elkton lurked just outside the boundaries of Eislander territory.

Typically, there existed a strained peace. The lycans in the foothills kept to themselves, and the humans respected the large "nature reserve" nearby. No need for compulsion or bribes to go unnoticed.

Roughly nineteen or twenty years ago, things hadn't been so civil. Eric could remember the time vaguely—one of the few who'd ever entered the heart of the small town in person. His destination had been the same then as it was now.

The sheriff's office. The second he parked, someone was already exiting the building to greet him.

"This is a surprise," the man called. Balding, roughly sixty years old, he had been a patrol officer in those days. A gleaming badge affixed to his crisp shirt proclaimed that he'd been promoted since then. "I don't think I've seen you around these parts in over a decade. Eric, wasn't it?"

"Yes. And you are deputy—now Sheriff, it seems—Varl," Eric replied, impressed the man could recall his name. Some of the tension left his body as he continued to advance, sporting a strained smile that he hoped passed as genuine. "Morning. I wanted to know if you remembered an incident that occurred a few years ago involving a spate of murders in this area."

"Oh, the Dansforth killings. Of course, I do. Everyone around these parts does. Why would you want to bring up something like that?" The man raised an eyebrow, but Eric sensed no hostility.

Just curiosity. Apparently, that time had left its mark on the humans the same way it scarred his kind—though some details had been blurred throughout the years. What the mortals recalled as a serial killer had, in actuality, been a rogue belonging to a pack of vicious nomads.

"I wanted to know if I could look at those files," Eric said, still maintaining a smile.

It was a hunch, but it wouldn't stop niggling at his mind. The killings had brought unwanted attention to their territory. So much so they'd been forced to work with a band of outsiders to come to a resolution.

One of them had been a female, young, blond. He could barely remember her name.

But he could remember her attitude well enough.

"I could send them your way," the sheriff said. "You want anything in particular?"

"I do," Eric replied. "I would like all of it."

9

"*S*he marked you."

Bill wasn't surprised when, the second he tiredly mounted the back porch steps, Sonia appeared from the shadows.

It was just after sundown, but she looked as exhausted as if he'd been gone for days. Her hair hung loose and unbrushed, while she had arms crossed over her chest, lips pursed with an emotion he couldn't place.

"Where is she?" he asked, ignoring the question: *Close by.* His nostrils were already flaring, impregnated with her scent.

"Inside—" Sonia inclined her head toward the house. "I didn't answer any of her questions, if that's what you're worried about, but it's time that you do. She marked you," she repeated. "I saw it. Don't lie to me."

"I won't," Bill admitted. Hours of running and his head felt no clearer. If anything, the instinct Loren had unintentionally awoken was stronger than ever, howling for relief.

"How far did it go?" Sonia began tentatively. "Did you… Bill, please tell me you didn't give in to impulse. Please. Especially if you plan on cutting her loose! Have you stopped to consider how this will affect her? Have you?"

He grimaced. Three years his junior, and Sonia *still* had a way of making him feel like a kid about to get scolded.

"I wouldn't take advantage of her like that," he began.

Liar. The wound on his chest throbbed in disagreement— recalling the sting of her teeth, sinking deep. The primal beast within him still seethed at the challenge and craved to return the wound tit-for-tat. He'd come close. A groan escaped him at the memory of her skin, plush and pliable right between his own canines. If Sonia hadn't come when she had…

"Tell me," the woman prodded. "How far did it go?"

"She couldn't control it," he blurted, trying to rationalize it himself. "The bond is too strong. I should have never—"

"That isn't what I meant." Sonia advanced as he mounted the top step, barring his path. "I'm asking why did *you* let her?"

She could have punched him in the chest right then and there, and it wouldn't have hurt any less than that simple question. *Why?*

"I didn't," he insisted gruffly.

Liar, the wolf in him hissed. He could have compelled her to stop. Let her run off while her emotions were heightened. Bringing her to Connors' house in the first place was a risk —especially after her nerves were already frayed due to the presence of Naomi. He had pushed her too hard—she was bound to snap eventually. And, damn it, he had *wanted* her to. A sick, twisted part of him embraced her rage. Craved her mark.

And the sad part was…that even now, with Sonia staring at him horrified, he didn't feel one damn ounce of guilt. *Mine.*

"Do you know how much harder it will be for her now? For you?"

He frowned at her mournful tone. It was the same question he had avoided answering himself.

"It won't matter," he explained, shaking his head. "I'll tell her the truth. Teach her our ways. The more she learns, the easier it will be for her to understand why I did what I did."

Sonia didn't look convinced. She always wore her emotions on her sleeve. Currently, her frown was so pronounced it resembled a crescent moon. "You should get started, then. While you're at it, what exactly *do* you plan on teaching her?"

It was the million-dollar question.

"How to hunt," he said, choosing to list the safer topics first. "How to master her instincts. How to fight. Our customs, the most relevant ones, anyway. Our history."

"And the mating bond?"

After a pause, he nodded.

"And how will you explain abandoning her once you take on Lukka?"

He winced. "Low blow, Sonia."

"Is it?" She squared her chin, and he internally groaned, recognizing the stance. Like a dog with a bone, she wouldn't let this go. "Let's say you win and then decide to leave; she won't be welcome on Black Mountain. Especially if someone like Kyle takes over in the aftermath—"

"Don't even go there." The mere prospect irritated something inside of him, and he turned away, gritting his teeth. "I don't need that mental image."

"That's what could happen," Sonia countered. "Kyle or someone else just as ruthless and cunning. Can you imagine what state we'll be in after that?"

Bill grunted. It was a good question, recalling the truth she let slip earlier.

"I know you can only dance around the issue," he began. "But it's time to come clean. What's been really going on since I left?"

It was her turn to grimace. "Our territory has shrunk, for starters. No one will say why."

So much for her reluctance; he couldn't hide his shock. "Shrunk? What the hell do you mean?"

She shrugged helplessly. "What else? We used to find plenty of fish in our rivers. That's changed. Same with the deer. The bears. Even the birds seem fewer these days. It's gotten so scarce, in fact, that Lukka has all but given permission to push into Eislander territory to—"

"Encroachment," Bill snarled. The polite term for what was, in essence, stealing. It was unheard of. He wouldn't have believed the claim if Sonia didn't appear to be in physical pain. Breaking Lukka's trust to divulge this much must have taken monumental effort on her part. So, he softened his tone. "Seasonal shifts happen all the time. That doesn't necessarily mean mismanagement."

"I thought so, too," Sonia admitted. "But it's been three years, and it's getting worse. There's more—" Her eyes shifted toward the shadows as if she thought someone might be lurking within them, listening. "There was a forest fire a few years back. It was small, relatively contained. Only a few acres were damaged, and no one was injured. Afterward, the affected territory had been marked off as a forbidden zone, at least until the natural balance returned."

"That's protocol," Bill said. Out of tradition, they avoided wounded parts of the forest and allowed them to regrow with little disturbance.

"It's been years, but the ban hasn't been lifted. Rumors have run rampant, of course. Some of them claim that, in actuality, the land has been sold off. For development—"

"No." Bill couldn't believe it. Lukka was many things, but to sell off their ancestral lands? That was a step too far, even for him. "Do you have proof?"

Sonia shook her head. "Of course not. Can you imagine the uproar that would cause?"

He could, in fact. Even the threat of a sale would be enough to foment an outright rebellion, if not a direct challenge from any number of elder lycans within the pack. But while Lukka had never been much of a fighter, the bastard was smart. Smart enough to cover his tracks.

"What aren't you telling me?" he demanded of Sonia. Her eyes were darting again, avoiding his gaze. She wasn't merely nervous. She was being evasive. For her to play coy now, after everything else she'd revealed, there could only be one explanation. "You *can't* tell me. There is something he compelled you directly not to reveal."

Her lips twitched. Suddenly, she jerked her chin toward the house. "That boy you let stay here. I saw him around Black Mountain before."

He raised an eyebrow at the change in subject. "Micha. He was with Kyle when he came for her. He claimed that he wasn't a part of what happened. I believe him."

"Well, there are a lot of boys like him around lately," Sonia continued. "Young. Wild. Strong. Eager to fight. Loyal to Lukka. He's accepted them from all over. Dozens."

She said no more, but Bill could fill in the blanks. Despite his resources presumably strained to their breaking point, Lukka was welcoming in rogues with open arms. He'd heard the rumors, even out here, but he'd thought it was a sign of arrogance. A prideful young Alpha eager to show off the abundance in his territory.

Now, thanks to Sonia's obvious skepticism, another explanation seemed more plausible.

"He's building an army," he said. "If anyone speaks out, sale or no sale, he has a team of young pups ready to put them down. Does he even know how dangerous a game he's playing?"

But that was the point—of course, Lukka knew. He didn't care. To him, the position of Alpha was all about power and control. For his benefit, no one else's.

"There have been some good things," Sonia added bitterly. "There seems to be no end of money with which Lukka can expand his lodgings. To supplement the lack of fresh resources, he's been importing processed foods from the outside. You're angry hearing this…" She raised an eyebrow at his expression. "I'm surprised you care."

"Sonia! Of course, I do!" Bill hissed through clenched teeth. He may have left Black Mountain behind, but that didn't mean he didn't give a shit as to what happened to his old home. "And, despite all this shit, *you* remain loyal to him."

"I don't have a choice! I can't survive out here like you can. You put on a good show, but admit it—being a rogue feels no different to you than being under an Alpha. Pack life has always been a conscious choice for you. Some of us aren't so lucky. We need an Alpha for guidance. It isn't our place to question his intentions. Do you know how hard it is for me to even tell you this much?" Sonia's voice echoed, high pitched and broken. Unshed tears glistened in her eyes.

Bill winced. "Yes, I know. I'm sorry. Come here." He pulled her into an embrace that lasted barely a second before she pulled back, swiping any tears from her face.

"Don't worry about me. You told me before that Loren refused to submit to you," she said. "I wonder if it's because of your calling? Somehow, she's tapped into that part of you and it's shielding her."

"I don't know," Bill admitted.

It was a plausible explanation, but he outright scoffed at it. Loren wasn't utilizing his own instincts to resist him. That rebellious impulse came from her alone. Despite the "calling" being a rare gift, he had stumbled upon the one meek, brutalized girl who had the same instinct.

He wanted to write off the suspicion at first. Laugh at it, even. But he couldn't shake a part of him that warned it wasn't so farfetched. He had sensed her long before he even knew of her lycan side. She intrigued him in a way no other woman had. Not even Emma.

There had to be a reason for that.

Though, maybe the truth was that he was no better than Frank Connors, sensing easy prey and eager to take a bite.

"You'll learn soon enough," Sonia said tiredly. "Once you break the bond, she'll have only her own instincts to rely on. For better or for worse."

Bill grunted. This time, Sonia wasn't subtle in her attempts to sow guilt. "I've made up my mind, Sonia. It's the only way."

"No, it wasn't. You didn't have to intervene at all. You made that choice all on your own. I warned you what could happen."

Bill heard the creak of the floorboards as she shifted closer. Warm fingers gently ghosted the back of his neck before settling over his shoulder.

"And I don't know why you're fighting so hard to deny the obvious. You're attracted to her—"

"No, I'm *not!*" Scowling, he pulled away and stalked to the opposite end of the porch. "She's too young," he grunted, though he didn't know if it were to himself or Sonia. "She doesn't know what she wants. You're right. I shouldn't have intervened."

But the half-assed excuses just made the whole thing that much worse. She *was* young and naïve and so damn innocent he sometimes wondered if she were more *Bambi* than Lycan.

Though, she wasn't all innocent. He dragged a finger across his lower lip feeling the stinging marks left over from the assault of her teeth. Even Emma had never kissed him like that—but *Emma* had been fully in control of her own emotions. Loren wasn't. The various complications of the bond made his head ache. Still, there was no use dwelling on it now.

"She's young, maybe naïve, but she's not stupid," Sonia pointed out. "She might feel loyal to you because of the bond, yes, but it can't create love—"

"Don't go there, Sonia. Please. Besides, it's too late," he said, turning to face her. "I appreciate everything you've done for me so far, but you don't have to—"

"There's one thing you haven't factored in." Sonia crossed her arms, eyeing the sky. "You act as if going against Lukka would be some desperate last-ditch effort you have to undertake all on your own. You don't understand that plenty in the pack will rise up in support of you. What of them if you walk away after that, huh? To hell with us?"

"Us?"

He didn't even need to see the determined gleam in her eye to know that Sonia hadn't included herself by mistake.

"I never asked you before." She moved closer, forcing him to meet her probing gaze. "Why you left. I assumed it was because you couldn't bear being in a place that held so many memories of you and Emma. I thought you'd last a year at most before you came back. I don't care if that makes me childish," she added as he cocked an eyebrow in surprise. "I hoped you would come back. Every day, I hoped for that. But now that it's been several years, I have to wonder if it were always more than grief. So, I'm asking you outright. What drove you away?"

He gritted his teeth. There was no point in dredging up that part of his past. Some things were better left unspoken. "Sonia…"

"Tell me the truth. I know you never tolerated Lukka. You could have beaten him easily if you wanted to. The fact that you haven't… It's like you're *punishing* yourself. Staying away not out of apathy, but masochism. It hurts you more to be out here, alone. You *want* it to hurt—"

"Lukka may be a bastard, but if you don't hate me after all this time, then even that bastard has kept his word," Bill countered. "He never revealed the truth."

Sonia eyed him warily, her brows furrowing. "What are you talking about?"

"It's no mystery why Emma was killed. She died because I failed her. The same way I've failed you, the pack, and Loren."

"Is that why you were so desperate for her to be taken in?" Sonia said with an accusatory tone in her voice. "You think you're not worthy of helping her yourself."

"It would have been best for everyone," he muttered, ignoring the part of him that scoffed at that. "What's happened otherwise? I killed on enemy territory. I turned a human—"

Sonia flinched, but he could tell from the way she clenched her jaw that she knew he was right.

"I deserve my judgment. Always have."

"Emma was killed by hunters, wasn't she? How is that your fault?"

"I should have been there, and I wasn't."

There was more. More that Sonia wasn't ready to learn, and he wasn't willing to say.

Still, she wouldn't go down without a fight. "Running away hasn't helped solve anything, but you know what might? Facing your problems and demanding what is your right. You want time to train Loren? I can buy you some time, but in return, you promise me something."

"What?"

"You let me feel out support for you among the pack. If I can prove that it's there, that there are some of us who will stand by you, will you take that into consideration when you make your challenge?"

"*You* don't count."

"Enough to field a true challenge, then," Sonia said. "You take him on with the backing of others in the pack with the intention to become Alpha should you win. No running away. No more self-doubt. You lead us the way you were always meant to."

"And if I fail?" An outcome that even he could admit was a possibility. "You'll suffer the consequences. That would be treason. I can't let you take that on for me."

"And what do you think it's been like all this time? Not easy. Not one damn bit. Promise me that much, and I'll do whatever I can to help."

"And in the meantime, Lukka will just let me frolic in peace?"

"I can give you time at least," Sonia said. "Enough to train your ragtag pack to survive on their own, anyway. And to prepare Loren for whatever happens next. Plenty of time to transition her properly and avoid causing her any more trauma or pain."

"While you play politics," he countered. "Do you even understand the risk you'll be taking? Lukka probably has you under a microscope already."

"Don't worry about me. I can handle him."

"Fine. Do what you want, but I can assure you that nothing will come from it."

"I wouldn't be so sure," Sonia said, jutting her chin. "While you've been off playing rogue, I've come up with a few tricks of my own. You're not the only one who's had to learn to survive. You've always had your brawn, but I have some skills, too."

"I'm sorry." He nodded in deference. "You're right… You know, Lukas always said that leadership was mostly bravado—"

"But human nature was mostly politics," Sonia finished for him. "Wow. I don't think I've heard you talk about him since… Not for a very long time."

She was right. After his death, Lukas had been regulated to the same part of his mind where Emma dwelled—a cache of memories he rarely revisited, his strained relationship with Kyle included. What triggered him to do so now? Loren? Perhaps.

"He would know how to handle this," he admitted. A wave of guilt slammed into him and nearly took him off his feet.

Sonia reached out, placing her hand on his shoulder. "I don't know why you always seemed so determined to place yourself in his shadow. You are not him. Remember when we were kids? We would play for hours, all of us together. You and Kyle dominated any game requiring physical strength like wrestling or tag."

He nodded. "But anything requiring an ounce of brainpower and you would easily win."

She laughed. "I lost to Lukka a fair share, though. Emma too… That's my point. You have your strengths, and he has his. I know Lukka isn't your favorite person, but the way his father would pit you two against each other… I think you've grown accustomed to seeing yourself only as he did —as his prodigy, nothing else. But, you are *not* Lukas."

"I know," he rasped.

That was the point—Lukas would have never found himself in such a mess.

"He would have found a way to have Loren accepted, politics be damned."

"I wouldn't be so sure." Sonia turned away from him, but from the set of her shoulders, he could tell that something was on her mind. "I know you idolized the man, but I think you would have made for a very different Alpha."

"How so?"

She eyed him, biting her bottom lip. "You are fair and just, and you are willing to risk everything for what you see as right. The old laws deserve respect, but you won't let yourself be restrained by them."

"You think Lukas was restrained?"

Sonia shrugged. "I think he's gone. You're here now, and you shouldn't punish yourself because you didn't do things exactly the way he would. You want to know how I think you should handle this? Your way. No one else's. If you didn't kill that Eislander, you need to prove it. Find out who did. Contact their Alpha if you can. They're fond of the old ways. Use that to your advantage and think of some way to prove your innocence."

"How?"

Her eyes glittered with that cunning intelligence that made her a dangerous opponent in any game of wits. "I'm sure you can think of something."

"And what about you? Do you need to head back now and tell your Alpha to shove his summons up his ass?" He felt an irrational urge to find any excuse to make her stay. At least for a few more hours. A full-blooded female lycan was a much-needed buffer between a half-breed and a newly made wolf.

"I'll stay until tomorrow night to help you as best as I can," Sonia suggested. "Then the rest is up to you."

Bill didn't know how to interpret that comment. As a threat? Or encouragement?

"I need the help," he said, rather than question.

"That's an understatement," Sonia said with a playful grin. "You went from no women to two within the space of a week. You have no idea what you've just taken on, do you? I tried to keep them occupied as best as I could. I made dinner, too, if you want some. And I gave the boy some old clothing I could tell you haven't worn in a while."

"Thanks, Sonia. You have no idea how much I appreciate you."

"Then prove it. Go in there right now and talk to Loren."

He groaned. Anything but that. "Buy me a few more hours. I need to think, and whether I reach out to them or not,

I'm sure the Eislanders will be back soon. I should scout some more, just to be on the safe side—"

"Then you tell her." From her tone, Sonia wouldn't drop this subject any time soon.

He hung his head in defeat. "Then I'll tell her."

"Good. The least I can do is hold down the fort. And I'm sorry to tell you that your fridge is practically empty by now. I'll head out and grab some groceries if you want."

"Thanks. And, I hate to use you as my middle man, but—"

"I'll tell the blond one to go home tonight. She should tell no one, blah, blah, blah. As for Loren, I'll handle her as well."

He felt like a coward for running. Maybe he was. A selfish part of him couldn't resist holding onto the lone rogue status for even a few hours longer, putting off the growing responsibility that had fallen onto his lap. A run would do him good, if only to give him time to convince himself that breaking the bond, and avoiding the pack were the only decent outcomes in the end.

Even if they went against every fiber of his being.

oren lingered near the kitchen window, fighting for a glimpse of McGoven and Sonia between bouts of pretending to do the dishes.

It was wrong to eavesdrop, not that she could hear much from here. Her only consolation was that their conversation didn't seem to be intimate. They stood near the center of the porch, and Bill had his arms crossed while Sonia intermittently shook her head.

Eventually, they stopped speaking altogether and just stood there, gazing at the darkened tree line. Was there something out there? Loren craned her neck to see more and wound up dropping the plate in her hand.

It didn't break, but the clamor shattered the silence, loud enough to be heard outside.

Caught! Both figures turned toward the window, and Loren barely managed to duck out of view. It was too late.

Footsteps approached the backdoor, and Loren raced into the living room, her cheeks flaming.

"It's about damn time he got back," Naomi sniped from the couch. "Does he expect me to just wait around like some homeless vagrant? No offense."

"None taken," Micha chirped. He sat on the floor across from her, a pile of clothing scattered around him. Sonia had fished them from the recesses of Bill's closet and invited him to take his pick. Under the guise of inspecting a sweatshirt with a faded logo, he looked up, meeting Loren's stare. "Hear anything interesting while you were eavesdropping?"

Loren blushed. In the end, she just shook her head and took up a post near the window.

It wasn't long before noise echoed in the kitchen, and someone warily poked their head through the doorway. Loren's heart sank as she saw Sonia's exhausted smile.

"Bill went out again," she said—a polite way of phrasing what Loren knew to be the truth—*he's out avoiding you.* "I thought I would get some groceries for you guys. At least, so you aren't living on tuna for the next few days."

"Thanks!" Micha chirped.

"Naomi, Bill fixed your car's battery while he was out, so you can go home tonight," the woman added, turning to the blond. "If you have any questions, he will talk to you tomorrow, I promise. Come on, I can follow you there just in case you have any more mechanical issues."

If she were disappointed, Naomi excelled at hiding it. Instead, she stood and headed for the door after Sonia.

The second both women were out of earshot, Loren turned to the window, hunting for any hint of a figure racing through the trees. It was too dark to make out more than shadow.

"Looks like I'll crash here, tonight," Micha declared, heading for the couch.

Rather than head upstairs into the empty bedroom, Loren remained by the window.

Just watching.

Loren woke up on the living room floor, curled into a ball. Her entire body ached in protest, and she sorely missed the comfort of the mattress.

At least she could get some sleep without the simmering tension of yesterday. After Naomi left, things felt strangely…normal. McGoven staying out all night was nothing new. In fact, the only change from the previous few days was that Micha was currently snoring on the couch with his folded pile of new clothing on the floor beside him. She assumed he planned on sticking around.

It was strange. Bill hinted that lycan bonds were different, and already she could sense that. In Bill McGoven's world, relationships were formed instantly based on subtle nuances. Strangers could become allies overnight. And friends could become lovers?

The image of him and Sonia wouldn't leave her mind, taunting her while she drifted in and out of restless sleep. The latter decided to sleep in her car, rather than take his bedroom. Still, Loren wasn't convinced their relationship was entirely platonic. Though, now might be the best time to ask.

She could sense his return before she even crept to the window. Sure enough, the sight of the dark figure picking his way through the trees made her heart beat faster. In relief? Or dread? He moved easily but Loren could sense the exhaustion his steady stride disguised.

A part of her wanted to lurk inside the house and wait for him to approach her first. Play coy. Pride wasn't her motive, but sympathy. So much unsaid lingered between them—too much to unload on him now. Still, those logical arguments didn't matter to that growing instinctive impulse that had her out on the front porch before she even realized it.

The cold air was a shock, and she regretted not grabbing a jacket. At least until a pair of gray eyes met hers from across the front yard and all fears of frostbite vanished. She was on fire. One look from him set her entire body alight with an emotion she couldn't name and didn't want to. It was unnerving and electric, flooding her veins with every breath.

He took his time, lumbering up the front walkway at a pace that conveyed more than anything else how reluctant he was. She could see the hesitation written clearly in his gaze.

That didn't stop her lips from flying apart the second he came close enough.

"Can we talk?"

He flinched, raising a dark eyebrow. He seemed just as confused by her sudden bravery as she was.

"Later," he said in a neutral tone. "I promise. But first…"

He mounted the porch steps and palmed the space beside the front door. "There are some things we should discuss. All of us—" He slapped the wall repeatedly until a startled Micha darted to the screen door.

By then, McGoven was already bounding toward the west fields. "Get dressed," he called back. "Then meet me near the paddocks."

Micha didn't seem to think the first command applied to him, and he rushed after Bill barefoot in only a pair of sweatpants.

Loren scrambled to put on her boots and grab her borrowed windbreaker from the hook by the door. When she finally trudged toward the paddock, Micha and Bill stood facing each other. While tense, their posture wasn't hostile. Instead, they looked as though they were preparing for something.

Once she reached them, Bill acknowledged her with a curt nod. "It's time I let you both in on the risks you've unwittingly taken by staying here. What happened with the

Eislanders was only the start. They'll come again, most likely with more reinforcements—"

"We can take them," Micha insisted with a confidence Bill didn't seem to match.

"We can't," he conceded. "Not alone. With that in mind, I've decided… My situation here is no longer tenable. If any of us are to have a shot at survival, regardless of what happens with the Eislanders, we can't remain here. If you're willing, I can teach you everything I know. After that… I've concluded it's time for me to leave the area. For good."

Leave? Loren didn't understand the word choice.

Micha did, though. His eyes widened. "You mean, you're going to challenge your status? Seriously?"

Bill nodded. "By creating a made lycan I've broken one cardinal rule too many. There won't be a choice. I either leave or surrender to punishment."

"Wow." Micha bowed his head as if overwhelmed by the severity of that possibility. "And then what?"

Bill shrugged. "I go north. Somewhere far from here, at least. Either way, if you attach yourself to me, you'll be signing up for the same fate."

"Wait?" Micha shook his head as if unsure he heard correctly. "You mean you won't challenge for Alpha status?"

"No. I only want the ability to cut all ties for good."

Cut ties. Whatever they were referring to, it sounded important. Desperation grappled with her long-honed need to remain silent. In the end, one impulse won out. "What does that mean?"

Loren flinched as both men turned to her.

"It means he's going to fight Lukka," Micha blurted in a rush. "That's a big deal! Huge! I mean, if he wins, he could take over. Become Alpha. But if he loses, it'll probably mean—"

"The point is," McGoven said over him, "you should know the danger you're in should you stay. If you don't agree with those choices, you are free to leave."

Micha squared his shoulders and appeared to dig his heels into the muddy earth. "I know you didn't kill anyone who didn't deserve it," he said in a tone an octave deeper than his usual cheerful chirp. "And if you fight for your freedom, then I will too. I don't think Lukka was ever a good fit for me anyway."

Bill winced. Obviously, he didn't expect this reaction. "You'll walk away from the security of Black Mountain for what? To follow a rogue you don't even know?"

"Not only that," Micha countered. "If what you say is the truth, then they used me. They used me to put a female in danger. Do you think I would stick around people like that?"

Bill frowned, but a new understanding flickered across those pensive gray eyes. "Fine. As for you..." He inclined his head in her direction, and Loren held her breath. "You have a choice in this, too," he said. "You can choose to go with the pack if you want. Leave with Sonia. Otherwise… You need to understand the danger you'll be in. If the Eislanders come again, I will protect you, but it is more important than ever that you grow into your lycan instincts. Learn to shift. Learn to fight. It's a monumental ask. You may have to push the limits of what you can handle. I can't deny that it will be hard. Dangerous. If you want to leave, I won't blame you."

And he did want her to leave. She could see the silent plea written clearly across his gaze. *Please go.*

Anger prickled inside of her, hot and irrational. Holding his stare, she lifted her chin and said, "I want to stay."

He visibly flinched, but disguised any disappointment behind a stern frown. "I won't go easy on you."

It was a warning. One that made her heart lurch at the sincerity. At the same time, something in her twitched as if eager to take him on. Prove her worth.

Fight.

Suddenly, Bill cocked his head as if picking up a far-off noise. Not even a second later, a pink car zoomed down the main road and parked in front of the house. As Naomi climbed out, dressed in a T-shirt and loose-fitting pink pants, McGoven nodded in approval.

"Now we can begin," he said.

Already, Naomi was advancing toward them, and Loren felt a flicker of what could have been jealousy flare in her chest. From the knowing glance McGoven sent her way, it was apparent he had communicated his intentions to her beforehand. Last night, even?

But then he'd avoided the house—and Loren altogether. She tried not to seethe over that fact as he moved to the center of their makeshift ring.

He took his time, inspecting each figure assembled before him with varying degrees of concern. He seemed reluctant while observing Micha and Naomi, but Loren noted that he seemed the most worried when he finally turned his gaze on her.

"Micha, you take Naomi to the northern boundary and help her practice shifting into her lycan form."

Both took off without argument, and Loren once again got the sense that this was primarily for her benefit. He was speaking in terms she would understand.

"As for Loren. You'll come with me."

He didn't explain his plan for her, and she couldn't suppress a shiver of apprehension as she followed him up to the hill that overlooked the property. This far out, she was grateful for his jacket as a barrier against the cold.

Not that the chill seemed to bother him. He stood tall, easily picking his way through the underbrush. Once they neared the crest of the hill, he stopped.

"I know you're frustrated."

His words seemed to penetrate beyond the surface tension, cutting to the irritation she could feel swirling within her.

"Loren, what happened the other day was my fault—"

"You keep saying that." She didn't know where the impulse to argue came from. She couldn't control the anger. The rage. It felt irrational, centering on the way he kept his gaze averted as if he were afraid to face her while isolated from the others.

"Loren, I need you to listen to me." His stern tone cut through her aggravation like a knife. She could think clearly for a split second and sense the sincerity in his voice. *Listen.* Whatever he intended to say, it was important to him.

"It's time I gave you a crash course on everything lycan. We won't have long, so we can start with the basics—pack structure. Every pack, big and small, consists of an Alpha at the head. Then a subordinate, usually called a beta, and finally several other members to fill the ranks. A lot of it is formal bullshit, rooted in tradition. In essence, you only need three to constitute a pack."

"Is that what you have now? You, Micha, and Naomi?"

He exhaled, not seeming to like that characterization. "Technically, yes."

"But then, what does that make me?"

He turned to face her, and the expression in his gaze smothered what little resentment she still felt. He looked so…torn. Conflicted.

"Whatever we are, you count as one of us."

But there was a reason why that was. A big one. Something he wasn't saying.

"What happens to me when you leave?" her voice caught at the prospect.

"That's up to you," he said evasively. "For now, I want you to only focus on what I tell you. These next few days will be hard. I'll have to push you to your limits. It's vital we get you to shift as soon as possible."

"Okay," she said, nodding. "I'm ready."

He didn't look convinced. In fact, Loren wondered if that were why he'd brought her out here alone. To warn her. From here on out, things would change. That talk about the pack wasn't mere information. It was a warning. In their unspoken hierarchy, she was at the bottom. No longer was he solely her protector but the Alpha of this ragtag pack. His job was to enforce order. Ensure survival.

By any means necessary.

"I want you to know that my main goal—my only goal from the start—has been to help you." He turned, catching her wrist before she could react.

Her heart lurched as she watched his larger fingers manipulate hers until they rested against his calloused palm.

"If you are to reach your full potential, then I need you to trust me. Without question. Can you do that?"

She didn't hesitate. "Yes."

"Good." He released her and took a step back. In that instant, something in his expression changed. His eyes? They were too bright. Molten silver.

"Then run."

11

"*Y*ou're dead." The cheerfully voiced statement came from Micha, who stood over her, his lips parted into a dazzling smile. "Try again?"

Loren groaned at the prospect. "Trying" seemed to be the only word capable of describing what exactly she'd spent most of the day doing. Trying to be patient. Obey. Learn. Put up with whatever McGoven threw her way without argument.

But she wasn't like him—or even Micha and, to an extent, Naomi. She was slower. Weaker. The equivalent of her "trying" to keep up turned out to be epic failure across the board.

She never knew it was possible to feel so sore. All over, she ached. Her hair was caked with mud, her body slick with a mixture of sweat and earth. Her legs trembled at the thought of taking another step.

But still…

Beneath the exhaustion was a thrill of excitement, she couldn't deny. It grew stronger with every second she spent out beneath the wavering branches and in the rolling fields. A hunger almost. For more. More freedom. More running. *More!*

Though, perhaps that excitement was nowhere near Micha's. He beamed as she extended her hand and allowed him to yank her to her feet.

"Again," she choked out. Then she ran.

Her eyes were on the white barn in the distance—her target destination for the past two hours of this "training."

This attempt, she barely made it two feet before she wound up on the ground again, coughing up dirt.

"That makes it ten deaths in a row. I think we should head back," Micha said tiredly.

Loren followed him without comment. Her mind was a whirl during the entire trek toward the house. McGoven seemed to think this would help her. But how?

After their talk, he led them to join Micha and Naomi— only to leave with the latter while she remained with Micha. Since then, the younger man had her run laps and try to evade him, only for her to fail each test miserably.

Beating herself up would change nothing—she knew that. Still, she couldn't resist seething over her lack of strength and speed. If McGoven had danced around the issue before, this brief training session had all but cemented his fear. Of the four of them, she was the weakest link. The one who wouldn't survive an attack should those men return.

The one holding him back.

No, a part of her growled. *We aren't weak. We held our own once. We can do it again.*

But whatever happened in the field that day with the intruders seemed to have been a fluke. She hadn't felt that same impulse around Micha. Not even McGoven. The only animalistic tendencies she'd shown so far today had been an uncanny ability to wallow in the mud.

But she was the outlier. Naomi apparently had already mastered whatever task Bill had given her, sans the dirt bath. Both figures stood on the back porch, watching them approach.

"We'll stop for today," Bill called as Loren mounted the porch steps after Micha. "Sonia made lunch. We can eat and then figure out the rooming situation for the next few days."

Apparently, he wasn't a fan of everyone sleeping on the floor of his living room.

When he entered the kitchen, Loren expected him to pull her aside and explain what went wrong. How to improve her instincts. Something.

Instead, he vanished, ceding the spotlight to Sonia, who greeted them with a mass of hot food waiting on the center island.

While Micha and Naomi didn't show their exhaustion as much, they ate ravenously. Even the normally chatty Micha was too busy shoving food into his mouth to spark any conversation. Between the three of them, they wolfed down their first helpings and were already onto seconds. With a nervous laugh, Sonia remarked that she would have to scrounge up something for Bill.

A pang of guilt struck Loren at the thought of him going without, though food seemed to be the furthest thing from his mind. Like a shadow, he appeared in the doorway to the living room, his arms crossed, his gaze thoughtful. He was sizing them up again, reassessing whatever judgment he had made earlier that morning. Micha and Naomi had apparently passed their tests.

But her… His gaze lingered in her direction, and she fidgeted beneath the scrutiny.

"Well then." Sonia seemed to pick up on the tension and seized the moment to change the subject. Despite spending the night in her car, she looked bright-eyed and well rested. Sometime during the day, she'd dressed in a blue sweater and jeans and smoothed her hair into a ponytail.

"We've tried to figure out a sleeping arrangement for the next few days," she went on. "The house is pretty small, but, Micha, there is a cot around here somewhere. You can take the living room."

"Cool!" he exclaimed around a mouthful of pasta.

"Loren, you can take the room upstairs, along with Naomi, should you decide to stay here."

Loren instantly felt her appetite wane. Not only at the thought of sharing a room with the prickly blond, but because of what that arrangement meant without stating it outright. Someone else wouldn't sleep beside her.

Her gaze was drawn to him, but he was no longer looking her way.

"I'll mostly keep watch," he explained grimly, "and find sleep when and where I can."

"So, is no one going to say it?" Naomi blurted. "Why we're all risking our lives like this is some war or something. We still have no idea what will happen when this is all over. Do you expect us to just do whatever you say without question?"

"I will," Micha declared before taking a bite of bread.

Naomi shot him a quizzical look before she squared her chin. "The point is I don't know anything about what's going on. I have school. A life. My friends."

"You agreed to come here," Bill pointed out. "But you're right. All you need to know is that you'll get your answers when you can better understand them. We'll stop for tonight. Tomorrow we'll pick up again. Micha, you should work on your stamina. Naomi, you need to hone your instincts."

Loren noted that he avoided her altogether as he headed for the door.

"I'm going to patrol—"

"Again?" Loren croaked. It was her turn to cause an outburst. "You haven't even slept."

And they hadn't talked the way he promised they would. *Three days.* She clung to that deadline like a mantra but still. She couldn't ignore the feeling that he was putting off being alone with her at all. Longer than to dish out his orders anyway.

"I'll be back tonight," he grumbled. By then, he was already bounding onto the front porch, taking off toward the west fields.

"Let's get everyone settled in," Sonia said cheerfully.

"And where do you fit into all of this?" Naomi demanded. Loren didn't know whether to be annoyed or relieved that someone else seemed just as disgruntled with this situation as she felt.

"I'm an old friend." Sonia's beaming smile never wavered. "I won't be here for much longer. Just visiting. But that doesn't mean that I can't tell you some things Bill hasn't." Suddenly, her blue eyes took on a serious gleam. "He probably glossed over it, but what he's done for you—all of you—has basically ruined any chance he has of ever returning to our pack. His pack. I know it doesn't make sense to all of you, but trusting him is the only course of action available."

Naomi scoffed. "What does that even mean?"

"It means we're a pack now," Micha declared. "Even if it's not for long. We need to have each other's backs and watch out for Bill."

"Exactly," Sonia agreed. "The time for doubt is over. Bill may not have admitted this outright, but I will—if he loses this challenge, Lukka won't let him go unscathed."

"What do you mean?" Loren asked, though a part of her already suspected the answer before Sonia voiced it.

"It means that if he fails, Lukka will decide his punishment. What that means, I can't say. Nothing good, I'm sure." That bothered her. Her blue eyes shone with a frantic desperation she couldn't disguise. Suddenly, she turned to Micha. "Can I speak to you for a moment?"

He shrugged. "Sure."

Sonia led him outside, out to the barn, and Loren could only watch from the window while Naomi grumbled beside her.

"She moves fast," Naomi said disapprovingly. "Looks like she wants all the men wrapped around her finger."

Loren didn't waste her breath replying. For what it was worth, Sonia and Micha's conservation didn't seem romantic in the slightest.

He looked tense, and Sonia…

She looked devastated.

12

Sonia's warning cast a grim pall over the rest of the evening. In a strained silence, Loren and Naomi showered and occupied the living room, while Micha prowled the kitchen for leftovers before eventually taking up vigil by the window, watching them both.

"I have to admit," he said once the sky darkened, and they turned on the lamps throughout the house. "This is the strangest pack I've ever been a part of. To be fair, I was born into the first one, and not really a member of the second. Still. This is really freaking weird."

Naomi looked up from the screen of her cell phone—the only fixture of the room she'd paid any attention to for the past few hours. "What is that supposed to mean?"

Micha shrugged. "My pack… My *dad's* pack was really old-fashioned. We did things by the book. Rogues weren't tied to the pack like they are here. They're driven out. As far away as possible." His grimace revealed that he had experienced that personally. "If I ever wanted to go back, I'd have to do what he's doing—" he jerked his chin toward the woods where McGoven prowled. "And make a challenge. To do that, you need to face the leader out in the open and get a witness to vouch for you. Someone who will oversee the fight, so to speak. It's a tall ask of anyone."

Naomi set her phone aside. Grudging interest flitted across her gaze before her lips pressed into a thin line. "If your dad was the leader or whatever, why didn't you take over?"

Micha winced. "I was too young. When the Alpha dies without naming an heir, the law dictates that those eligible fight for the right to lead. Otherwise, you grovel for acceptance or get driven out."

Loren recognized the tale. He'd told her this story before.

"You have a sister," she added, remembering as much.

He nodded. "Violet. I think she wanted to challenge Levi, but she wasn't strong enough. She stayed as close to the territory as she could. The last time I talked to her was maybe a year ago. It's hard communicating on the outside from this distance. When you're driven out, you aren't given money or a place to live. You have to make a living on your own any way you can. I came here because I'd heard rumors that Black Mountain was open to outsiders."

"So what about him? McGoven—" Naomi seemed to whisper the name as if fearful he'd overhear. "He has a house. A job. Whatever he is, it doesn't seem like he's had it as rough as you have."

"No." Micha shook his head sadly. "I'd say he's probably had it worse. I was never the strongest or the fastest, even around packmates my own age. But him? McGoven was poised to take over when the old Black Mountain Alpha died. Even though Lukka was his son and all."

"What happened?" Loren asked, hoping he'd reveal more details than the last time he recounted this story.

Micha cast a wary glance toward the window. Then he shifted to face them. "I wasn't around then. I only heard rumors. They say Bill was a born Alpha. He had more promise than most, and even Lukka couldn't hold a candle to him. Lukas, the old Alpha, named him as his successor outright—which meant that when he died, there should have been no battle for supremacy. The pack should have been Bill's to lead with no dissent."

"But," Naomi prompted. "What? Was he too bossy even for a bunch of wolves?"

"No," Micha said. "I heard that after Lukas died, before Bill was accepted as Alpha, there was a breach on the territory's perimeter. Hunters." He shuddered as if the term referred to unspeakable horror. "They aren't common, but they roam the territories sometimes, and they don't care who they kill to make a point. I heard that they even kidnap people like us and torture them and run experiments."

"Great," Naomi said tightly. "Just great. I went from worrying about graduation, to worrying about creepy werewolf hunters. I'm sorry, *lycan*."

Loren felt her eyes narrow. Bill must have educated her on his preference of the latter term.

"Well, to be fair, I've never seen any," Micha admitted. "But in the attack that day, several people died. One of them was Bill's own mate. After that, I guess Lukka accused Bill of not heeding a warning and allowing the attack to happen out of fear. That gave him the premise to challenge him for the position of Alpha."

Naomi scoffed. "And Bill lost?"

No, a part of Loren growled even before Micha replied.

"No. That's the thing. He didn't contest it. He just declared himself a rogue and left. Whatever happened, he must have felt guilty enough to pledge himself to Lukka and remain on the outskirts. Around here, they use rogues to watch the wilder ones who can't be trusted among human society unsupervised."

Like Fred Connors, apparently.

"McGoven's been out here for years. He never even tried to reinstate himself or return to Black Mountain. And if he truly means to challenge Lukka, well, that's a big fucking deal. Pardon the language."

"Why?" Naomi demanded, though Loren was just as curious.

"If he wins, he can take over the pack. To go from a rogue to an Alpha… That's almost unheard of. He'd be welcomed back with open arms—if he could prove his standing fair and square, that is. Or he could earn the right to leave for good."

"And then what happens to the rest of us?" Naomi snapped, crossing her arms. "We just get left behind or dragged behind him like baggage? Some of us didn't sign up to howl at the moon for the rest of our lives. I need space."

She stormed from the room while Micha stared after her sheepishly. "I forgot that you two aren't exactly used to this," he said.

Loren didn't know what to say. In the end, she just shrugged. "We'll get used to it."

According to McGoven, they would have no choice. Sooner or later, danger would come for him again, and if they couldn't keep up…

You'll be killed, that inner voice said gruffly.

Micha seemed to pick up on the mood and said nothing else. Eventually, Loren spied him nodding off in the armchair by the window. While Naomi didn't return, she could sense her stewing somewhere close by. Was that by choice? Or because she didn't have permission to leave…

The thought made Loren's head ache. There were too many topics demanding her focus. Rather than face them, she put on her boots and retreated to the one place that remained her refuge despite all the upheaval in her life recently.

The horses nickered warmly as she slipped inside the barn. If she wasn't mistaken, she could sense that they missed her.

Then she remembered how Bill had characterized their reactions to him—they saw him as a predator. With multiple creatures on the property who smelled the way he did, who knew how stressed they'd been?

Like always, they didn't react negatively as she approached. She had felt a stubborn pride at that fact before. But now? It bothered her. If she didn't smell like the others, did that mean she wasn't like them either? Lycan, perhaps, but different somehow. Broken. Corrupted.

That's why he's been avoiding you, that voice whispered, louder, more persistent. *You disgust him. You aren't good enough.*

It could have been paranoia…if it weren't for the many instances of his behavior that seemed to bolster the fear. He seemed pained every time he touched her. Their kiss or any similar embrace had been followed by abject horror after. There was no way around it—he seemed to be fighting something within himself whenever she was around.

And he's been lying to us, that voice hissed. Maybe not outright, but despite all his explanations of the lycan way of life, she couldn't escape the sense that he was avoiding something. Whatever it was itched at the boundaries of their every interaction, but he deliberately ignored any mention of it.

Why?

Was it something about her true nature?

Did he know why she was so…broken?

The thought consumed her. She couldn't even bring herself to return to the house and pretend that nothing was wrong. Instead, she sought out a corner of the barn and curled up on a bale of hay. Out here, she would know when McGoven returned, and she could confront him in private, away from the others. Maybe if she asked him outright, he'd tell her whatever it was he was holding back?

It was the only tempting course of action.

Resigned, she waited, letting her eyes drift shut as the gentle murmurs of the horses lulled her into a fragile sleep. She wasn't sure how much time passed when a sound finally broke the quiet, startling her awake. Blinking, she stared through the darkness, trying to get her bearings—someone had turned out the lights in the barn without realizing she was inside.

That same someone sighed heavily, his pure exhaustion, so palpable Loren swayed, dizzy with the feeling. Apparently, his intention to nap had fallen by the wayside—he'd been out for hours. Securing the barn must have been his final act before retiring for the night.

Yet, here she was, waiting to pounce like a stalker.

Guilt and dread weighed her down as she mulled over how to make herself known without startling him. That was the strange part—he hadn't noticed her yet—he was *that* exhausted. Creeping to her feet, she prepared to approach the door to the barn when she stopped short as a light, feminine aroma reached her nostrils.

He wasn't alone.

"It's about time you came back," Sonia said disapprovingly. "I was worried sick that you'd pass out in the fields somewhere. You should be conserving your strength, you do realize?"

"You didn't have to wait up for me," McGoven replied gruffly.

"Don't look so surprised. Besides, I was already in my car. I'll have to leave soon, but I wanted to say goodbye first."

Loren clenched her teeth against another wave of irrational anger. She almost couldn't stop herself from barging through the doors. Then she heard Bill sigh, and her irritation instantly diminished.

"I'm sorry. I didn't intend to be gone this long, but I can sense it," he said. "Something's off. The Eislanders should have returned by now. The fact that they haven't doesn't bode well. Fuck, this is bad—"

"How do you mean?" Sonia's alarm matched Loren's.

"I thought about what you said, and you're right. It's time I approach them directly. Loreck, anyway. The only problem is…"

"You can't go near their territory without causing even more trouble," Sonia surmised. "I know you won't like it, but you could ask Lukka to vouch for you—"

"Bullshit. You don't think Loreck would go after one of Lukka's own rogues without his blessing? The men he sent here said something about one man I killed. A member of their pack—but he mentioned only one. Claimed he was innocent."

"I'll see what I can find out," Sonia said. "In fact, there's something else I wanted to talk to you about. I wasn't sure how to address it, but I'll just come out and say it. Remember when you asked me to look into Loren's mother?"

Loren held her breath. Did it bother her that he'd asked Sonia to delve into something so personal? Yes.

"You did? What did you find?" McGoven demanded.

His curiosity matched the desperate impulse Loren felt lance through her heart. She held her breath, paralyzed by anticipation.

"Nothing," Sonia said. "That's the thing. There was never any woman, lycan or otherwise, by the name of Eveline Connors on Black Mountain. Not only that, but all records indicate that Fred Connors was unmarried when he left the territory, and he never took the equivalent of a mate. I even talked to some of the men who were around back then. They said he was a recluse. Kept to himself and rarely got along with anyone else."

"That doesn't make any sense," McGoven replied. "He was listed on Loren's birth certificate. I saw it myself."

"I don't know," Sonia agreed. "He was exiled only a few years before you were. Maybe six, seven years ago? I dug into the reasoning, and it seems he lost control, strayed off territory, and attacked a human. They weren't seriously injured, but given his nature as a made, he was harshly punished."

"I'd heard that," McGoven admitted.

Loren frowned. She didn't know that tidbit of her so-called father's history.

"Things from that time are hazy at best," Sonia went on. "We were young, but I remember a little of it. The murders that went on in that human town nearby? You remember? I was five, I think. So you had to be eight or nine—"

"That was nearly twenty years ago, Sonia," McGoven grumbled. "But yeah, I remember."

"Fred Connors was made during that time. One of the victims. That just makes everything that happened with that poor girl far creepier."

"Yeah, but Loren's eighteen, almost nineteen. She was born long before the bastard was exiled, but after he would have been turned."

"It's quite the mystery," Sonia admitted. "But that isn't all. I never realized it until now, but given that Fred Connors was turned so long ago. Bill, that means that the Alpha who welcomed him into the pack was—"

"Lukas," Bill said tightly. Loren vaguely recognized the name. Micha had mentioned it. *Lukas, the old Alpha.*

"Yes," Sonia said softly. "If the man did father a daughter in that time, the Alpha would have known. There is no way he wouldn't have. I've tried to probe Lukka for what I can, but he hasn't exactly been welcoming of me as of late."

"I'm sorry, Sonia," he said. "I've gotten you into this mess. I didn't even stop to think how hard this must be for you."

"Don't apologize. If I didn't want to be here, I wouldn't be. But… I want you to think about what I said. Not because of me, or Loren, or anyone else. I want you to think about your future. What do *you* want? If it's to be on the outside for the rest of your life, fine. I won't like it, but it will be your choice. But if that *isn't* what you want… If you've been living this way out of some misplaced sense of punishment—"

"It's late," Bill said. "You should head back if you want to get there in time to put your plan into action."

"Don't sound so skeptical. You were always destined for more than life as a wayward rogue, and you know that. If it takes committing treason to prove it to you, well… I'll just have to do that, won't I?"

"Call me as soon as you get back, or when you have any updates," Bill said. "I mean it, or I'll go there myself to check on you. Promise me."

Sonia sighed. "I promise to call as soon as I can. But you make me a promise in return, huh? Talk to Loren. Tell her the truth. Can you do that?"

Loren heard the thud of a heavy set of footsteps. "Goodnight, Sonia."

Sonia's voice was barely audible. "Goodnight."

Loren sensed rather than saw her retreat. The same way she knew that Bill lingered behind. At first, she suspected that he'd caught her lurking in the shadows, but as the seconds ticked by, she realized that he might have been savoring the quiet.

Whatever was happening was taking a toll on him. He disguised it well while around Micha and Naomi but seemingly alone, he groaned, and Loren could picture him leaning against the barn door as the weight of the world bore down on his shoulders.

A part of her was tempted to lurk and savor his nearness. At the same time, something about it felt voyeuristic. Wrong.

Clearing her throat, she stood and crept toward the barn's entrance.

"Loren?"

He was there to meet her in the doorway. Even in the darkness, she could see how tightly his jaw was clenched. For perhaps the first time ever, she had caught him off guard.

"What are you doing out here?" Whatever he saw in her expression made him sigh. "Apparently, you've been here long enough to overhear that, huh?"

"You didn't tell me." She didn't mean to sound so accusatory. "About my dad—Fred Connors. I mean... You don't have to. I can understand. I just don't want to be in the dark, please."

His upper lip twitched in a way that might have betrayed guilt. She couldn't tell. Abruptly, he marched toward the paddocks, and a sharp tilt of his head was her only clue to follow.

He moved to where a lone lightbulb affixed to the side of the barn cast a puddle of illumination. There he faced her, an eyebrow raised.

His nostrils flared, sensing the air. At first, she wondered if he had picked up the scent of one of the intruders. He didn't stiffen in alarm, though. Slowly, his eyes widened as if he'd come to some startling revelation.

"I never noticed until now," he said softly. "I can pick up your scent from miles away. But here? I can't smell you at all among the horses."

She resisted the urge to sniff herself, unsure if his observation was a compliment or an insult. Yet another example as to how she was different, perhaps?

The longer he watched her, another puzzling detail seemed to creep to the forefront of his mind. "I'm sure you heard what Sonia said. About your mother?"

She nodded, suddenly overwhelmed by grief she didn't expect. It hurt. Not knowing more about the woman who gave birth to her. All she had left were a few scattered memories, none of them clear enough to cherish.

"What does that mean?" she asked.

He crossed his arms and eyed the sky. "I don't know. It just deepens the mystery surrounding you. I swung by the station earlier and dug up your file. I kept a printout. It's in the truck. We can look through it together, if you want. When you're ready."

Loren nodded, though she wasn't sure if she was ready at all. Not now, at least. Her heart pounded the same way it had when she stood at the threshold of her father's house. There was something lurking in her past she wasn't ready to face.

Though why was that? He had something to do with it. She could feel it. When she looked up at him, she swore he tensed, as if he knew the question that might leave her mouth next.

"I… I feel like you've been avoiding me."

Again, she didn't mean to sound so pathetic.

Bill, however, didn't shy from the accusation. "You're young," he said firmly. "You're scared. I don't want to overwhelm you. I know it seems like I'm being evasive. I'm being cautious."

Loren noted the subtle wrinkles etched into the skin around his mouth. They alone hinted that he was far older than she was. Just how old? She sensed that even if she asked, he would never tell her, using the information as a wedge to force even more distance between them.

And suddenly, she felt that irrational anger again. It wasn't his choice to make.

"I'm eighteen."

His eyes flickered, sensing the challenge conveyed in that statement. "You're young," he repeated. *Don't question me.*

The air between them shifted as a subtle dynamic came into play. Loren imagined it was something similar to a set of scales, swaying from one side to the other with the slightest provocation. They were weighted in his favor now.

But…

"You kissed me."

Just like that, the balance shifted, and she was on dangerous ground. Picking a fight with him was a battle she would never win. And yet, at the same time, a part of her insisted that she had to fight. Challenge him. Provoke.

It was the only way to make him listen. *No one controls me.*

"A mistake." The heat in his voice startled her. He meant it. Kissing her was a mistake.

Stung, she moved to run, but his hand latched onto her wrist before she could take a step.

"Wait—" The word seemed ripped from his chest. Against his will. He wanted to release her. But something deep within wouldn't let him. Wouldn't let her go.

She turned to face him, caught off guard by his expression. Pained was the only word for it. Her very presence was a knife stabbing through his chest. An agony he couldn't evade.

He *had* been avoiding her. It was all he could do to restrain himself…

Until he couldn't. One hard tug yanked her closer. Their lips met, and it was lightning. Shocking. Punishing. Even as he broke the kiss in the next breath and backed away.

"I don't want to fight with you, and you don't want to fight with me." His voice broke, reducing the threat to an outright plea. *Don't make me put you in your place.* "You should go back. Get some sleep—"

"Is this a lycan thing?" Loren's chest heaved with the effort it took to breathe. "That I can feel your emotions. That I feel… Is this what it's like with everyone?"

"No." He looked pained again. "Your emotions are out of control. I can't imagine how confusing this is for you, but I need you to trust me—"

"Why? You're lying to me!" Where did that come from? She didn't know, but she felt it. The same way she could feel her pulse surging like mad through her veins. "There's something you aren't saying. I know it."

"You're right," he admitted. "You promised me three days, remember? Give me two more."

Her head swam as that impulse rose up, demanding she resist. Argue. He owed her respect, not coddling. She wasn't a child.

"I am not a child."

His eyes flashed. "You think I don't know that?"

Snap. She could almost hear one bastion of his self-control breaking. Another cracked as he shifted his weight to the balls of his feet.

"You have no fucking clue how hard this has been for me." Suddenly, he whirled on his heel, closing the distance between them in a heartbeat. "No clue. I can smell you every second. Your thoughts. They're driving me fucking insane."

"I can feel it," Loren admitted in a whisper. More than that. She could feel his anger then and there. All of it. His frustration. Pain. Confusion. Desire—

Wait. That emotion was the most foreign of the tangled mass, taking more effort to decipher. It was something she rarely felt for herself. The closest comparison she could make was when she desperately needed a new pair of shoes. She'd risk a beating just to get them. The thought of going without was…unthinkable.

And he felt that. Every waking minute, the feeling seemed to grow, transforming from mere desire into… Hunger. Craving. Desperation.

Then, all of a sudden, she felt nothing as if the tenuous, invisible link to him had been closed off.

"Go to bed." He stormed off, marching toward the forest. To hide, she realized. To run away and avoid her for another night. More hours. At least until he could get rid of her. Break ties. Cut her loose.

"No." The voice didn't even sound like her, but her ears rang with it. Her throat ached, her lips parted.

And he stopped short. She could count every ragged breath he drew in. Each one was a hallmark of how fiercely he grappled to regain control. He didn't want to shout. Argue.

He couldn't help himself. "Loren, I told you to—"

"You said it yourself," she stammered over him. It was like she was possessed. This wasn't just her saying this, but that inner voice finally making itself heard outside the confines of her mind. "You aren't my Alpha. You aren't my guardian. You didn't even want me here. So, what are you to me? Because you certainly aren't in charge."

Something dangerous flitted across his gaze, gone in an instant. Her breath stuttered regardless. If she had been on thin ice before, it just shattered, plunging her into a place from which there was no turning back.

"Who am I?" He advanced slowly, but the contrast in his posture—even the way he breathed—made her pulse race. She took a step back. Then another, retreating inside the barn, driven by an instinctive warning to run. Or fight.

At the thought, her feet stopped, bracing against the concrete flooring just as he reached the doorway.

She took a step, and he ruthlessly followed, matching her movement for movement. Only this time, when she retreated toward a corner of the barn, far from the horses' stalls, fear wasn't driving her. Just anticipation.

An electric foreboding so thick she couldn't stand it. The only cure was him. His heat as he lumbered closer, towering above her, blocking her in with sheer bulk. His breath fanned her throat as his hands palmed the wall on either side of her hips. But not close enough. He needed to touch her.

"Please," she croaked. What exactly she was begging him for? She didn't know.

But he did. His teeth gritted, a curse grated between them. "Fuck."

The muscles in his arms twitched with the effort he exerted to fight whatever impulse he felt. Until he couldn't. His fingers found her waist, feathering together over her lower back.

Loren's mind went blank. Nothing in the world could describe the feeling—none of their previous embraces came close. This wasn't a volatile reaction out of impulse. This was deliberate on his part, his way of answering her via the only method that mattered.

Touch.

Who are you? she'd demanded. The possessive brush of his calloused fingertips, easing beneath the hem of her shirt, satisfied that question more definitively than words ever could.

I belong to you. You belong to me. Don't question it—don't even fight it. Just trust me. Accept me. I know you. I need you.

That reassurance alone might have been enough for the scared little girl from over a week ago. But now? She needed more.

Unbidden, she reached up, lacing her fingers through his hair. It was wrong. She didn't know him.

That didn't matter. She continued to explore him, and the second her fingers made contact with the planes of his jaw, all doubt left her mind. *Yes,* a voice within her exclaimed, though it didn't feel entirely hers. *This is right.*

More than right. Vital. Only breathing felt more natural.

Yet, he still hesitated, his arms tensing. "I can't—"

"Please."

His mouth was on hers again before she knew it, prying her lips apart for his tongue to probe deep. This was different. He didn't test or goad her into fighting back. She relented to him, inching closer, inhaling as much of him as she could.

But it wasn't enough.

She needed more. Everywhere. She needed… Ownership. The greedy way he started to touch her next. His fingers curled around the waistband of her pants, grazing the flesh beneath, but fear didn't even enter her mind. She arched her hips to assist him, eager to get closer. Feel more.

Her eyelids fluttered as the roughness of his palm met the bare skin of her thigh, but the sound he made…

It ripped through her like a current, awakening nerves she never knew existed. Feelings came from nowhere and struck like lightning. She was only vaguely aware of his fingers inching higher along her thigh. Higher…

The first brush of his knuckles against the tender space between her legs made her head rear back against the wall so hard sparks exploded before her eyes. Almost instantly, his free hand was against her scalp, cradling the aching area— not that the pain was any match for the sensation of him.

A harsh voice, dripping into her ear, finally responded to her initial question. "You wanted to know who I am to you?"

Her heart panged—he'd never sounded like this before. This guttural. Primal.

"I am everything you'll ever need. Everything you could ever want. I am…"

There was a note in his voice some small, buried part of her didn't ignore.

He was *everything*.

Whether she wanted him to be or not.

$\mathcal{S}$*low Down.* Bill felt like a bystander, screaming helplessly as a tragedy unfolded before his eyes. There was no stopping it. He could only witness the inevitable—and, in this case, he was both watcher and perpetrator.

You fucking monster. The moniker haunted him as he mouthed the pulse in Loren's throat while his fingers breached a part of her he had no right to take. Guilt didn't diminish his awe one damn bit. He groaned instead, his heart lurching at the feel of her.

If only he could stop his body's reaction there. Rebelliously, his cock swelled, straining against the thin cotton of his sweatpants. There was no ignoring the pure, biological response she inspired so innocently. She was molten, her body broadcasting in every way it knew how that she was ready for him. Aching for him.

No. The thought belonged to the one bastion of control he had left—like a drowning man, Bill clung to it.

Drawing back, he sucked in air and tried to refocus. His hand withdrew from her thigh, his teeth clamping down over any impulse to kiss her.

"No—" Her nails lashed at his chest so hard she drew blood.

He saw red. The next second, he had her slung over a bale of hay. She was so much smaller, but her body concealed its strength like a jackknife. One minute she seemed weak and ineffective. And then, as though with the press of a button, she transformed. Grew claws. Lashed out.

Her eyes blazed at him, her chest heaving as she clawed at his forearms, dragging him back.

"You don't want this." He tried to reason with her.

Her reply came in between harsh pants. "You don't know what I want."

But he did. He could feel her desire in every pore of his being. The tumult of emotions emanating from her felt poisonous in their intensity. Confusion. Desire. Greed. Lust. She wanted him so badly her entire body throbbed with the need.

He could smell it. Taste her arousal in the air. The scent had him crouching, nostrils flaring as he sought out the source. Something hampered him. Her pants—so he ripped them off, baring her legs to him as well as a pair of pink panties.

The thin strip of fabric irritated him. He needed to see her. Every inch. Take stock of her body in full. Like the pale, creamy skin of her inner thighs, marred with scrapes and bruises that drew a growl from his throat. There were other marks. Ones she'd wanted to hide from him. On her lower back. Her wrists. Her stomach.

Years of abuse and neglect scarred her like words on the pages of a book. Inspecting them made his heart ache. She was so strong. So frail.

But, as far as he was concerned, no one would ever hurt her again. Ever. He cemented the promise by nipping at the nape of her neck in an act only the most primal part of her would recognize as both a marking and a warning.

She was his…

But they weren't alone.

Noises scratched at the periphery of his consciousness. Shrieks. Cries. The horses? And something else. Voices, growing in intensity.

"…going on in there? I don't know… Going to see…"

"Fuck!" His common sense returned, allowing him to pick up two pairs of footsteps rushing in their direction. Probably because the horses were going haywire. The black one kicked at its stall while the two mares issued blood-chilling cries. He had no idea how he hadn't heard them until now.

"Shit." He lurched to his feet, scrambling to snatch an item of clothing from the floor. Her pants. Only they were torn.

He looked down to meet her gaze and went cold. The lust that consumed them both had faded. Now, Loren watched him horrified, and the guilt hit him so brutally he staggered with the force of it.

"Fuck… I… I'll hold them off," he told her. "When we're gone, get to the house."

He didn't give her the chance to argue. Already, he'd stepped from the barn, surging to meet Micha and Naomi. Just paces from the door, he barred their path and prayed they couldn't sense Loren within.

"What's going on?" Micha asked, an eyebrow raised.

The horses were still agitated, their cries drowning out any other noise.

"I think they smelled a predator," Bill said. "We should all take to the perimeter to be on the safe side. You two head south. I'll go north."

Micha and Naomi shared a look.

"What about Loren?" the blond asked, displaying an uncharacteristic but genuine concern. "She isn't in the house—"

"She's out doing a bit of training on her own," Bill lied. "I'll find her and tell her to head back. Now go!"

They both took off in the direction he indicated. Already, he was impressed with their skill. For a new made, Naomi had a decent grasp of her instincts. He just hoped both were far out of range when he finally took off, clearing the way for Loren to exit the barn. Despite every cell in his body warning him not to, he circled back and watched her leave while keeping his distance.

The darkness shielded her well, but his enhanced eyesight still caught the pale, milky limbs, bared to the elements. The sight made his jaw ache, his erection unbearable. Invoking the shift was the only method of relief—and even then, just barely.

He ached to follow her and finish what they'd started. Soon. Before…

Before he could even think of breaking the bond. If he cemented their joining for good, it would be too late. There would be no undoing it.

Enough! Groaning, he shed his clothes and took off for the north field. It was a good idea to patrol anyway. With Micha and Naomi, he could cover more territory in half the time.

Already, he could sense them both on the other end of the property, moving parallel to his position. Within minutes, they cleared most of the land, presumably finding no hint of a predator who could have spooked the animals so badly.

Because there wasn't one, of course. As he ran, Bill struggled to compose a more convincing explanation. He could always blame the weather. A rodent. Something other than the truth.

Though Naomi and Micha, to an extent, may have been naïve, they weren't stupid. Sooner or later, they would sense the bond between their Alpha and his mate. Already, Micha seemed to recognize it. For all their sakes, he needed to address the reality. And soon.

Though, there was always the possibility that he would fail in his challenge to Lukka, and everything afterward would be a moot point. Perhaps death wasn't a bad thing in that case…

No. He shied away from seriously considering that possibility. Turning his focus to the feel of the earth beneath him, he ran faster, clearing the full perimeter and gaining on Micha and Naomi. They were moving slower than he would have expected. Had they decided to wait for him?

Suddenly, his hackles raised as he picked up a scent that didn't belong. Not here and not now.

Shit.

He bounded through the trees in the direction of it, alarmed to find that Micha and Naomi were in the same location.

And they were in danger—there was no mistaking the animalistic musk that grew thicker with every yard he gained. *Fuck.* So much for training.

His ragtag pack was about to be tested for the first time—
and he could only pray that this altercation went far
differently than the last.

14

Chilled to the bone, Loren tore into the house and latched onto the first piece of clothing she could find—a pair of sweatpants in Micha's prized pile of hand-me-downs. With a mental note to replace the garment later, she pulled them on and struggled to regain control of her breathing.

The house was empty, but the loneliness resonated more intensely than even the days in her father's house. This felt…

Intentional. She had no doubt in her mind that Micha and Naomi would return first, but McGoven would stay out as long as humanely—or lycanly?—possible, if only to prolong facing the inevitable.

They kissed. They did far more than that…

Once again, he'd made a mistake.

No. The voice was so loud it was as if someone was growling into her ear rather than inside her head. *Not a mistake. He owes us more. So much more.*

Her skull ached as the thoughts swarmed into a chanting drone. They were painful. Almost as if something were fighting to claw its way out of her very soul. The dichotomy between Loren Connors and the creature strengthening inside her had never been stronger. They were two entities grappling to exist in the same body.

Or, as McGoven put it while referring to his lycan form, two halves of the same coin. For the first time in her life, she could feel the difference in mindset. A change. Something animalistic lurked within her.

And it was angry.

As awkward as the strange emotions felt, she didn't want to be alone with them. Alone with herself. She almost cried with relief when she heard the sound of footsteps bounding up the front porch.

At random, she snatched more clothing from Micha's pile and headed for the foyer, averting her eyes to the ground.

"Here—" Even before she realized that the muddy boots of the figure on the porch were too big to belong to Micha or Naomi, she knew something was wrong. She could…smell it. A scent like sulfur wormed into her lungs, proclaiming alarm. *Stranger!*

Though not exactly. One look and her eyes widened. She knew this man, with a haunting brown gaze that glimmered in the glow of the porch lamp.

The man from the day Naomi had been attacked.

"I'm not here as an enemy," he said as she drew back. His voice was harsh, and yet… Something in her could parse out the grudging truth in it. He wasn't here as an enemy.

Not that it mattered one damn bit.

"Go away!" She stood firm, possessed with a strength she never knew she had. Or perhaps she just hadn't felt often enough to recognize it. Whatever it was, resembled the confidence that took over that day in the clearing. When she bellowed a word that seemed ripped from her very core.

Admittedly, this time, the feeling was different. When it came to this man, that inner voice was more cautious. *He's too strong,* it warned. She would have to fight.

Her gaze darted to the kitchen, where a drawer near the stove held knives. Not that she could make it that far.

Already, the man had taken a step forward, blocking the doorway with his sheer bulk. That smell intensified, and she coughed. It was cloying. Suffocating.

"We intended to meet your rogue until I saw that he left you alone. I apologize for the crude measures—" He gestured to his body. The plain jeans and dark shirt he wore appeared more formal than what he sported in the clearing, but she wasn't put at ease. If anything, his approach seemed…bold.

Dangerous.

"All I want to know is the name of your sire," he said, advancing another step. "You're heritage. Family line. Legacy?" Her confusion seemed to confound him even more. He raised an eyebrow and swept his gaze throughout the empty hallway behind her.

Run!

She pivoted into the kitchen, and lunged through the back door. She wasn't anywhere near fast enough.

She didn't have to be.

A monstrous sound rattled the house to the very foundation. A growl. Several. Loren barely made it onto the porch before a large, black shape bounded from the darkness in her direction. She knew, before she registered the graceful outline of a familiar wolf, that she wasn't in danger from him at least.

"I meant no harm," the intruder said. He warily advanced through the back door, his hands held in front of him.

An answering growl revealed what McGoven thought of that assertion. He remained crouched, feet from the porch, and though she didn't know exactly how, Loren was sure she could sense his intentions. Hear them inside her head.

Come to me. Now!

She descended the steps and crossed the distance. Instantly, Bill moved to stand in front of her while two fellow wolves that she assumed were Naomi and Micha closed in on either side of her.

But there was another wolf, lurking just off in the shadows. Only a pair of glowing, yellow eyes revealed their position —but an overwhelming hostility came from that direction. They didn't belong here either.

"We aren't here on official business," the intruder in human form said, taking responsibility for the presence of the other wolf. "We merely wanted to talk. A parley of sorts. Between the rogue and me. No one else. This changes nothing regarding the justice you have yet to face, however. We merely want to discuss the topic at hand. Nothing more."

Silence hung for several seconds as both figures eyed each other, saying nothing. Despite the lack of words, Loren suspected that plenty of unspoken sentiments were being traded between them, too quickly to track. She couldn't tell which way the pendulum swung. Then, in a beautiful and violent shift of muscle, the black wolf seemed to distort and Bill McGoven appeared in its place, rising to his feet, starkly naked.

"You have some damn nerve coming here," he said, his voice bellowing. "You sneak onto my property. Attempt an ambush. Took efforts to cloak yourself in what? Deer piss? That isn't a very friendly gesture."

The intruder squared his jaw. "I wanted answers. I thought your mate would have them—"

He turned his gaze to her, and Loren flinched. *Mate.* That word had been uttered more than once—and each time, it seemed to hold more importance than a term of acquaintance. Way more importance.

"You wanted to talk. Then talk," Bill growled, sounding equally as ferocious as he had while in animal form. "Now."

"In private," the man specified. "I think it would be better for all involved if we did. My man will stand guard, as will your people. If I am to believe that you didn't attack Jamal in cold blood, those rules should be simple to abide by."

McGoven cocked his head, his posture unreadable. "And then you'll walk away without attacking another human on my property?"

The man laughed. "We will walk away. Tonight. I guess your Alpha didn't inform you as to the terms of our truce. Though, it looks like his liaison has left empty-handed."

Loren struggled to keep up with the conversation. Liaison. Sonia?

"Time is running out for you to do the right thing, rogue," the man added without explaining the reference.

Bill remained tense. For a second, Loren was sure he would transform again and go for the man's throat.

"Micha, Naomi, stay with Loren," he barked out eventually. "As for you—" he raised his voice so the other two figures could hear him clearly. "You want to talk? We do so out in the open. Afterward, you leave. Understood?"

The man descended the porch steps. "Lead the way."

Loren couldn't ignore a sense of aggravation as the two men headed for the west fields. Their conversation would involve her. She knew it. And yet they seemed more than content to leave her out of it as if she didn't matter. Had no say. No voice—

Something nudged her side, shocking her from the thought. The culprit felt cool against her hand. Wet—the snout of a large brown wolf, she realized. Its eyes glowed an electric green as they met hers with unmistakable energy only Micha could exude. *Don't worry,* he seemed to say. Then he nudged her again and inclined his head toward the house.

Her curiosity aside, Loren didn't need to be told twice.

The second they entered the back door, she moved to barricade and lock the front and close all the windows on the first level. The barriers wouldn't do much if the large wolf still lurking outside decided to attack, but it was something.

Because, if things did go south, she couldn't shift. She couldn't run. She couldn't even smell the danger until it was literally under her nose.

The pity party helped distract from her concern for McGoven—though not for long.

When she finally had the sense of mind to get her bearings, she noticed Naomi in the corner of the foyer, quietly scrambling into a set of clothes. Micha remained in the kitchen, and the confines of the relatively spacious room helped to illustrate just how massive he truly was while in lycan form. There was barely enough space for him to comfortably crouch between the center island and the wall.

"Are you okay?" she croaked. He couldn't be comfortable.

Comically, he snorted and shot her a glance that seemed to say, *I'll keep watch.*

Until what, exactly? An invisible pressure ratcheted up with every passing second, and she suddenly had an idea of exactly what Bill had been afraid of. Another confrontation with these men.

Another fight in which she was a liability.

Even if all went well and the intruders did leave tonight, it was only a matter of time before they returned.

And no matter how many days Bill had them running in the fields, they would never be a match.

She would never be able to hold her own.

And he would have no choice but to fight for her.

"*I*nformation wasn't the only reason I came out here, rogue. I wanted to see it for myself," Loreck Eislander's man called as Bill led the way from the house. "The bond between you and that girl. Your sick, twisted imitation of it."

Bill clenched his jaw so tightly he was surprised bones didn't crack. Respect wasn't his motivation but tact. Staying silent was his best bet. Indulging the bastard would do more harm than good in the long run. Still, he felt the urge to reply. "See what?"

"If our worst fears were true and you really are beyond help."

Bill scoffed. "And the verdict?"

The man didn't answer, not that Bill was particularly keen to hear one. Instead, he focused on testing the air, hunting for any sign of another player who might have ventured out to attend this little party. So far, beyond the two trespassers, he couldn't catch a trace of anyone else.

That meant nothing considering the man closest to him had cloaked himself in deer piss just to go unnoticed. It was an old trick. Something Loren had unintentionally taken advantage of by lurking within the barn. Similarly, the animals' scents had cloaked hers, obscuring her unique aroma.

Trick or not, he would need to learn how to combat the effect. Right after he dealt with the welcome wagon.

Walking in front of the bastard was a risk, but one he was more than willing to take. It meant he didn't have to school his expression, and for a few brief seconds, his true emotions could break through.

Fuck. This was bad. Sonia was gone, and with her went the slim chance of settling this diplomatically. Otherwise, he didn't have a real game plan should this visit turn out hostile.

The only course of action was to go on offense. "Well, you came here to talk," Bill began, turning to face the man directly. "So, talk."

He had to admit that he didn't resemble the bastards who attacked Loren. He was cleaner, for one. He didn't reek of booze or illicit substances. Just earth and the traces of his home pack beneath the piss.

Unexpected jealousy stabbed at him. He didn't miss life on Black Mountain—he couldn't. But there was something in the man's confidence he envied.

"The girl—"

Bill couldn't help the part of him that lurched at the unsaid insult. The man had deliberately avoided using the term "your mate."

"Who is her sire? I'm sure you learned that much, even if you did take her against her will."

"And why do you care?" Bill countered. "I don't remember you asking about her family tree when you tried to kill her. Neither did the *men* who attacked her on your land. I don't think you or your Alpha truly give a damn. What do you really want?"

He expected another threat. The man's raised eyebrow caught him off guard.

"Is that your way of saying you don't know?" Rather than hostile, the man sounded…concerned. "Your Alpha seemed to think her father was a previous rogue known to the area, but I made some inquiries. The man wasn't a born lycan. Either your Alpha wasn't aware of that fact—" the man scoffed, revealing that he didn't buy that belief. "Or he doesn't know her true heritage. He didn't seem too concerned to find out, either."

Bill frowned, curious despite himself. Was that disgust in the man's voice? "That doesn't answer my question," he countered. "Why are you here?"

"Frankly, this conversation isn't for your benefit, rogue. I came here as a courtesy but don't think for a second that anything you've done has been condoned by anyone in my pack. Your crimes are too numerous to list. If you want even a shred of mercy, you will relinquish the girl to me now."

Bill curled his hands into fists, hearing each knuckle crack. "And with that, I'm afraid you've worn out your welcome. As for my crimes? Humor me. What proof do you have?"

Besides four dead bodies, of course. Though again, Bill got the sense he was only seeing a small fraction of the actual picture here. *Jamal.* In his previous tirade, the man had only mentioned one murdered lycan he was supposedly responsible for. He doubted that kind of oversight was by accident.

"Evidence?" With a cold laugh, the man raised his hand. "A knife with your blood on it, drawn by the man you killed. That man's body, slain by a cowardly act. And your scent on our territory, far from your assigned post, rogue. Then we can touch on the fact that you took an unwilling, innocent female as your mate. You didn't try to have her integrated into a pack… Some might say that on the surface, your actions could be interpreted as an underhanded way to subvert your status in a desperate bid to regain power."

"It seems you've gotten everything you need from Lukka," Bill spat, shifting his stance in case of an attack. "So why come here? Unless…"

A sudden suspicion replaced some of his anger with pure confusion.

"Unless you don't believe him."

The man disguised his reaction to that statement well. Only a furtive glance toward the house gave him away. He was curious about Loren. Too curious for his own good.

"I'm assuming your Alpha doesn't know of this little visit?" he guessed.

The man's cold stare proved it. He had to be high ranking to speak with such authority. Perhaps even as powerful as Eislander's beta. Someone with that much to lose wouldn't make the trek out here on a whim.

Against his better judgment, Bill put off retreating a few seconds longer.

"The girl. Do you recognize her? Could she be a descendant of one of your men?"

Though, even as the words left his mouth, Bill doubted them.

The man's scoff proved he was thinking along the same lines. "We don't lose track of our females, and we certainly wouldn't let a full-blooded pup grow up on the outside." A growl edged his words. He wasn't lying. But…

Bill decided to take a chance and reveal what little he did know. "You were right. Fred Connors was a made from Black Mountain, and he's the one listed on her birth certificate. I thought her mother might have been a human, but there is no record of her ever living in our territory. Not even on the outskirts. Connors was only exiled seven years ago and turned over a decade before that. If he had sired a child, the woman couldn't have lived far away. We didn't allow outsiders unfettered access back then, and Connors wasn't high ranking enough to have traveled outside the territory unaccompanied. Though…"

Bill hadn't made the connection before, but something Sonia dredged up came back to him.

"Connors was supposedly attacked by a rogue who rampaged in your area twenty years ago. From what I know, the Eislanders dealt with that situation. Did you know the lycan responsible?"

He was rambling, but he couldn't help it. When said out loud, the mystery of Loren Connors was more perplexing than ever. It was as if the girl had come out of nowhere. In fact, that would make more sense than where the facts seemed to lead—in circles.

"I don't see how a rogue has anything to do with this. It seems as though you got your information wrong," the other man replied. "The mother could have changed her name to avoid drawing notice. Sometimes, humans who stray too close to our kind feel the need to take drastic measures if they decide our ways no longer appeal to them."

"I thought of that," Bill snapped. "But with every search in every goddamn database, Eveline Connors is the only name that turns up—"

"Eveline?" The man's entire demeanor shifted on a dime. His eyes flashed, his jaw clenched. "That was her name? Eveline?"

"You recognize it?" Bill asked. "Someone from your pack?"

He couldn't be sure. Already the man had schooled his expression into a blank mask.

"You mentioned Connors was turned by a rogue. You think it was connected to the attacks twenty years ago. Why?"

Bill felt his eyes narrow. "Connors might have been a victim. If your pack dealt with the rogue, then you know who it was. Could he have been Loren's father?"

A crazed murderer wasn't ideal, but it was better than the alternative. Loren needed answers, and Bill was willing to entertain any avenue to find them—even if he had to beg an enemy outright.

"Tell me."

"The girl should know her upbringing. Have you asked her?"

Bill couldn't silence an exasperated snarl. "She doesn't remember—"

"Or she doesn't trust you enough to tell you."

"You think I took her forcefully as a mate, but you don't think I'd take advantage of my access to her memories?" Bill laughed coldly. "That doesn't make very much sense, does it?"

The man hid his disappointment well—but not all of it. A hint of alarm flitted across his gaze before vanishing. "Either you're lying or…"

"Or someone hid her memories deliberately." The prospect sounded insane out loud. And yet… Fuck, it made sense. Too much sense.

"If that is the case, there are ways to recover those memories," the Eislander murmured, seemingly to himself.

Bill didn't bother to suppress his disgust. "You turn up your nose because I mated her, but now you casually suggest I break into her mind to satisfy your curiosity. That tells me you know more than you're saying."

The man turned away. "We're done here." He surged forward, continuing toward the property's boundary. Whatever he knew, he was choosing to keep it to himself. "If you care about that girl, you'll release her. Soon. Her presence here is the only reason we've shown you mercy until now, but we won't extend that grace for much longer. Sparing her the pain of your death would be ideal—but not a deciding factor. You can have two days to break the bond and send her to a pack. No more."

He sounded so damn smug. As if he were offering him a lifeline.

If anything, the bastard had just given him more of a reason to act on the very course of action he'd been trying to talk himself out of.

"In two days, I'll be on your doorstep. You can take up my punishment with Lukka right after I've dealt with him," Bill spat without parsing through the consequences of revealing that part of his plan.

It was too late.

The intruder stopped short, his head cocked as if he didn't trust what he'd heard. A slow, rich laugh echoed back, and Bill scoffed in return.

"I thought you were brazen, rogue—but this is outright foolish. You aim to challenge your Alpha? As if they will accept you now."

It stung to admit the bastard had a point. That was a hurdle he would overcome later.

"I don't intend to sit around waiting to be executed for a crime I didn't commit. I won't let Lukka spin the narrative, either. I killed no one who didn't deserve it."

The man hissed. "Maybe we will wait and let fate deal out your punishment in due time, rogue? If Lukka doesn't rip you apart, your own packmates will."

Bill didn't even waste his breath arguing. There was no point. Instead, he watched the man fade from view before he bounded toward the house—though a nagging voice at the back of his mind warned that the bastard had been right.

Loren would be better off without him.

Alive or dead.

----

*P*atrolling the boundary wasn't his excuse for staying out all night this time. Just reluctance. Oddly enough, rather than fade beneath the trees, he lurked outside the house in plain view without ever leaving the yard. Loren even caught a glimpse of him from the living room window, prowling in the form of a black wolf. Naomi and Micha must have sensed him as well, but they said nothing—and no one made any move to go outside and see for themselves.

He obviously wasn't in the mood to talk.

His irritation prickled the air like the scent of smoke mingled with his usual aroma of pine. He didn't want to be bothered. Not yet. For the first time, his presence wasn't a comfort, though. Loren barely slept, curled up by the window.

McGoven's vigilance contributed only partly to her unease. The nightmares were more intense than ever, descending the second she closed her eyes and haunting her until she wrenched them open again. No longer was her pursuer a distant shadow. He was closer, visible just beyond her peripheral vision.

Watching.

Waiting.

Ironically, much like McGoven.

Only when a tendril of pale daylight pierced the darkness did she find the nerve to creep into the kitchen. On the way there, she passed a snoring Micha who lay sprawled in the middle of the floor and Naomi, who slept soundly on the couch.

Before she reached the doorway, she could sense someone prowling in the room beyond. The scent of pine gave his identity away in a heartbeat. He must have entered the second she'd gotten up—though he managed to find a pair of sweatpants at least. For now, his back was to her as he rummaged through the food Sonia had stocked the fridge with. In the end, he resurfaced with a packet of tuna and moved to grab a loaf of bread resting on the counter. He silently assembled two sandwiches, but Loren didn't refuse when he abruptly offered her one.

"You have questions," he declared before taking a ravenous bite. "Ask them. I'll answer what I can."

Nothing regarding whatever happened in the barn. She knew without asking that topic was off-limits. Thankfully, there wasn't a lack of pressing issues needing to be addressed.

Squaring her jaw, she picked one issue at random. "Those men. What did they want?"

He frowned and took another bite. "I don't know." He admitted after swallowing.

"But they aren't going to leave you alone." She could sense the tension in the air. Even the way he moved screamed vigilance and hostility. He was on guard more so than before.

"No," he said gruffly. "You either. But believe it or not, they aren't the biggest threat facing us at the moment..."

Us. She swallowed at the word choice. Though, what did he think was the main threat they faced? He seemed unwilling to voice it out loud. Instead, he glowered at the window. The sky seemed perpetually gray these days—a stormy hue the same color as his eyes.

"That man," he began. "You didn't smell him before you entered the house, did you?"

Shame flooded her cheeks. "No," she admitted—but when she inspected his expression, she didn't find any blame or anger there.

"There was a reason for that," he said with a nod. "Can you explain why?"

It was a question dangerously close to the one her father always uttered, "Care to explain?" Only, his tone lacked any malice.

She knew in her gut that he wouldn't strike her for a wrong answer, either. With that in mind, she took her time, parsing through every interaction. One glaring oddity stuck out.

"He smelled strange," she said, cringing at the memory. "Like sulfur. It was awful—"

"Or, to put it bluntly, it was deer urine," Bill said with a harsh scoff. "It's a dirty trick. Something young boys might do to sneak out of the territory unnoticed. The scent of prey overpowers anything nearby. It's instinctive, you might say. When we hunt, it allows for us to zone in only on our target and let nothing else distract from the pursuit. But it can also be used as a double-edged sword outside of a heightened environment. Especially in a place like this where prey animals live full-time. You've grown accustomed to the scent of horses, for example, and it allows other lycans to cloak themselves and mount a surprise attack. Or," he added dryly, "it allows a lycan to hide in a barn and overhear a private conversation."

"I didn't know..." she trailed off as she recognized what he *didn't* say outright but merely alluded to—he knew her scent thoroughly. There was something primal in that knowledge that made her shirt feel tighter, and her throat constrict.

"There are other little nuances," he continued, oblivious to how her thoughts had wandered. "Interactions you wouldn't understand outside of our culture. Like, for instance, that deer you found on the porch the other day."

Loren stiffened. Apparently, the grisly carcass hadn't been left by a hunter after all. "They put that there?"

"They did," McGoven admitted. "But it's more complicated than that. Keep in mind that we don't kill for sport. Never. Only to feed. To leave a carcass like that is a warning. One of the most severe our kind know how to issue. Think of it as the equivalent of spitting in someone's face and rubbing their nose in it."

All in all, far more serious than he'd led her to believe.

"Why did you lie?" Her voice sounded calm enough but the anger she felt caught her off guard. He lied. He didn't trust her.

"I didn't want to worry you." From his tone, she couldn't discern any deception, but he was no longer looking her way. Instead, he once again inspected the horizon. "But it was wrong to lie to you. If I want you to trust me, then it must go both ways. I shouldn't hide anything from you. Starting with the truth of the full extent of the danger you're really in."

Loren swallowed. If she weren't mistaken, those words sounded like an invitation. One she'd be a fool to turn down.

"So, tell me the truth. What did those men really want?"

He sighed in defeat. "They asked about who your father might be. I don't know what Lukka told them, but they seem to think I... That you're here against your will. Finding your real father would go far in discovering how you grew up the way you did, though. Where you belong. I don't want you to take this the wrong way, but you present an aggravating puzzle. Nothing about you makes sense. Nothing."

Loren marveled at the characterization. She was used to feeling like a burden. But a puzzle?

She flexed her bare toes against the tile floor and awkwardly fidgeted with the hem of her shirt. McGoven had retreated inside himself, dwelling on whatever mystery he thought she presented. Unlike last night, she couldn't sense any emotion directly. Navigating this conversation felt very much like flying blind.

But getting the man to talk at all was such a rare occasion she didn't dare waste it. Clearing her throat, she tried a neutral question. "So, what now? Will they come back?"

He nodded. "They will. Not that I plan on us sticking around to greet them."

Because he still intended to fight for his freedom. Then what? He hadn't been exactly clear on that part. For whatever reason, that was a question she wasn't eager to ask.

Instead, she fixated on another aspect of what he'd revealed.

"You said you hunt. Do you mean you…"

"It's not a violent act," he said plainly. "Get the grisly images from horror movies out of your head. We are far more humane than human hunters with their guns. It is one of the most sacred acts a lycan partakes in. It might seem savage to you, but to us…"

He sighed again, wistfully this time.

"It's beautiful. Natural. I can't even describe what it feels like. But the hunt… Such a tradition is what has allowed our kind to survive for so long. Few wars. No famines to decimate our numbers. We could subsist during the harshest times, and everyone could feed in harmony."

It certainly sounded more wholesome than the cruelty she'd been exposed to in her short life outside of the pack and their laws. Hearing him describe even that small fraction of their customs made it sink in just how little she knew. About lycans. About him.

"You said you don't need the moon to change," she began, seizing upon his rare willingness to speak openly. "So then how? You said the Alpha calls it forward—"

"When we are children, around the ages of four and five—it differs depending on the pack and their traditions—we are gathered before the Alpha under a full moon right before that month's hunt. Around us, the others shift. For some, it might be the first time they ever see their mothers, brothers, fathers, and sisters in lycan form. Then, one by one, the Alpha approaches each child and presses his snout to their chest. That alone is enough to waken the instinct in most cases. Keep in mind that it's a bit more ceremonial than I'm making it seem."

He laughed, but not even a heartbeat later, his customary frown returned. "Afterward, the children are encouraged to submit. They join the fold and partake in their first hunt that very night."

"But you didn't," Loren said softly. "You resisted."

"For three years," he said thickly. "I'm sure you can imagine that made me a bit of an outcast in those days. I was well past the age of most when I finally accepted my Alpha and undertook the change. So believe that I, more than anyone, understand your struggle. It's easy to interpret the things that make you different as a sign of weakness. Don't."

A new emotion colored his voice, softening the rich baritone. Fondness? Pain? There were moments when he referred to the pack with such disdain. Then times like this where he recounted those memories almost reverently.

"But I am different," Loren said softly. "I can't shift…" Her voice broke. Only as she uttered the confession did she realize how much it actually stung. "Naomi can, but I can't, and I'm supposed to have inherited this. What does that mean?"

"It means that you are not Naomi," McGoven replied. There wasn't an ounce of judgment in his expression. "You will shift when you're ready. Sometimes being different isn't a bad thing. If you were in the pack, some would shun you. Others would support you."

"Like Sonia?"

He laughed. "Like Sonia. Though the most important thing to remember is that, at the end of the day, you can't always rely on anyone else. There comes a moment, when the only person you can rely on is yourself."

His eyes were downcast, his jaw clenched. That seemed to be a lesson he had learned the hard way.

"What is it like?" Loren asked. "Living with the pack?"

He shot her a questioning glance. Then he leaned against the counter and inclined his head. Just when she thought he might not answer, he sighed.

"It could be considered regimented by your standards, I suppose. Everyone has a place there. A role to play. Much like our lycan and human forms, we carry on the dichotomy in our daily lives. You might be surprised by how…normal our lives are for the most part. By day, some work in a communal kitchen or in private fields to grow vegetables. At night, we partake in various rituals to embrace our primal side. We develop very little of the land, to leave most of it untouched. Wild. The animals we hunt have been born and bred within our borders but roam freely."

"You miss it." She didn't know what possessed her to say as much. Still, his curt nod gave confirmation.

"It's hard not to. I grew up there. It wasn't perfect, but I can't say it was terrible, either."

The question of why he left in the first place was poised on her tongue. Just as she gathered up the nerve to ask it, a shrill sound pierced the quiet.

Bill stiffened, warily eyeing the landline phone attached to the wall near the fridge. He moved cautiously, reaching for the device as though it were a poisonous snake ready to strike.

"Hello?" Almost instantly, his expression softened, and his tone lost the hard edge. "Yes, sir. I'll make it in today. I may not be able to stay long… Yes, due to that family emergency I told you about."

She recognized that tone of voice—the one he used while in uniform. Apparently, a "family emergency" was the lie that had allowed him to miss work the past few days. When he hung up, he raked a hand through his hair.

"I need to go into the station today for a few hours. Just to tie up loose ends. But while I'm there… I would like your permission."

Her belly flipped at his serious expression. "For what?"

"When I reviewed your file, I did so intending to keep your privacy intact. But things have changed. We need to know anything I can glean from your past. Anything."

Deep down, Loren knew she should have been horrified by the prospect. Something bad lurked within those memories. Horrific. But when it came to recalling exactly what—or feeling the fear at full force… She couldn't.

So, she consented with a curt nod. In the same instance, she blurted out a question that seemed just as pressing as her murky past. "Do lycans feel emotions differently?"

He raised an eyebrow. "What do you mean?"

"Ever since my father… Fred Connors. Ever since he died, I haven't been able to feel… What I should feel. I can't even remember what happened."

She tried…

Nothing came to mind. Not even the night before his death.

"It's shock," Bill insisted. He stood fully upright and headed for the hall. "I'll get dressed and head out. In the meantime, I'll leave some exercises you and the others can work on. Basic training."

In other words, nothing requiring a lycan form.

"Is it time for breakfast?"

Loren turned to the living room as Micha appeared in the doorway, rubbing at his eyes. Without a word, she headed to the fridge and made him a few tuna sandwiches, along with one for Naomi.

By the time Bill returned downstairs, fully dressed in his uniform, all three house guests had eaten and were waiting awkwardly in the kitchen.

"I need to go out for a few hours," he said. "Naomi, you should go check in with your parents. While you're at it, see if you have any clothing you can spare for you and Loren. Then come back here. Micha, you and Loren run a few laps around the property. Stay away from the boundary. You can answer whatever questions she has, but try to stay on topic."

"Yes, sir," Micha replied with a mock salute.

On topic, Loren assumed, meant "no personal history" regarding McGoven or anyone else involved in this strange saga.

Not even ten minutes later, she and Micha were traipsing across the fields. Or, more accurately, Micha was traipsing while she struggled to catch up.

"Any questions?" he chirped. "Ask away! I'm an open book. We can talk about anything from moon cycles to pack dynamics—"

"What is a mate?"

Micha stopped short, so suddenly, Loren nearly ran into him. Instead, she tripped, landing on the dirt.

"Oh, I'm sorry!" Micha was by her side in an instant to help her to her feet. However, when she dusted the dirt from her knees, he wouldn't meet her gaze directly.

"Why do you want to know about a boring subject like that?" he asked. "I can think of ten topics off the top of my head that are way more interesting. Like scent marking and what it's like on the mountain, and—"

"Why won't anyone explain that to me?" Loren couldn't help the desperate frustration in her voice. She supposed it had been building since the very day she woke up to Sonia and Bill whispering about her, refusing to tell her outright what was going on. She hated it. Being treated like a child. An idiot.

A burden.

Something in her expression made Micha wince. "Okay! Okay! Don't make me the bad guy. I'll tell you."

He shot a wary glance over his shoulder as if hunting for McGoven. Then he conspiratorially lowered his mouth near her ear.

"A mate is like… Humans might compare it to marriage or something, but it's more than that. A connection. It outlasts any other bond—even between a lycan and his Alpha. A mate will always come first. But it's… complicated. You can't just walk up to someone and give them a ring like humans do." He laughed, only to trail off awkwardly once he realized she wasn't in on the joke. "It's a sacred bond," he said with a solemnness Loren had only seen in him a handful of times—the day the intruders attacked Naomi in the fields and again when he pledged his life to Bill. "Lycans who are mated to each other… It's like they have two brains instead of one. Two sets of senses. Two strengths. They're one and the same, and not everyone can handle that kind of connection."

Butterflies came to life within Loren's stomach. "What do you mean?"

"There are downsides," Micha added. "A bond like that… If one mate dies, the other can go insane from the pain. It's like having their soul ripped in half."

The words felt way too eerie. Was that why she could feel McGoven's emotions? Sense his thoughts? Was he her…

"How?" she asked hoarsely. "How can you tell if someone is your mate?"

Micha fidgeted, suddenly fixated on the waistband of his pants. "You know what? Why don't we do one more lap before blondie gets back and brings down the mood with her pouting—"

"Please." Her voice lacked any true emotion, but Micha deflated as if she'd shouted.

"It's not random," he said thickly. "It's a choice. Two lycans meet, and they willingly share themselves with each other. Usually—" he cleared his throat. "With an intimate connection as well, but I've heard that's not necessary. It's a mutual acceptance."

Loren frowned. So much for that theory. She couldn't recall Bill McGoven ever asking her outright to be his mate.

"There is no other way?" she prodded. Was that disappointment fluttering in her stomach? She had no right to be.

Micha sputtered. "Well… I ah—"

"Tell me, please."

"I've heard stories of some really fucked-up lycans forcing a mating bond. It's… It's the worst violation you can ever think of. You force your way into someone's mind. Their soul. We are taught to never do something like that without consent. Ever. B-But," he added hastily. "Sometimes, in rare cases, it might be better for a female—a lycan—to have another lycan forge a mating bond to help them transition. Especially if they've been traumatized. The mating bond can offer relief from fear. Pain. Bad memories. If done with the right intentions."

He was dancing around something, but suddenly Loren didn't want to know. Whether with good intentions or not, the thought of someone else having control of her emotions and fears felt…

No better than Fred Connors using his fists to accomplish the same thing.

And yet. If her attraction to McGoven was just a fluke. Unrequited… That thought stung just as badly.

$\mathcal{I}$n the five years Bill worked for the New Walsh PD, he had never received a less than stellar evaluation. Though, if a skilled investigator happened to dig into his past, they would discover that he had no university or academy training to speak of. In fact, he had no credentials other than the ones he left the pack with all those years ago—which, to say the least, weren't much.

Luckily, an unnatural sense of smell, reflexes, speed, and an ability to plant "suggestions" within human minds went a long way to fill any educational gaps. Besides, New Walsh was such a quiet town that most calls centered around silencing rowdy neighbors or finding lost pets.

Until Loren Connors. Tackling her case was the first time he'd ever felt out of his element.

In more ways than one.

Damn Fred Connors and the bastard's secrets. Bill had hoped that his death would end his hold over Loren, but that was turning out to be wishful thinking. The visit from the Eislander bastard cemented his gut feeling that something was off. More than questioned paternity. Loren's true origins had been…hidden somehow. Fred Connors had merely been a scapegoat.

But for who? And why?

Therein lay a wealth of suspicions that made Bill's stomach churn. Connors simply wasn't smart enough to plan such an elaborate ruse on his own. No… To have his name listed on Loren's birth certificate eighteen years ago, and though reluctantly, take her in without questioning her paternity, there weren't many explanations for that. Either Fred Connors grew a sliver of a heart in his time as a rogue, or he'd had no choice. Someone far stronger had compelled him to maintain the lie.

Bill didn't like where that possibility led. Not one damn bit.

Lukka was still the lead suspect—but he had already shown an inclination toward more violent routes to get his way. Beyond him, there were only a handful of other figures powerful enough to arrange such a scheme—but Bill cut off the thought then and there. Rampant speculation would help no one.

He needed real answers.

With that goal in mind, he left his truck and entered the modest station near the heart of the town. His first destination was the small room where they kept case files. Instantly, he realized why he'd been called in so abruptly.

"Hey, Bill," Mindy, the clerk, greeted from her desk posted near the door. A slight woman with curling blond hair, she'd been one of the few friendly faces to make his post here bearable. Usually, the only thing she kept on her desk was a mug of coffee. This morning, something sat beside it, glaringly out of place—a square package roughly the size of a textbook, bound in brown paper.

"Sorry to call you in from your vacation," Mindy went on innocently, "but this came over from Elkton with specific instructions to give to you ASAP. I don't even know what's inside it. They didn't say."

"Elkton?" Bill felt his brows furrow. "That's a town up north, isn't it?"

Fuck. Very north, in fact—not far from two large lycan territories nestled within the mountains.

"Yep!" He barely heard Mindy's reply. Jaw clenched, he fought to refocus. "A ways away," she went on. "Maybe five hours on a good day with light traffic. Do you have any idea why they might be consulting with you all the way down here in New Walsh?"

"No idea." Bill fought to school his expression. While the Elkton police had no business with him, he could think of someone who might. An entire pack, in fact, who happened to live just outside the town's boundaries.

Unease made him eye the package warily, suspicious of what might be inside it. Would Loreck Eislander really stoop to involve humans in whatever feud simmered between them?

Considering the man's supposed beta had the balls to trespass onto his property the night before and issue demands, who knew what the bastards were capable of.

When he finally took the package and entered the case file room, he didn't feel confident it contained a harmless missive. It was heavy, with only his name written across the front. His nostrils flared, hunting for any trace of a nefarious substance the package might contain. Another carcass? Whether it was a good or bad omen, he couldn't smell anything.

When he ripped off the paper, all he found inside was a battered file that could have come from any one of the cabinets in this very room. Written on the front was one name. *Scolera.*

Bill frowned. He had heard the name before. It belonged to a pack somewhere out west. Nomads, to be more specific. They were less organized than Black Mountain or the Eislanders, preferring to roam their territory seasonally in makeshift caravans. That, however, wasn't what gave them their infamy.

Scolera wolves were wild and vicious. Rather than follow a single Alpha, they formed small, scattered clans with no real hierarchy. Due to that unorthodox nature, they weren't welcome in most spaces. In fact, he only knew of them through rumors—most notably, the belief they fed on humans.

Though, on second thought, they weren't entirely unknown to this area. If Sonia hadn't brought up the incident, he might have forgotten it completely—twenty years ago, a spate of human murders had been attributed to a rogue prowling the area. Things had gotten so bad that Lukas Grehmaine and Loreck Eislander had joined forces to tackle the threat before it brought unwelcome attention to both packs.

Bill barely remembered that time—he'd only been a child. All he could recall was the tension that had infected everyone for those tortured few weeks. Once the rogue had been caught, things went back to normal.

He'd said as much to the Eislander as a cruel joke, but maybe it was the truth. Could that monster have been Loren's father?

Puzzled, he flipped through the first few documents contained within the file, questioning the sender's motives. Was this some backhanded attempt at a warning?

Perhaps.

Though, when he skimmed over a particular line, his eyes nearly fell out of his head. It was buried within a list of names that seemed to document various Scolera family members known to the area.

One, in particular, stood out—Eveline Branshaw.

Loren's mother? Bill's first impulse was to doubt it. Scolera wolves, what little he knew about them, were rabidly fierce to their loosely connected clans.

Then again, nothing involving Loren had made sense up until this point.

He skimmed the rest of the file, finding nothing that stuck out. One mystery, however, was answered soon enough—at the very back of the assorted documents was a note. The ink smelled fresh, presumably written by whoever sent the package in the first place.

We need to meet, rogue, it said. *Wolfie's bar in Withead, outside of Elkton. Come alone. Bring any trouble, and you will regret it. This is about the girl, nothing else.*

Bill scowled, picturing the Eislander lycan from the night before. Apparently, the bastard had lied—he had recognized the name of Loren's mother after all. Enough to place her identity, at least. Did the bastard know who her real father might be?

All signs pointed to that farfetched scenario—a crazed rogue Scolera who fed on humans, Fred Connors presumably being one of them. It was a sick twisted bit of irony.

Sadly, it wasn't even the most tragic of turns in Loren's case.

Bill had spent all morning trying to ignore the inevitable— the Eislander bastard had a point. There was a way to enter her memories. A way to learn the truth without traipsing out to Elkton…

Though, he wouldn't have long to weigh the ethics of such a method. Sonia had to be back by now, but she hadn't called him. Putting Loren aside for a second, he tried her cell phone, but no one answered. To say her silence was bad news was a grievous understatement.

Either Sonia was in danger, or Lukka had tightened his leash. The bastard was planning something.

Bill groaned as the threats against him stacked up. His head ached. Would the visit from the Eislanders be capped by a direct assault from Lukka? Who the hell knew?

For the time being, he needed to focus on one dilemma.

Without letting himself overthink the act, Bill cleared a space on a table near the back of the room, fetched the file they had on Loren Connors, and prepared to read.

18

"Let's do one more lap," Micha insisted.

Loren groaned internally. He might as well have asked her to jump off a cliff for fun. They had been at it for hours, and he barely seemed winded, despite speaking almost constantly in addition to running.

"It's good to get some exercise," he chirped. "It can clear the head, you know. Put things into perspective. I used to run at least two hours every morning—"

To conserve her sanity, Loren tuned him out, though she couldn't deny feeling some guilt for his sudden chattiness. It seemed to be his desperate attempt at preventing her from asking him anything else. Like about mates and how that particular connection was forged.

But she needed to know. The craving for information burned beneath her skin, growing into an almost painful ache that plagued her every waking second. Contrary to

Micha's insistence, running didn't distract her any. Neither did his steady stream of conversation. She was almost grateful when Naomi's sports car zoomed down the main road, and the blond stormed out, carrying a pink duffle bag slung over her shoulder.

"Who does he think he is?" she demanded as Micha and Loren approached. "Lie to your parents. Gather up some of your designer clothes to hand out to the paupers. Don't ask any fucking questions, and certainly don't waste time on preparing your college admission essays or community service projects. You know, the things that actually matter in my life? Though, hell, I guess I'm just lucky that school went on break this week, or he'd have me blow that off too just to squat in a house with a loser freak and wolf boy."

Micha whistled through his teeth. "Bad day?" he asked without a hint of mocking in his voice. Either Naomi's insults went right over his head, or he had way more patience for cruelty than Loren gave him credit for.

Naomi scoffed at him anyway. "Here—" she practically threw her duffle at Loren. "Make use of my charity. Though I suppose you're used to it by now. Living off the kindness of others. Crawling around like a sniveling little worm afraid of its shadow. You know, he told me you're lycan or whatever. I'm calling bullshit."

"Naomi…" Micha's voice suddenly dropped an octave, though Loren wasn't sure what caused his sudden alarm. She didn't smell any outsiders nearby. Just the cloying stench of Naomi's perfume.

"Oh, what is she going to do?" the blond demanded with a harsh laugh.

Only then did Loren realize she'd impulsively taken a step toward her.

Not that Naomi seemed cowed one bit. "She can't even change. As far as I'm concerned, she's totally fucking useless!"

Micha sprung toward her, sensing something Loren didn't. "Naomi, don't!"

Ignoring him, the blond lunged. Loren felt a pair of manicured hands collide with her shoulders. She went sprawling, nearly losing her balance. Then everything went black.

Her next coherent observation was watching her own fingers lash at a beautiful, tanned cheek. Again. Again.

The scent of blood tinged the air, beautiful and vibrant. It drowned out the sickening perfume—but barely. She needed more.

"Loren, stop!"

She couldn't. It was as if her body moved separately from her mind, wrestling on top of a squirming Naomi. The only action she consciously had control over was shouting. Screaming. The words echoed nonsensically, and only snippets actually registered.

"Kill you… I'll kill you!"

"Enough!"

Suddenly, a force hooked around Loren's waist, wrenching her back and off her feet entirely. *Micha.* He barely managed to insert himself between her and Naomi before the blond charged again.

Loren forgot her rage for a heartbeat, and genuine awe rendered her frozen. There was something undeniably beautiful about the way Naomi threw herself forward, and a golden wolf took her place.

It wasn't an instantaneous transformation when viewed up close. More…violent. The muscles in Naomi's slender jaw protruded and burst. Her green eyes widened while her body expanded three times its normal size, and her designer clothing shredded around the lupine form. Even so, it was a breathtaking thing to witness. So much so that Loren missed the moment Micha transformed as well.

He was the only figure large enough to inhabit the brown wolf that came from nowhere to pin Naomi's smaller form just beyond her reach.

Logically, Loren should have run. She was no match. One bite from those wiry jaws could rip out her throat. That logic couldn't penetrate the rage consuming her, though. She shifted her weight to the balls of her feet, ready to fight anyway.

Then…

Nothing. It was as if an unseen force smothered her emotions, rage, and all. She went still, surprised as Naomi whimpered, pressing herself to the earth.

Once her breathing slowed enough to register the scent in her lungs, Loren easily placed the culprit behind the sudden shift in the mood. *Pine.* Heart pounding, she scanned the fields wildly for the sight of a scowling Bill or snarling black wolf. Apart from Micha, there was no one else around.

But he was here. She could sense him as surely as she knew her own name.

And she wasn't the only one. Micha shifted back into human form, crouching—out of modesty for her, Loren suspected. He shot her an apologetic glance, but said nothing.

Not even a minute later, a patrol car turned the corner and parked halfway to the house. Bill emerged in a silent display of power, so effective Loren swallowed, rooted to the spot.

He didn't yell. He didn't storm across the fields in their direction. He merely stared for what felt like a solid minute. Then he silently reentered the patrol car and drove to the house.

"We should head back," Micha said with a weary sigh. As he turned to Naomi, the girl breezed past him, still in wolf form. In a graceful display of speed, she loped back to the house.

By the time Loren traipsed up the back porch steps, a hint of emotion tugged at her conscience, stopping her in her tracks. It wasn't the mixture of dread and guilt flooding her own mind, but… Something different. Not anger, but a darker and more brooding emotion.

Much like whatever lurked within Bill's gaze a moment ago.

"Get changed," he called from the kitchen the second they entered the foyer. "Then, we need to talk."

All four of them? Or just him and her? He didn't specify, and Micha herded Loren into the hallway before she could ask.

Already, the shower in the downstairs bathroom was running, and presumably, Naomi was inside it. Whether intentionally or by accident, the girl had left her duffle outside the bathroom door.

Loren hated the thought of wearing anything of hers, but she didn't exactly have a lot of options. Reluctantly, she fished a sweater and jeans from Naomi's bag and retreated upstairs to get dressed.

When she finally returned downstairs, at least one question became answered immediately.

This conversation was meant to happen only between her and Bill. He waited for her in the living room alone. Through the window, she could see Micha and Naomi in the field by the barn. Both were in human form, having a conversation of their own.

Loren couldn't tear her gaze away as a pang of jealousy stabbed at her. Would Micha's mindless chatter be preferable to this overwhelming tension? Maybe.

As if sensing her unease, McGoven sighed. As she turned to him, Loren noted that his expression was carefully blank.

"Sit," he commanded, nodding toward the couch.

She took a step, only to hesitate. It felt wrong to relax when he seemed so tense. Especially when his mood was very much her fault. Fighting with Naomi was such a stupid, childish diversion in the grand scheme. She deserved to face her scolding without cowering on the couch.

Oddly enough, Bill didn't question the disobedience.

Instead, he sighed and cut to the chase. "I found some new information regarding your mother. What do you know about a place called Hillmarrow?"

She blinked, shocked by his blunt tone. Taking his advice, after all, she sat down and tried to form a coherent response. "I don't think I've ever heard of that—"

Wait. Something itched at the back of her mind. A memory? It wasn't cohesive. Just a fragment.

Bill latched onto her discomfort. "What's wrong?"

"I think…" All at once, the truth dawned on her. She *had* heard of it. Once before, maybe years ago. She couldn't remember the context or what it meant. Only who said it. A voice like rich honey that made her heart ache to recall.

"I think my mother mentioned it one time," she croaked. "But I can't remember. I don't even… What is it?"

"Interesting." Bill leaned against the window and raked his hands through his hair. "It's the name of a territory out west," he explained. "Home to a clan of lycans known as the Scolera. I don't know much about them, but I have reason to believe your mother might have been from there."

Her mother. It was a drastic shift from teenage drama. Overwhelmed, Loren stared from the window and tried to process the new information. "How do you know? What does that even mean? If she was from that place, then…"

"It means she might have been a full-blooded lycan," Bill finished for her. She couldn't tell if that prospect relieved him, or unnerved him further. Probably both, judging from the taut line of his mouth. "Scoleras are reclusive. They don't tend to stray this far from their territory. I need to know more about her. Whatever you can remember."

The urgency in his voice made her breath catch. She wanted so badly to please him. Remember something. Anything. As the seconds passed, she could only lift her shoulder in a helpless shrug. "I'm sorry. I don't… I can barely remember what she looks like."

All that remained was just a heart-wrenching mixture of features. Blond hair. Blue eyes. Kind smile. The overall picture was blurry—as were any memories attached to her mother directly. All she could clearly recall was an overwhelming sense of peace. Love. Protection.

Sometimes, if she tried hard enough, she could still hear her laugh…

"I need you to remember," Bill commanded. "Try."

Loren flinched. Try. But how? She closed her eyes and attempted to fixate on those old memories and bring them into clearer focus. It worked…slightly. She could remember a small house on the outskirts of Ridgerton. The scent of spring flowers and fresh air. A beautiful laugh. A smile…

Then nothing.

"You can't."

Bill didn't sound angry as she opened her eyes to find him watching her. Instead, his lips were pursed, his head cocked thoughtfully to the side.

"I know you're trying," he said, easing some of her doubt. "One reason why those memories elude you could be that you were so young. Another reason…"

"What?" Loren prodded, desperate for any explanation. "Why? Because I can't shift. Is it my fault because—"

"No. It wouldn't be your fault at all." However, he seemed reluctant to voice this theory. For a few seconds, he said nothing. "The truth could be that you've been *told* not to remember. But that wouldn't make sense…" He started to pace, thinking out loud. "Only a powerful lycan could issue a command strong enough to last over a decade. It's a long shot, but at this point, I'm betting the answers we're looking for are obscure for a reason. They've been hidden."

"Hidden…" It was a strange way to refer to her own memories. "How? By my mother?"

"No." He shook his head. "Even if your mother was a Scolera, I don't think she had the experience to issue a compulsion this strong. It would need to be someone older. Stronger. An Alpha. But who?" He formed a fist that made every muscle in his forearm bulge. "This doesn't make sense."

"Maybe it's better if I don't remember." Loren couldn't believe the words came from her own mouth. As they resonated, however, she didn't feel the need to take them back.

Her mother's death was a blur on her psyche, but the pain was so fresh she could feel it now… It hurt—until suddenly, the discomfort vanished.

"I know this is hard for you," McGoven murmured, sitting beside her. Though they weren't touching, his breath tickled her neck. Awed, Loren watched as his thick fingers entwined with hers. He didn't seem to realize he even moved. The need to comfort her was instinctive. Irresistible.

As was her desire to respond to him.

She almost felt guilty. Nothing should have mattered in the face of discovering her true parentage, but one pressing issue broke loose anyway. *Mate.* Everything Micha described, she felt. All of it. All of him.

And yet, there had been no fancy, romantic ceremony. No willing acceptance. So, he couldn't be…

"I need you to focus."

Gingerly, Bill disentangled his fingers from hers and stood back up.

"There is a way to break through even a hold that strong. We can try it, but..."

Whatever this plan was, he didn't seem eager to put it into action. His entire body was angled away from her, his jaw clenched, eyes on the window.

"Tell me," she whispered.

"*But*, we would need to be careful," he said tightly. "I'll need your trust, and your...restraint. Patience. Fuck, I shouldn't even consider it. I shouldn't..."

"What?"

He pivoted and met her stare with a probing gaze that took her breath away.

"It's better if I don't explain it. Not yet. But... We'll do it tonight," he said. "But I want... I need you to remember what I said. Can you do that for me?"

Something in his expression made her bite her tongue against any questions—and she had plenty. She nodded instead.

"Good. But first... I can't take this tension. Whatever it is between you and Naomi, we squash it. Now."

He entered the kitchen and exited through the back door, leaving her to catch up. When she did, Micha was sitting on the bottom porch step. Almost comically, Naomi stood across from him, her eyes in their direction.

"What the hell is this?" she snapped. "The Spanish Inquisition?"

"Enough." Bill's tone was so sharp Naomi swallowed, her tan complexion a few shades paler. Even Micha flinched and jumped to his feet.

"You two," Bill went on. "Muck out the stables and come to an understanding. You are *not* to fight. You talk. All this hostility is giving me a splitting headache. I need to sleep. By the time I wake up, I expect some semblance of harmony. Understood?"

"Yes," Loren whispered. The thought of causing him pain, even unintentionally, smothered any irritation she felt toward the blond. For now.

To her credit, Naomi had the sense to look guilty as well.

"Good. Now go. Micha, you can patrol the perimeter if you don't mind."

"Sure thing!" The younger man shot off while Bill headed for the kitchen.

His voice reached back to them, slightly less stern. "Both of you aren't as different as you think and not to be a downer, but we have bigger things to worry about than teenage drama for the time being."

He was right.

But that didn't make facing this showdown any more appealing.

19

"I don't care what he says," Naomi snarled from her end of the barn. "Don't expect me to sing kumbaya and hold hands. As far as I'm concerned, our relationship doesn't have to extend beyond this stupid house. He's planning on ditching us, anyway, remember? No need to play happy family."

Loren let the vitriol fly unchallenged. Anger still simmered within her—though she could admit that mixed within Naomi's ranting was some small shred of truth. Either way, she lacked the energy to fight. Bill's plea might have been partly responsible, that and the overwhelming exhaustion she could feel lurking just beyond her own consciousness. It seemed crazy to even think as much, but… Could it be his? What *he* felt?

If so, he had minced his words. This tension wasn't merely exhausting him. It was draining him of everything he had left. Or, it was at least partly the reason.

While she wasn't sure if psychic abilities were part of the lupine power set, even the possibility distracted her from everything else. She was able to overlook her disgust for Naomi and purely focus on shoveling manure from the stables. Eventually, Naomi took the hint and pulled her weight, matching Loren wheel barrel for wheel barrel.

Finally, every stall was clean, but rather than guide the horses from the paddock where they nervously grazed, she and Naomi lingered in the pasture instead. Their unspoken directive loomed overhead, though neither party seemed eager to address it.

Finally, Loren sighed and faced the blond first. "I don't know what your problem with me is."

While not an apology, it seemed to be enough of a catalyst to garner a response.

"Problem?" Naomi threw back her head, her hands on her hips. "That would imply you were important enough to ever matter to someone like me. Newsflash—you don't."

"Fine." Teeth bared, Loren turned on her heel as fresh anger strained her sympathy for Bill. So much for a truce. "I won't bother. Be a selfish bitch then and hold onto your stupid grudge—"

"You have no idea, do you?"

Reluctantly, Loren turned back. "What do you mean?"

Naomi's scowl was still firmly in place. Her eyes, however, sported a hint of an emotion she wasn't used to seeing there. Pain?

"Innocent, princess Loren. Drawing sympathy and attention wherever she goes. With one look, you have the whole world eating out of the palm of your hand. I could respect that. But not the game you play. You scurry away as if everyone is out to get you, when hell! You bat your lashes, shed a few tears, and boom. Men like Officer McGoven are rushing into battle to defend you while those of us who aren't blessed with the damsel gene get treated like the enemy."

For once, the blond's voice boomed without the aggressive flair that made her such a cruel bully. In this instance, she was ranting, driven by pure emotion. Loren didn't even know how to counteract the tirade.

"I don't know what you're talking about."

"Oh really?" Naomi crossed her arms. "That's the point. I bust my ass to get good grades, make a decent impression, succeed where I can. Then little Miss Loren comes in and gets top marks within three months. Even with this whole teen wolf thing, I can't even have that. You want to know what he—" she jerked her chin toward the house. "Told me after he mutilated me and turned me into a monster? He said it might be hard for me to adjust, but I was lucky. Perfect Loren Connors was also a wolf freak, and we could bond over growling and shit."

Loren fought to keep up with the convoluted argument. "So, you hate me because you're jealous?" It sounded ridiculous.

Naomi, however, wasn't laughing.

"I hate you because some of us can't just play the victim and crawl through life knowing we'll be protected. We don't have that luxury."

Loren raised an eyebrow. "Playing the victim? You act like you know everything about me just because you heard about 'my case.' You have no damn idea what I've been through, so don't pretend to understand me."

So much for Bill's plea. Her anger flared hot, and it seemed impossible they would ever come to anything other than blows. Still, she fought to find some shred of a logical argument to respond with.

"You talk about me," she bit out, "but *you* have everything you could ever want." It stung to admit that. She used to pray for even a fraction of what someone like Naomi Tanner possessed. "How is your life any harder than mine?"

Naomi scoffed and stomped her foot in exasperation. "When will you learn, Connors? Open your eyes. You aren't the only person in the world with problems. Like him, for instance? Have you even noticed just how stressed he's been lately? Because of you. No? Or that weird guy, Micha? He's terrified of something, and I bet you don't even care. You're so caught up in the poor, sad girl narrative. Wake up!" She clapped her hands for emphasis. "There is more going on in the world than Loren Connors and her pathetic problems. Now, if you don't mind, I think that's enough friendship bonding for today. He wants us to come to some sort of truce? Fine. You stay out of my way, and I'll stay out of yours."

She stormed toward the house, but Loren watched her go, startled by a puzzling realization. Naomi…had a point, albeit an obvious one. Her issues with reconciling her lycan nature aside, Loren knew that she wasn't the only one struggling. Something was off, evident in Bill's recent moodiness and constant vigilance.

Her one shining bit of hope was that he promised to enlighten her. Hopefully soon. Curiosity alone was what finally drew her back to the house in Naomi's shadow. True to her word, the blond said nothing before storming to her car. She barely climbed inside the driver's seat when a voice boomed from the house.

"Get some rest," Bill said from the front porch. "Come back tomorrow morning. I suggest you pack enough clothing for a few days."

Naomi acknowledged him with a curt nod before driving off. As she finally disappeared from view, he turned his focus to where Loren stood.

She gritted her teeth in sympathy. He looked only *slightly* less tired. Despite his promise, she doubted he'd slept any. Dark circles lined his eyes, and he raked his hand repeatedly through his hair, tousling the strands into an increasing state of disarray. Like always, his own discomfort seemed an afterthought to him.

He fixated solely on her. She could feel it—like an invisible hand extending in her direction. A wave of comfort followed, though he never said a word. His only action was to beckon her closer with a tilt of his chin.

Loren swallowed hard and mounted the porch steps on trembling legs before following him inside. A quick glance through the kitchen doorway revealed that Micha wasn't in sight, presumably still outside patrolling.

They were alone.

Rather than remain in the neutral territory of the downstairs hallway, Loren was shocked when Bill approached the stairs and took them one at a time. Near the top, he hesitated.

"Undoing whatever block is on your memories is the most important task at the moment. Whatever it takes."

His tone made her stomach lurch. She still didn't understand exactly what he wanted from her. "How can a…" She scrambled to recall the word he used. "A compulsion from a lycan. How can that keep me from remembering?"

Frankly, it sounded too fantastical. Crazy. She intended to wait for him to answer, but despite herself, she was already mounting the stairs after him. Just as she came within reach, he continued ahead, entering the lone bedroom first.

"It's hard to explain." He sat on the edge of the mattress, smoothing a hand along the planes of his face. Behind him, a tendril of waning daylight pierced the bay window, casting shadows over his rigid features. Loren's belly flipped at the sight. Naomi had been right. Something was bothering him, far more than the tension with the hostile pack.

Her past? It seemed doubtful her problems could weigh on his mind so heavily—but something was. Speaking at all seemed to take an immense amount of effort on his part. Finally, he cocked his head to observe her.

"There is so much I haven't told you about our kind," he said, subtly changing the topic. "Our gift for 'persuasion,' for instance."

He paused as if gauging how she would react to that word.

A bubble of excitement fluttered through her belly. "Persuasion?"

He nodded and stretched out his legs while he leaned back, bracing his hands at his sides. Taking the stance as an invitation, she inched forward, leaning against the door frame.

"It's far more nuanced than the term suggests," he began. "Compulsion is the slang for it. A blunter way of saying that we can exert our will over others, even our own kind. It's how the Alpha maintains control. Order. There is a hierarchy as well, but it extends well beyond any physical constraints. It's internal. A lycan with a strong will can plant suggestions into the minds of others, as well as manipulate thoughts, feelings, even memories. If you're good enough, you can even see those exact recollections as if they were your own—though typically, only an Alpha can master that skill."

Loren went cold. An Alpha… Or a girl who felt a need out of nowhere to tell a much older, much stronger man to submit. Her mind kept replaying that day over and over again, but she couldn't bring herself to voice it. Besides, she had another example of this "compulsion" in action.

"Is that why I listened to you?" She was referring to their first few meetings in particular. Certain phrases from him had resonated like commands, compelling her to respond against her will. To refuse, she had to consciously resist him.

"How do you mean?" He raised an eyebrow, prompting her to explain.

"When you would say things, it was like I couldn't ignore it. I had to obey."

His lips contorted into something that might have been a smile on another man. "Yes. In retrospect, I apologize. It's not something regularly done among… Equals."

She squirmed, suddenly hot all over. He had deliberately substituted that word for another. Mate? Regardless her cheeks flamed at the thought of being on the same level with him in any context. Though, he was being generous. This close to his domineering bulk, they seemed the furthest thing from similar. He was all solid muscle, pure strength. And she…

"I could feel it, though," she croaked as a sudden thought took hold. "I remember what it felt like. I don't remember meeting anyone else who had that effect over me."

Because that was what he was suggesting. Wasn't it? Someone had told her to forget. As much as she respected him, she just didn't buy that explanation. A magical command gave her way too much credit. The truth was her mind was fragile, shying away from those dark memories out of cowardice. Nothing more.

"You wouldn't remember," he said tiredly. "Not if they didn't want you to. It's a tricky concept. Think of it as though your consciousness is a room. Inside it are various boxes where you've stored your memories and experiences. At a glance, it seems neat and orderly—but the reality is that some of the boxes have locks on them. You have no access to what's inside. You may not even be able to pick them out among your normal recollections. Time doesn't erode those locks, either. The only way to access whatever those boxes contain is for the person who originally stored them to grant you access. Or…"

"Or?" she asked as he trailed off.

"*Or* you break in." His grim expression sent a shiver down her spine—he didn't mean those words purely as a figure of speech. "You find a way to access those memories no matter what it takes. Even if you must shatter the box, lock, and all."

She winced. "That sounds painful."

"It is. More than you can imagine. Sometimes, agony is a necessary evil if the potential outcome is regaining control of your own life."

He was speaking more than just theoretically.

"Have you had that happen?" she asked. Though, it was hard to picture anyone having any semblance of control over him. "Did someone ever tell you not to remember something?"

"No," he said tightly. "Though I'll be honest. There are some things in my past I wouldn't mind having erased."

For a second, her thoughts drifted from her own dilemma to something he'd only hinted at. Never said. "Like what happened to make you leave the pack?"

His startled grunt answered her question before he even voiced a response. "Yes..."

From the way his eyes widened, he had surprised himself with that admission. How long had he suppressed a yearning for home? Loren wished she could empathize.

Her time with her mother was too hazy to yearn for completely. The horror that had come after... She didn't know what it was like to have a place to truly call home. Barring this exact farm, anyway.

"Maybe it's a good thing," she said softly. "Maybe it's better if I don't remember."

For a long moment, Bill said nothing else. The shadows around them grew and distorted, lengthening like fingers reaching from the corners of the room. Loren wasn't sure if unease or sympathy drew her closer, but before she knew it, she was standing beside him.

"Those memories aren't hidden from me like yours are," he went on, his voice hoarse. "I can access them and the pain they cause every single day. There are days that I wish I couldn't, but you should have that ability with your own memories."

He stood, facing her, his hands held open at his sides.

"I can help you access that locked box in your mind, but I need you to trust me. More than you ever have before."

This had to be the third time he used that exact phrasing. Loren wasn't sure if it were overkill, or his desperate attempt at a warning. Either way, he was giving her more than enough time to back out. Refuse.

And, even as her belly flipped with foreboding, she couldn't bring herself to do so.

Instead, she licked her lips, prepared to ask exactly what he planned, but he stepped forward before she could voice a single word.

"Those nightmares you've been having," he said, fixing her with a probing stare. "Tell me about them."

Loren blinked, caught off guard by the abrupt change in subject. "I'm running," she said haltingly. As she spoke, the images flashed across her mind in chilling clarity.

"Someone's chasing me. I don't know what he wants, but… I just know he can't find me."

A cold sweat coated her skin. Even while awake, the fear was ever present, paralyzing in intensity.

"They're just bad dreams," she added in response to his frown. "It could be what happened with my father. I can't remember that night at all. I've tried to, but I can't."

She expected him to react with alarm, maybe pity. Anything but nod once as if he knew exactly why that was.

"You need to trust me," he insisted. "Because to break through that hold, you need…encouragement."

Her heart sank. "Will you chase me again? Push me down. Make me—"

"No." He snatched her waist, yanking her closer. Their chests met, her wide eyes finding his. The expression on his face wasn't the dangerous, predatory grin he'd sported during their chase. He looked somber, as if his next act would hurt him far more than it could ever affect her. "I need you to relax," he warned, securing her shoulders in an iron grip.

The next second, his mouth settled over hers. At the back of her mind, she recognized that this wasn't a kiss. It was a method of attack. His lips parted, easily prying hers apart. In the same instant, he utilized her shock to shove her back.

She fell and couldn't even cry out before a firm surface broke her fall. The mattress. Something heavy enough to support their combined weight as he settled over her without allowing her to regain her bearings.

"W-What are you doing?" Her heart hammered, trying to beat its way from her chest. She couldn't breathe. The oddest thing, though, was her overall lack of fear. All doubt vanished. Every trace of concern ceased to matter. His weight wasn't a restraint, but a welcome pressure she arched her hips to experience in full. As his heat seeped beneath her skin, a sigh ripped from her lips.

But, if anything, her acceptance seemed to irritate him. He lunged, utilizing his weight to pin her down and crush the remaining air from her lungs. His thighs, pressing into the mattress on either side of her, became a prison. All the while, he consumed her within another kiss—only one far deeper. Ravenous. One of his hands fisted through her hair, using the contact as an anchor.

But the physical touch was just one prong of his approach. She could feel him…inside her head. The sensation was akin to a battering ram slamming against her skull. The wielder's intentions weren't malicious, but that didn't negate the pain of his actions.

It hurt.

"Ow!" she whimpered, resisting the embrace. "W-Wait—"

"Loren, trust me." His lips met her forehead with a desperation she could feel, almost like a coherent thought. *Let me in. Please. Just let me in.* The plea echoed faintly at first, growing stronger and stronger. Clearer. Belatedly, she realized the pain was gone. All that remained was a fervent desire that consumed her from the inside out.

They needed to know. Needed to know. But he didn't want it to hurt. Couldn't let it hurt—

"Trust me," his voice, grated against her earlobe, was the catalyst needed to unlock something within her. She went limp. Panting and breathless, she could only obey his next command.

"I need… You need to be relaxed for this to work." His tone was gentle but with the slightest trace of commanding authority. Her body reacted instantly, and some of her alarm eased.

But not all of it.

The pain in her head quickly faded away in contrast to the growing realization as to how close he was. How heavy. His heat crept beneath the fabric of her borrowed clothes, but muffled. The material felt more like a nuisance than anything. She needed it off. Now.

His eyes seemed to darken with the same understanding. He reached for her sweater first, moving slowly as if to allow her plenty of time to recoil.

She didn't. When his fingers finally slipped beneath the thin wool to brush her skin, her eyelids fluttered at the sensation. *Right.* There was no other word to describe it other than perfect. Natural.

Her body was his to touch. Explore.

But, still, he hesitated.

Her thoughts swam as she struggled to look up. He stared down at her, fully clothed, his jaw tight, those eyes a stormy gray. Some moments, he seemed almost predatory in how he looked at her, like a hungry beast savoring a wounded bit of prey.

But others, he looked…guilty. Like he hated himself for giving in to the attraction she knew they both felt.

"It's okay." Her voice wavered, but resonated more strongly than she would have thought. "I'm… It's okay."

His eyes flashed as if to challenge that. Then he lunged. What happened next occurred so quickly she could barely track the progression. He kissed her first—*really* kissed her—so fiercely her lips stung in the aftermath. Then he pulled back. Snatched her sweater. Fabric tore. More kissing. Heat. Sensation. Skin on skin.

Wait. The little voice of reason spoke up from the back of her mind, only to be drowned out by the rush of warmth that replaced Naomi's designer clothing.

Her pants were gone. Panties too. A rugged, harsher surface replaced the thin fabric, running up her inner thigh before contacting the space between them.

Her breath caught. It was as if all her life she'd gone without something vital, never knowing what it was. Until now. His touch. His warmth. His possession. They cleared her mind of everything but the need for more. All of him.

Her nails raked over his forearm as she gripped it tight, still processing the foreign sensations wafting through her.

He went rigid, giving her that time, she realized. Then just as she relaxed again, he rocked his hand.

A sound she'd never heard tore from her throat, only to be swallowed by his mouth. He did it intentionally, smothering her gasp as a thick finger eased inside of her. She recognized the shape instantly, coated in warm, calloused skin.

Her cheeks flamed as her knees buckled—but there wasn't time to panic at the intrusion. As if from far away, she felt that probe against her mind again, but there was no pain. Just acceptance. He picked through her thoughts gently. Recalling that analogy he made, this room was his to explore as he wished. With single-minded focus, he fixated on only a handful of memories in particular. Her mother…

Suddenly, the agony returned tenfold. Wincing, Loren ripped her mouth from his, sucking in air. "W-Wait—"

"It's okay." He stroked her again, igniting a trail of fire that lanced up her spine. Her hips arched off the mattress, her mind adrift.

"Loren." Guttural and soft, his voice was her only anchor to the present. "Relax. I won't hurt you."

He wouldn't…

The discomfort was entirely her own. A part of her didn't like this. Those memories couldn't be unearthed. They were dangerous. Excruciating.

"Just a little more," he breathed against her parted lips. More gently than he had the right to be, he caught a sliver of skin between his teeth and nipped. It should have hurt, but it didn't. If anything, her body craved the sharp sting. Wanted him to bite down harder. "A little more, then it's over."

Memories flickered through her head in a torrent. They were old. From when she was six. Eight? As one image sharpened in clarity, she gasped. The woman was a stranger, but one so familiar, Loren questioned how she could have forgotten her in the first place. Her mother—so beautiful it hurt, with mournful blue eyes and pink lips contorted in a faint smile. Her heart swelled with an adoration she must have pushed to the back of her consciousness.

Then, without warning, someone else replaced her. A man? He was older. She'd never seen him before, or she couldn't remember.

Until now.

He was too close. She tried to run, but he pulled her back, gripping her arm. In the distance was a vaguely familiar living room with a simple couch and yellow walls. Her old house? She didn't know. Wherever they were, it was forever scarred with terrifying memories.

Panic rose up within her as her heart pounded, threatening to hammer its way from her chest. She couldn't remember! No! She couldn't!

But her will wasn't the force driving this recollection, and she could only watch in horror as it continued to unfold.

The unfamiliar man, wrenched her to face him as he crouched to her level. His eyes were so cold. A hue of blue like winter ice, devoid of all warmth. Humanity.

"You are never to access your lupine side." A harsh voice echoed throughout her skull, radiating so much power she cowered internally. *"Not even if your life is in danger. Not when you are afraid—"*

"Please," a woman cried. Her face appeared beyond the man's shoulder, contorted with pain. Agony, the likes of which Loren couldn't imagine. *"She's just a child. She doesn't know. I never even told him—"*

"Enough!"

It was only when she heard the scream resonate throughout the room that Loren realized it had come from her. She was crying. Sobbing openly and Bill stood paces from the bed, his expression horrified.

"I'm done," he insisted, his hands raised before him in a gesture of surrender. "It's over."

"I can't… I can't." She cradled her head, rocking back and forth, but already the pain was subsiding. All that remained was nauseating exhaustion. She couldn't keep her eyes open. Couldn't think.

We can't remember. Her mind seemed to conspire to suppress those memories again, burying them deep down to never be accessed.

We can't. Can't...

Overwhelmed, she slumped onto the mattress, squeezing her eyes shut. Even as the tiredness took over, she was aware of him. Bill.

Rather than relieved, he seemed...furious. His anger lashed through whatever tenuous link existed between them. The wrath wasn't directed at her—she knew that much.

It had flared the second he saw the face of the man from her memories. Her nightmares.

ell, his plan had backfired spectacularly.

If he had been confused about the origins of Loren Connors before, Bill was downright perplexed now. While he was no expert in recovering memories, they'd broken through, alright—and without fail, all the clues led to the same damn place. Black Mountain. Ironically, Lukka wasn't the man in the center of this chaos.

Damn. Bill loathed to even consider the alternative suspect. While there were many things he regretted about leaving the pack behind, they could be boiled down to recent events. Lukka. Emma. Kyle.

Never did he think he would ever question the one man whose presence had been a constant positive influence throughout his life. What he saw… It had to be a mistake. Someone else had starred in Loren's memory—not *him*.

But how many random men sported those features and happened to be an Alpha who spent decades honing his skill?

No… Only one could have been the figure who commanded Loren to forget.

Lukas Grehmaine, the former Alpha of Black Mountain.

Bill loathed to even consider it—the tooth fairy seemed a more likely culprit. There had to be an explanation, but there just wasn't time to think of one.

Her pain took precedence over all else. Though he tried to rationalize against it, he couldn't resist the primal urge that made him hold her afterward. Comfort her, even if it meant strengthening the bond. Enduring her heat. Savoring the feel of her arousal on his fingertips like the sick monster he truly was.

Only when she finally drifted off to sleep could he do anything else.

Even if it meant literally running in circles.

After an hour of patrolling the property boundary under the guise of hunting for Eislanders—or any other enemy—Bill felt no calmer than before. The physical exertion was merely a way to stall. Otherwise, there was nothing to distract from the reality of what he'd done.

And learned.

Predictably, once the shock wore off, doubt set in. Then guilt.

The quest for answers aside, the method he utilized to retrieve them was…

Beyond dangerous. He had played with her head, extending a game that no one would win in the end. Hell, he'd had no right to enter her mind in the first place, good intentions or not. Either way, it was too late for regrets.

He could only pray that she recovered quickly enough with no lasting side effects. At best, she would be exhausted and drained for a few days. At worst, she would be prone to irrational outbursts and mild paranoia—to say the least of any emotional damage he might have done just by touching her like that.

His fingers burned, unwashed, still drenched in her scent. *Damn.* It took everything he had to curl a fist and keep himself from bringing them to his nostrils and inhaling all traces of her.

Until he couldn't refrain any longer.

A strained hiss escaped him as guilt battled the arousal unfurling in his gut. Loren deserved so much better. Her first sexual encounter should have been with a man of her choosing—without the mating bond muddling her thoughts. His only consolation was that he hadn't gone any further than touching. Tasting.

But, *damn*… His entire body hummed for more. He couldn't get her scent out of his head, nor the memory of her writhing beneath him. If he could compel himself to forget, he would.

Nothing good would come out of this. The honorable man he claimed to be would go back now and break the bond, consequences be damned.

But how honorable could he be when he had based everything he knew on the example of the only figure in his life worth emulating?

Lukas had been his idol—and even that term was an understatement. That man gave him everything. His purpose. His place in the world. The knowledge he cherished and everything he admired about his lupine heritage. He wasn't related to the Grehmains by blood, but no one would have known by the way the Alpha treated him. Few men, lupine or otherwise, would have accepted him so easily.

Every interaction Bill could remember had been punctuated with nothing but the stern but kind man he'd known his whole life. That man wouldn't have compelled a child to silence. Not only that, but to deny her lupine side. It was…

Unheard of. Cruel wasn't a heinous enough word.

Monstrous came close.

Even if he had years to dwell on it, he doubted he could come up with a plausible explanation. *No.* Only one place held the answers, and they didn't have years to find them, but days. Maybe hours.

And if Lukka decided to preempt any move he might make… Well, that would certainly complicate things.

Feeding his paranoia was the fact that Sonia hadn't called him yet. The anomaly buzzed at the back of his mind, only to grow into full-blown fear by the time he finally returned to the house. He entered the kitchen and reached for the phone, dialing the number she typically called from.

No one picked up. On its face, that alone wasn't enough to cause suspicion, but he knew Sonia. Either she was too busy to call him, or she physically couldn't. The thought of her facing punishment on his behalf was too damn much.

Besides, he had another dilemma to worry about. Someone had summoned him to Elkton for a reason. The Eislander beta?

Their actual identity didn't matter. Venturing so close to a rival territory—let alone Black Mountain—was risky at best. Though, hell, if he did plan on issuing a challenge, there was no better time than now to do so.

Lukka wouldn't sit around twiddling his thumbs, waiting for his next move. In fact, the bastard was probably goading the Eislanders into doing his dirty work. Should they falter, Bill didn't doubt the Alpha wouldn't hesitate to come after him directly.

Suddenly, a shrill sound pierced the quiet—the phone, a sign from the universe if there ever was one. Warily, he answered it, unsure of what to expect. Lukka, issuing a summons?

"Bill?"

His breath caught. The voice was high-pitched. Not Lukka. "Sonia?"

"You need to leave," she said in a rush. "Leave New Walsh. Now. Leave the state if you have to—"

"What's going on?" He'd rarely heard her this unnerved. Her voice shook, and he growled at the thought of what might have happened to have her so spooked. "Tell me."

Static interspersed her words. "Lukka isn't… I think he knows what you intend, and he won't ever let you face him to do so. If he sees you even attempt to approach the territory, he plans to head you off and have you killed."

Bill formed a fist and slammed it onto the nearest counter. "Predictable." He'd feared as much, though he'd hoped that even Lukka would respect the old laws enough to play fair, at least in this instance. No such luck.

But if Lukka was on the warpath, who knew what he might do to anyone he perceived as an enemy. "Sonia, get somewhere safe—"

"I'll be fine. He can't risk hurting me outright. Please, Bill. Just go."

She hung up. Hissing, Bill tried to call her back to no response. He wound up pacing in frustration, torn between his duty to Loren—and the others—and the need to rush to his packmate's aid. In the end, he decided on a grim compromise that ironically would kill multiple birds with one stone.

No more stalling.

He would return to Black Mountain.

Whether he liked it or not.

oren groaned as a loud thud shattered the quiet, snapping her awake. Her head throbbed, and every thought felt like jagged glass slicing through her skull. There wasn't time to wallow in the agony, though.

Something was off. Her heart started racing before she could pinpoint the reason why. Tension laced the air. She could practically taste it—a scent like pine, but bitter. Colder. Winter. Alarm displaced her discomfort, and she stirred, fighting to make sense of her surroundings.

She was on a bed. In McGoven's room? Before she could be sure, another sound reached her ears, providing more clarity.

"…my truck isn't large enough. …need to use… Thank you, Naomi…" The voice came muffled from below. McGoven definitely, followed by someone with a higher cadence. Micha?

"This is so weird. All the stealth and stuff. I feel like we're going on a mission or something—"

"*We* aren't doing a damn thing," McGoven warned. His voice radiated quiet anger she suspected had been simmering within him since the two men from the rival pack visited. Only now it had seeped into the very atmosphere, tinging the air with that wintery chill. Whatever unease infected her—he was the source of it. "You pack up, stay close and stay out of trouble. That is all. Wait—"

Suddenly the voices went silent, and a pair of steady, quiet thumps echoed throughout the house, advancing in her direction. Footsteps.

Her cheeks flamed as she looked down, taking stock of her shivering frame crouched over the rumpled blankets. Throbbing headache aside, she was mostly naked apart from an oversized T-shirt she couldn't remember putting on. There wasn't even time to cover herself with the sheet. Not even a second later, a tall figure appeared in the doorway, and she felt her entire body resonate with relief instead of shame.

He wasn't…hiding this time. He faced her out in the open without the aid of nightfall or shadows to obscure his expression. The contrast was startling. Pale daylight bathed him in a soft, gray glow. It was morning—very early. Dawn? She must have slept right through the night, but judging from how her body ached, she could still use a few more hours. Every nerve and bit of muscle felt used and abused.

His nearness, however, soothed most of the uneasiness. She found herself shifting toward the end of the mattress, aching to get closer. It was all coming back to her now. What he'd done to help her remember.

His kiss. His touch…

She drew her knees together and swallowed at the memories. Looking at his face, however, made her blood run cold. He stood back, his arms crossed—the first sign that something was weighing on his mind. The second clue was that he was fully dressed for once, wearing a red and black plaid shirt that had to be the most colorful item she'd seen him in. A pair of dark jeans enhanced the look, and he resembled a lumberjack rather than an officer.

Or a lycan, for that matter.

Ironically, the hard gleam in his eye was reminiscent of a soldier ready to go to war more than anything else.

"Something's wrong," she croaked. "Tell me."

"How did you sleep?" he asked, skirting the question.

Loren tensed. She knew that tone—and that the harmless inquiry was merely to preface what he really wanted to say. Something unspoken loomed between them, suffocating her with every passing second.

"Fine. Now tell me what's going on." She drew her knees up to her chin and reached for the sheet, draping it over her front.

Whatever happened between them seemed over and done with. He was keeping his distance for a reason. Presumably, the same reason why his eyes never left her face, devoid of the hunger she could recall. By the second, the man who'd touched her so intimately felt more like a dream than reality.

"You should sleep for a few more hours. But…" He frowned imperceptibly. Then he sighed. "Tonight, we're leaving. There isn't time to pack much, but Naomi will bring some clothing for you."

"Where are we going?" she asked. Though deep down, a part of her already suspected the answer.

"To Black Mountain—"

"No!" She lurched to her feet, leaving the sheet behind. Her knees buckled, barely able to support her weight, but she gritted her teeth and fought to remain standing. This was a conversation she couldn't passively accept. "I'm not going anywhere. You promised!"

"You should rest," he suggested without so much as blinking—he'd been prepared for this reaction. "I forgot to warn you that there might be side effects from exploring those memories. You've been put through the wringer, physically and mentally. We won't leave until later tonight—"

"Why?" she demanded, horrified for cutting him off. But rebellious anger smothered the guilt. He deserved it for treating her like an afterthought once again.

"You're going to be emotionally raw for a few days," he explained, audibly straining for calm. It was the way he'd spoken when explaining why she needed to go off with a stranger like unwanted baggage.

Because he knew best.

"Stop treating me like a child. You said you'd let me stay. You said—"

"Will you listen to me?" He raised his voice by only a fraction, but she stiffened, her teeth slamming together. A familiar tingle raced down her spine—once again, she was experiencing firsthand his uncanny ability to manipulate and control.

But a part of her lurched, panicked. He wouldn't make her listen this time. The desire to move wasn't conscious. Her body took over, staggering past him before he could think to stop her.

"Loren, wait!"

Run! She tore down the stairs and ran through the front door before she did something stupid. Scream, punch, kick? Act like a spoiled child?

She just wanted to know *why…*

Why was he so intent on pushing her away? Eyes blurring, she made it out onto the porch, intending to run— disappear beneath the trees.

The second she took a step, someone appeared at the bottom of the steps, barring her path. McGoven. A twitching muscle in his jaw was the only sign of exertion. How in the world had he managed to move so quickly? She doubted she would ever understand.

"Loren," he said, still utilizing that firm tone. "Just let me explain—"

"Stop!" She slapped her hands over her ears, anything to keep that tone from penetrating deep. "I don't want to hear your rationale. I'm tired of you playing with my head. You've been planning this the whole time, haven't you? To throw me away again?"

He had the decency to look ashamed, at least. His lips moved, words distorted by the pulse rushing through her hands, but she didn't dare take them down.

She could guess his excuses. *It's for the best. You just need to understand…*

"Loren." He mounted the bottom step, and she scrambled back, throwing her hands out in front of her.

"Don't touch me!"

"Loren—"

"I'm eighteen," she shouted over him. "You can't make me go anywhere I don't want to."

His eyes flashed in a way that clearly said—*The hell I can't.*

"I'm not making you do anything," he insisted out loud, stressing every word. "We will go there together, so that I can contact the pack—"

"Screw the pack!" Loren didn't even recognize the sound of her own voice. It was loud, high pitched—the shriek of a crazy woman, but she felt too on edge to really care. All that mattered was the feeling ripping through her chest. Pain. Once again, she was being thrown away, pushed to the side like an unwanted toy.

"I don't want to go with *them*," she insisted. "I need to stay with you!"

He flinched as if she'd slapped him. The next second, those eyes narrowed, deepening to a dark shade of steel.

"No, you don't."

Nearby, a squirrel darted from the bushes and took off across the yard. Even Loren sensed the warning in his tone. Any other day, she might have backed down.

This wasn't one of those days.

"Yes, I do!" She raised her voice while his only got deeper.

"Loren—"

"I'm sick of you telling me what I want and what I need." The words seemed to just tumble out. She had no idea where they came from, but it was impossible to stop. "You don't know anything! I *know* what I want."

You.

He shook his head. "You don't have a fucking clue. And if you want to talk about this, then we're not going to have a screaming match at five in the damn morning."

Loren gritted her teeth, aware that her fingers were bunched into fists, nails biting into the flesh of her palms. The feeling pulsing through her veins wasn't *all* self-righteous anger—he smelled different. A low, prickly fury bristled off him in waves. It was in his voice. His scent.

I'm warning you.

The danger didn't frighten her. Not one damn bit. If anything, it was like a sick part of her fed off his rage. Her shirt felt tight. Whenever she breathed, all she could *taste* was fucking pine…

"Good." He seemed to take her silence as a sign that she was listening, giving in. "Loren, go back inside and—"

"No." The word seemed ripped right from the pit of her stomach. "I'm not going anywhere."

She turned, intending to march across the porch and jump off the other end, rather than pass him, but his voice yanked her back like a fish on a hook.

"You're not thinking straight. You need to sleep. Get back in the house."

"No."

"*Yes*—" his tone made her belly quake. "Whether I have to drag you up to bed myself, or—"

"Stop."

"Listen to me—"

"No!"

She remembered slamming the screen door and whirling to face him.

She remembered shouting…

But she didn't quite remember the moment she leaped from the porch and *lunged* at him. No logical thought ran through her mind, just action.

But the element of surprise gave her the edge to catch him off guard. Her hands slammed into his shoulders, and he fell back with a startled grunt. She saw him hit the ground hard.

But something more shocking distracted her from any concern—her hands, weren't really "hands," but paws topped by sharp nails that bit into his skin…and the words tearing from her throat, weren't "words" at all…

But growls.

oren Connors was gone, and Bill could only gape at the creature growling in that meek woman's place. It crouched over him, its body lithe, compact…

And purely lupine.

The wolf was barely half the size of his lycan form overall, but sleek and lean. A brown pelt covered her slender limbs, darkening to nearly black over a delicate snout. Her eyes were that same, unsettling shade of hazel—but both were wide with a horror he couldn't even begin to imagine.

"Loren…" He fought to keep his voice steady. "You need to listen to me. Wait—"

She took off, clearing his body in one long leap before darting for the woods.

Bill lunged to his feet, wincing as his shoulders stung, unintentionally scratched by her claws. Fear for her easily overrode any pain. "Loren!"

Already, she had disappeared beneath the trees with a quickness that took his breath away.

"What's going on?" Micha and Naomi rushed onto the porch behind him, but he only paused to shed his jeans before taking off.

He invoked the shift mid-step and hit the ground on all fours, growling in the back of his throat. Loren's scent pulled at him like a tether, leading him blindly through the woods, past the stream, and beyond.

Rather than chase her down, he kept his distance, giving her space to run freely. It was a risky decision. She could have gone anywhere—and a frightened, newly-shifted wolf was erratic at best and unpredictable at worst.

Either way, she didn't stay a beast for long.

He could sense the exact moment she shifted back into human form, near the boundary of his property. From yards away, he heard her startled gasp. After that, she just ran on foot, hurt, alone, and naked. His heart throbbed for her—at the same time, he increased his pace. If she made it into town, Bill knew that it would have taken all the skill of an Alpha to convince that many mortals to forget what they had seen.

In the end, her eventual destination didn't surprise him one bit.

With one last surge, he pulled free of the forest and entered the small, neglected backyard of a decrepit brown house. The location made for twisted, poetic irony—wolves were always drawn home.

Even if that place happened to be hell.

Heedless of any mortals who might have been strolling down the street a few yards away, he shifted and mounted the porch steps before his toes had even finished forming from paws.

"Loren?"

She said nothing, but he didn't need verbal confirmation of her presence. He could hear her heart pounding in a manic rhythm even from there. Regardless, he didn't relax until he finally caught sight of her crouched form through a gap in the back door.

She sat slumped against the base of a counter, face turned away from him. Her knees were drawn up to her chest, dark hair pooling on the floor. The sight triggered an unwelcome flash of *déjà vu*—he'd only seen her this upset once before.

The night Fred Connors attacked her and set everything after into motion.

"Loren." Cautiously, he entered the kitchen, but she didn't react as the rotted floorboards creaked beneath his weight. Even so, he kept his distance, hovering near the threshold.

"I should have warned you," he said gently. "What I did would leave you emotionally raw. You might be more prone to anger and fear. It's a normal reaction."

"Leave me alone."

Her toneless whisper affected him like nothing else. Her fear, confusion, and pain were like *knives*, driving deep into the pit of his stomach—drowning out that tiny voice in his head that proclaimed everything he'd done had been for her sake.

This was about way more than a misunderstanding. Still, for someone who had just phased for the first time, she seemed to be holding up well enough. At least she wasn't curled in a ball, cursing like Naomi had been.

"We need to talk," he went on softly. "I'm not sending you away, I swear."

"Oh, really?" Her voice came muffled. "Dropped the 'three days deadline,' have you?"

"You have the right to be upset," he admitted, gripping the screen door just to keep from reaching for her. "About a lot more than this misunderstanding. At least, let me explain."

Her head jerked up, and Bill sucked in a breath as those large hazel eyes stared from over the mountains of her knees.

"You want me gone. What more is there?"

Bill recognized her tone all too well. That wasn't the average talk of a scorned teenage girl. That was the lycan speaking.

The lycan who valued trust and safety and loyalty above all else. The lycan who was inherently pissed at the deception of her mate.

Even if she didn't understand the depth of it.

"I'm not sending you anywhere," he said, stepping fully into the narrow kitchen. "I'm going *with* you. If you want something to be angry for, though, I can give you a few reasons."

A lot more than a few. But there was no need to traumatize her further by spilling the whole truth while they were both exhausted and naked.

"We should go back," he suggested. "You can shower, and we can get dressed. Then, once you're rested, I can explain just what I plan to do."

She stiffened, wrapping her arms tighter around her body. Her hair was long enough to shield most of her. Even so… he had to force himself to look away. To move at all.

The wolf in him yearned to bask in the glory of his mate without a shred of remorse. Instead, he pushed past her, into the living room, where he took the rickety stairs to the upper level.

Things like guilt or respect for the dead didn't stop him from rummaging through the tiny room that had belonged to Fred Connors. He grabbed a pair of sweats at random from a dresser and pulled them on for modesty's sake, suppressing his disgust at the thought of wearing the man's clothing.

Loren's room was different.

As he headed toward that tiny space, no bigger than a closet, he had to pause before he could step inside and held his breath.

Not that it helped.

The stench of her fear *still* tainted the air. It was everywhere, itching beneath his skin. Invoking a fierce desire to protect. To destroy anyone who'd ever hurt her.

Kill…

He shook his head to clear the thought before he barged in and managed to grab a sheet from the bed. He had removed any clothing the morning after the attack, but even a blanket would be better than nothing.

He returned downstairs to find her in the same spot. After leaving the sheet within her reach, he stood back. Seeing her so tense and fragile made him realize that taking her back to the house and putting off their inevitable conversation would be cruel. What better way than to just rip the Band-Aid off now? "Loren…"

Funnily enough, he didn't even know where to begin.

I found you? I mated you? I let you stay with Fred Connors even when I knew he was hurting you?

Those indiscretions barely cut the surface. His biggest crime against her sprung from his lips before he could hold it back.

"I lied to you, Loren. About more than you could ever know."

There was no way to easily explain—but he didn't have to.

"There's another side to the lycan way of life." He sank into a crouch just beyond the doorway. "Sometimes, it can be the only option for someone who has grown up without the shelter of the pack. A way to integrate them while minimizing the trauma. It—"

He broke off, grunting in annoyance. *No.* He wouldn't give her some bullshit explanation or try to pretty it up. With a guttural sigh, he tilted his head back to eye the ceiling. The truth, as repulsive as it was, needed to be said. No fluff. No excuses.

"We take mates, Loren."

She reacted to that word. A ragged gasp escaped her lips. For all his insistence on coming clean, he couldn't even look at her. *Coward,* the wolf in him, scolded as he focused on a light fixture. *You fucking coward.*

"It's the highest form of connection," he went on gravely. "Something deeper than any human concept of a relationship. Once a man and woman mate, it..." He grappled for the right words and could only find three. "It binds them."

He didn't even realize that he'd fallen silent until the sound of the screen door swinging into the side of the house broke the quiet. The wind had picked up, heralding yet another storm. The rain would help cover their tracks, at least. Sooner or later, someone would come looking for him. That fact only served to drive in how little time they had, but he didn't say a damn word to hurry things along. Loren deserved to process this in peace. It was the least he could give her.

Once a few minutes ticked by, he soldiered on. "Taking a mate without consent is a last resort. But that doesn't excuse the fact that it's wrong. It's a violation of the most intimate kind. When lycans mate, they become in sync. They can access each other's thoughts, feelings, memories."

On Black Mountain, it wasn't that unusual for a member to offer to mate an outsider to make the transition easier. But he doubted that anyone could dredge up an example of someone mating a naïve young girl to protect her from the horrors locked inside her own head.

"How?" Her voice came so softly he barely heard it. "How do you…mate?"

He made himself look up and reluctantly meet those watchful eyes.

"You enter someone's core. Their mind. It's a bond, more intimate than even sex," he said, cringing at the thought. The crimson spreading across her cheeks told him that she knew damn well what he meant. "But the two must be willing…to an extent, to prevent any difficulties adjusting."

Or, in her case, stunned, traumatized, and barely conscious. His skin *crawled* with the memory of her, lying there passively beneath him—but trying to forget wouldn't help him any.

What was done was done.

"It's not just that," he added, clenching his hands into fists. "The mating bond is strong—stronger than any other connection in the world. It shapes those under its influence. Drives them to protect and defend each other at all costs. It's…"

All in all, it had proven to be a pain in his ass.

He could feel it, even now, bristling at the fear and unease that wafted from her like a bad stench. He had to bite his lip just to keep from reaching for her. Holding her. Touching her. Fuck, he had to drill his own nails into his palms just to keep from…

"What aren't you telling me?" Her eyes were sharp, picking up on his hesitation.

Bill choked back a groan. "I *can't* tell you," he said finally.

Call it weak or stupid—whatever. He couldn't say it out loud and watch her reaction. He *couldn't.*

"But…I can show you."

He rose and moved toward her as cautiously as a soldier navigating an active minefield. To his surprise, she didn't flinch when he offered his hand.

It hung in the air for a long while before she finally took it, pulling herself upright. Bill had enough sense to turn away as she stooped for the sheet and wrapped it around her trembling frame.

"Tell me," she whispered, facing him from beneath that curtain of hair. "Please."

Bill couldn't help himself. Fingers shaking, he placed a hand on her shoulder.

Just this once. One last feel of her delicate muscles flexing beneath his palm before he lost her forever. Her scent teased the air, and his nostrils flared, desperate for one last whiff. Against every ounce of logic in his brain, he leaned in, allowing his mouth to brush the corner of her jaw before settling near her ear.

"I'm sorry," he rasped.

And then…

He just let go.

Finally, releasing her memories was easier than he ever would have thought. It was like a weight being lifted off his shoulders. A relief. He could finally *breathe* without that darkness at the back of his mind. Though, he would have gladly kept that pain for eternity to prevent the strangled sob that broke from her.

Her eyes widened, glistening as the memories returned faster than she could handle them all. Even now, Bill couldn't bring himself to go through the worst of them— but he could guess fair enough.

It was too late to change his mind, but as her expression fell, he would have given anything to do just that.

23

*L*oren swayed on her feet, knowing that his grip was the only thing holding her upright. But rather than comfort, his touch repelled her, confused her, irritated...

She recoiled as a tangled mass of memories overwhelmed her all at once. In a distorted slideshow, they ran through her brain, each one more painful than the last.

McGoven. Fred Connors. Uncle Bart.

Punctuating them at random intervals were the recovered instances of her mother, and the terrifying figure from her nightmares, now with a face.

It was like waking up from a hazy dream when she hadn't even been aware that she'd been sleeping. She could only stare into McGoven's silver eyes and attempt to process the various emotions rising within her.

Everything was…

Too clear.

Too sharp.

Too *much*.

Rage. Anger. Hate. Pain. Fear.

More pain.

Fear, fear, fear, fear, fear.

She'd forgotten so many twisted, horrible things—and wished never to remember them. Abruptly, the last night in her father's house came back to her in snatches. *He dragged her out of bed…shoved her down the stairs…beat her.*

She remembered running, falling, screaming for help.

The knife. The woods. Her nightgown was gone, torn around her like broken wings. She was curled up on the ground beside her father's dead body…

Only now she had a pretty damn good idea of who killed him.

"Oh…God." Her fingers shook as she braced them against the counter—anything to stay upright as the world started spinning. McGoven had danced around her father's murder for a reason, but one too horrifying to fathom.

Some nameless criminal hadn't killed him.

"I did it." She *had* to say it out loud. Admit what she figured some distant part of her had known all along. "I stabbed him. I killed my fath—"

"He wasn't your father," McGoven said gruffly. Throughout her violent recollections, he maintained a grip on her shoulder, keeping her upright. Though his fingers flexed, as if expecting her to pull away.

"You protected yourself," he insisted. "I'm pretty sure that if you hadn't, he would have killed *you*—"

"Don't." Loren wrenched out of his grasp and staggered for balance. "Don't try to pretty it up because you think I can't handle the truth."

She couldn't—but his concern didn't make it any easier.

"I killed him," she croaked. "I stabbed him with a knife. And you—"

More visions filled her head, chilling her to the bone. He had been there. *Standing over her. Watching. Dragging her back when she tried to…*

God, had she really tried to kill herself? The thought seemed so surreal, like it belonged to someone else. A whimper tore from her throat as more images flashed through her head. *He had pulled her back…confirmed that her father was dead, and…*

"Loren, just let me explain—"

"No!" She squeezed her eyes shut, fighting to remember. *Him. He was in her head. Her soul. Taking. Obscuring. Controlling.*

"I only wanted to protect you." He'd taken a step closer, towering above like a wall of muscle, eyes so bright they practically burned. She had never seen him this tormented, as if every breath he took was poisoned, killing him from the inside out.

"Loren, please. Listen to me." He reached out, and she flinched.

"Don't touch me!"

"Okay." He withdrew, displaying his hands passively in front of him. "I just need you to know that everything I did was to protect you."

"Protect me?" She would have laughed if the thought wasn't so horrifying. "From what? Why didn't I remember? Why now? Why? *What did you do to me?*"

Because he had done *something* alright. Something that had ripped away the mental veil keeping the dark thoughts at bay. Something to block out these memories in the first place.

Then, it hit her.

Mates. That damn word everyone kept flinging around. It was the real reason why he followed her the night he sent her with Kyle. Why he kept her near him at all. Probably the same reason why the very *thought* of him being around any other woman nearly drove her insane.

He entered her soul—but that wasn't the horrible part that had tears springing to her eyes.

After forging such an intimate bond between them, and seeing her memories and thoughts for himself, he then deemed she was a burden he didn't want any responsibility for.

And he threw her away.

"You made me feel like I was being crazy," she said in a rasping voice, spinning to meet his gaze. "But you knew why I was attracted to you. I felt like something was wrong with me, but… If you didn't want me, why do that in the first place?"

"Loren." Something she couldn't name flashed through those silver eyes. Was it pain? Guilt? "You have every right to be angry with me. Let me take you back—"

"No!" Suddenly, the room felt too small. Enclosed. Suffocating. Panting for air, she staggered for the door.

"Loren, wait—"

"Get away from me!"

She fled onto the porch, feeling the wind whip her hair back and enhance the fact that she had left the sheet behind. Ignoring the cold, she raced down the stairs and took off, choosing a direction at random.

But she would never be fast enough to escape him.

"Loren!" His voice resonated through her skull, rousing a sudden need to go back. *No!* She slapped her hands over her ears—anything to tune him out. Make him go away.

Her memories, her fear, her horror—all of it was too much. The specters of Fred Connors and Uncle Bart loomed large, but the men themselves were already dead. McGoven wasn't the source of her rage—not by a long shot—but he was the only target she had left to focus on. And in this moment…

She needed to fear someone. Hate someone. Blame *someone*. For her past and for the horrific things she had yet to face.

She needed him to just *go away!*

It was as if everything she'd ever felt boiled within her all at once. Until… She stumbled, tripping over her own feet, and her hand went to her chest. It *hurt.* Her initial fear was that something had hit her—a bullet? What else could explain this pain tearing through her? Ripping her apart?

But…he felt it too. His agonized grunt made her whirl around, frozen by the expression on his face. Her first thought was that he'd been mortally wounded. Stabbed.

But there was no blood. No one else was in view, either.

"You broke it," he said hoarsely in between pants. "On your own. How did you even… Fuck!"

He collapsed to his knees, gripping his skull with both hands as if he felt his brain might burst from it.

Despite everything—the pain and the rage—she couldn't stop herself from racing to his side. "What's wrong? What did… What did I break?"

Something vital—though she never even touched him. Horror ripped through her, and she wracked her brain for anything she could have done. Any touch. Any errant word.

Her tantrum alone couldn't cause this. As he struggled to regain control of his breathing, McGoven hunched over. His eyes were tight with pain before they suddenly widened, meeting her gaze.

"I'm sorry," he rasped. "I'm so sorry…"

It seemed surreal that he cared so much about her even though he was the one in agony. Sweat beaded over his brow, and she was convinced he'd been injured after all. "Do you need a doctor?"

"No." He shook his head and stood disjointedly, lacking his usual grace. As he towered over her, she realized that he was just wearing pants while she remained naked, in full view of anyone who happened to be gazing into the Connors' backyard.

That possibility seemed to matter to him more than his own discomfort. Grimacing, he headed for the woods. "I… I'll explain later. Right now, we need to get back."

"To leave?" Loren didn't move as her initial reason for running came back to her. Her cheeks flamed. It seemed so irrationally childish—freaking out because he had even hinted at leaving her again.

At the moment, the fear had felt monumental. Like a betrayal.

And now? It was harder to grasp that prior rationale. Her thoughts seemed to come all at once, from varying directions. Fear. Shock. Alarm. Pain. Interspersed among them were images and fragments—memories.

Fred Connors. The night he attacked her. Her mother's death and the horror that followed.

She groaned, clutching her forehead. The mental assault was ruthless, unbearably painful. It took every ounce of control she possessed just to wrestle them aside and refocus on the present. McGoven—and one vital fact he himself had admitted. Looking up, she met his gaze, surprised as hot tears slipped down her cheeks unbidden.

"You're taking me back to Black Mountain."

"No… Not quite." He inclined his head in her direction, but she noticed that he winced as if moving at all hurt. "We're leaving *together*. All of us. That's what I've been trying to tell you. Lukka and the others… They'll come for me soon, and Sonia might be in danger if I don't act. Leaving now is the only way to stay ahead. Besides, Black Mountain holds the answers to your heritage, and we need to find them. Last night, the others and I loaded up my truck with whatever supplies we might need. All that's left is to hit the road before the pack comes calling."

"What if I don't want to know?" she asked in a whisper. "My past. What if… What if it's not important anymore?"

He squared his jaw, and she could see a bead of sweat drip down his forehead. "Well, I do. This isn't just about you anymore—I need to know. I have to."

Something in his tone warned that his motive was more than just curiosity. "Know what?"

"Why *my* Alpha compelled you to forget your lycan side and left you to be raised out here alone." His words registered in two distinct ways.

The first was that he was furious. So very angry. But, as she weighed his revelation, Loren couldn't process her shock. It was enough to diminish whatever mixture of confusion and horror she felt toward him.

"What? Do you mean…" The man from her memories. "You knew him."

Bill nodded, his expression darker than ever. "Yes. And the only way we are ever going to get real answers is to go and find them."

Loren didn't move, feeling her teeth chatter. Micha and Bill seemed rarely affected by the cold, but she was already shivering, and the prospect of walking the entire way to Baker farm made it sink in just how far she'd run in only a few minutes.

While a wolf.

"I just shifted," she blurted with a tattered laugh. That seemed to be an understatement. Amid that violent transformation of muscle and bone, she felt wild, untamed emotion she'd never experienced. Ever. Remnants of it lingered still, heightening her awareness of everything from her swaying stance, to the way her heartbeat surged beneath her skin.

Her nerves prickled, her knees buckling with unsteady energy. All over, her entire body hummed in a way that felt…

Primal.

Even his nearness resonated differently. His scent overwhelmed every ounce of air she drew in, and she could feel a shadow of his heat despite the distance between them. A part of her shuddered, drawn to him regardless of everything…

"Please," Bill called, snapping her back to the present moment—they were still in the middle of Fred Connors' backyard. "Come with me."

His tone alone coaxed her forward, and she followed him in a daze, still eyeing her thin, pale limbs. They looked the same, belonging to the frail Loren Connors, but within… It was as if her brain had expanded to twice its previous size. She was aware of so much more than her own fear, and discomfort. The sky seemed brighter, the wind far louder, rustling through the trees in a deafening clamor. Even her body seemed affected—her stumbling, unsteady movements were such a violent contrast to the way she'd moved while in wolf form. No wonder McGoven seemed to relish the change.

"Wait here," he said once they reached the boundary of the property. "I'll bring you some clothing. Then we'll load up."

"All of us?"

He nodded. "Micha and I will take my truck. You will ride with Naomi. It's safer for her to be with me than on her own. At least for now."

She couldn't bring herself to argue. "And then?"

"Then we get answers."

What he didn't say echoed in her mind, uttered by that shadowy inner voice—*By any means necessary.*

24

"You drive," Bill told Micha before tossing him the keys. He didn't even know if the kid knew how. Still, if he took the wheel himself, he doubted they could reach Black Mountain in one piece.

From the corner of his eye, he saw Loren and Naomi entering the latter's pink sports car. Admittedly, the flashy model would stick out like a sore thumb anywhere near the relatively rural outskirts of Black Mountain. Oh well. He'd regret the oversight later—among other things.

While he'd kept it together enough, to grab Loren a fresh set of clothing, focusing was a struggle. Funnily enough, the shock was more startling than the unexpected pain.

How damn ironic. He had been prepared to play the hero and break the bond himself, when Loren did so easily without even understanding what it was. On her own. He hadn't expected that plot twist, and it... Unnerved the hell out of him.

Perhaps she had inherited "the calling" as he had, but even so—from the very start, he'd sensed something abnormal in her. A duality of sorts, that allowed her to seem like a harmless human one minute, and a wild, feral lycan the next. Her unusual nature puzzled him, though maybe the horror inflicted on her as a child played a role in it all.

After being suppressed for nearly a decade, her lupine instincts had mutated, becoming just as unpredictable as the environment she'd grown up in. Hell, that might have been the only reason why she'd survived this long.

To protect her, the wolf within had learned to adapt and react however it saw fit.

Even against him.

The worst part hadn't been his own agony at the severance. No… It killed him to witness the pain on her face as she understood the truth. Being stabbed through the chest with a blunt knife would have hurt less. Only one other loss in his life overshadowed this mental anguish—Emma's. But while this pain was different in essence, it went just as deep.

And unlike Emma, Loren wasn't gone. Her scent lingered, taunting him even as they hit the highway, and all traces of her should have been diminished by the fresh air. He couldn't stop his gaze from straying to the rearview mirror, watching that pink car tailing them.

He pictured her inside it, but he couldn't even imagine what she might be thinking. Or feeling.

With the bond gone, he shouldn't have cared—not like this. Gritting his teeth and clenching his hands into fists couldn't suppress the urge itching through his veins. It didn't make sense. Damn it, he *still* wanted… To explain. Comfort her. Hold her.

Every damn thing he'd blamed the bond for.

It wasn't like he didn't have a frame of reference for how this *should* have gone. When Emma died, the pain had nearly hollowed him, but he had still been able to find shreds of himself within the wreckage. A hint of the person he'd been before.

This time…

A part of him still howled that the woman with the unusual scent belonged to him in a way that couldn't be erased— bond or no bond.

She was *his*, always. From that very first day she'd stepped onto his property, the wolf in him had craved her. Claimed her.

All along, he'd fed himself excuses and lies, but the grim truth was that he'd never had a choice. The moment he saw her desperate and in pain, there had been no stopping his instinctive reaction.

The worst part? He would do it all over again.

In a heartbeat.

"So, what's the game plan?" Micha demanded, sounding miles away. "Because, one would hope that, by us going up to Lukka's front door, you would have a strategy for how to announce yourself, and we wouldn't just barge in like lambs to the slaughter…" He laughed weakly. "You *do* have a plan, right?"

Bill gritted his teeth, fighting to refocus on the task at hand. His doubt, or whatever this feeling was, could wait. First things first.

"The 'game plan' is that we aren't going straight to Black Mountain. Not yet," he said. "First, we need to make a detour. I know a neutral piece of territory where we can camp for a night or two. Then we'll decide what to do next from there."

"That sounds…risky," Micha replied. He wasn't even trying to hide his nerves. He sat hunched over the wheel, his eyes bug wide. Every few seconds, he slammed on the brake as if afraid to touch the speed limit.

Bill's one consolation was that he might not have long to reconcile his feelings toward Loren if he died in a fiery car crash. Tentative driving aside, though, the kid had a point.

They couldn't just barge into Lukka's territory unannounced. Surprisingly, Bill had yet to think that far ahead. His gut told him that Lukka would be plotting a long, drawn-out plan to avoid confronting him directly. That's what the bastard excelled at—dirty tricks and underhanded lies. Not to mention Kyle. His thirst for misplaced revenge would play right into Lukka's hands. Bill had more than learned his lesson with Loren to never underestimate a lycan, especially one with nothing to lose.

Rather than dwell on the impending confrontation, he decided to change tack. "Tell me what *you* think we should do?" he asked.

"Well…" Micha cleared his throat. "I think your best option would be to meet with Loreck Eislander first. He's the main one gunning for your throat, and I can have your back. You didn't kill anyone who didn't deserve it. With him convinced, Lukka won't have a real reason to persecute you outright. Other than…well, Loren."

"At least that's one crime taken care of," Bill said tiredly. "Loren's broken the bond on her own, and I've already told her everything. There is nothing to punish me for."

"What?" Micha nearly drove off the road. Only his reflexes allowed him to regain control of the truck in time. "Sorry! I mean, wow. She broke it? Seriously? I've never heard of that before. That's…"

"Not important," Bill said. "What *is* important is keeping her out of my mess."

"Well, the no mate thing helps," Micha admitted. "Then it's Lukka and you on even footing. Though, I guess you don't really have a reason to fight him, if your mate isn't in question."

"Oh, I can think of a few reasons," Bill said quietly. "I've thought about it, and I've decided to challenge him outright. For my freedom…and for the pack."

"What?" This time, Micha slammed on the brake so hard they both almost went flying through the windshield.

"Maybe I should drive," Bill said with a wince. Still, he couldn't deny that Micha's shock was at least partly warranted. He scarcely believed it himself.

He was going home. Not to cut ties, but to reassert himself if possible and take control. Hearing it out loud only cemented how insane a plan it really was. Just twenty-four hours ago, he would have considered the possibility unthinkable. But here he was…

And there wasn't an ounce of doubt in his body. For years, he'd been so hellbent on running that he never stopped to ask himself why. Why had he spent so long on the outside, determined never to look back?

Emma was merely part of the reason. The whole truth was far more complicated. By failing her, he had failed Lukas and his teachings. In his mind, he'd lost the right to ever lead. Maybe taking up the role of a rogue had been his way of punishing himself?

But now…

The past was irrelevant. If his years on the outside had taught him one thing, it was that the world stopped for no one. By shirking the role of Alpha, he'd told himself that he was the only one who deserved to suffer—that he had been sparing the others. Only now could he admit the truth.

He'd been afraid. Afraid that Lukas had pegged him wrong. He was no Alpha. No leader. Just a flawed bastard who couldn't protect the one person he loved the most.

And here he was, letting history repeat itself. If he studied the reasons for his change of heart intently, Loren Connors was the main culprit. Watching her process her newfound lycan abilities made him realize how important community truly was. As Alpha, he could show her exactly what her life was meant to be.

From a platonic distance, of course—though something in his chest pulsed as if in argument. *Mine...*

Logic couldn't quell the possessive impulse. No matter how he tried to reason his way around it, his wolf rebelled at any thought of a future that didn't include her.

As more than just a packmate.

Whenever he envisioned keeping his distance, his mind would replay their every interaction. Every kiss. Every stolen, guilty bit of pleasure.

Every greedy gasp she'd uttered in response.

"I'll be honest," Micha said quietly, drawing his attention. "I don't know if this will work, but I've got your back."

Bill raised an eyebrow. "If you were smart, you would take off and try to rejoin the fold. Lukka won't show you any mercy."

"About that..." Micha squirmed in his seat, and Bill sighed. He knew that look. Today was the day for uncomfortable revelations, it seemed.

"What is it?"

"She made me promise not to tell you. Not until you made up your mind—"

"Sonia?"

Micha nodded.

"Tell me what?"

The young rogue exhaled. "That Lukka is planning on making a play for Eislander territory. Soon."

Bill was thankful he hadn't taken over driving, because now he would be the one running them off the road.

"That greedy son of a bitch. He wants to overthrow Loreck Eislander." Sure, he'd already suspected as much, but to hear it stated so plainly… What the hell was the bastard thinking?

"I had no solid proof," Micha admitted. "Just a gut feeling. That's one of the reasons I didn't want to go back. I got the sense that something bad was going to happen."

"Something so bad you would rather take your chances with a rogue who has an entire pack on his ass?"

Micha laughed. "Actually, yeah. I can't explain it. No one said anything, mind you, but there was something about the way we would ignore the boundaries between the Eislanders and us. It felt off."

"Like provocation," Bill said grimly. "Luckily for Lukka, I've given him all the reason he needs to tighten his borders even more under the guise of vigilance. He did something to Sonia. She told me to run before he came for me."

"So, what's your *real* plan?" Micha asked. This time, the question had a more pointed meaning. "Try to warn the Eislanders? Let's say they *don't* kill you on sight. What then?"

"It's too risky to count on them alone," Bill admitted. "And besides… If Lukka has gotten himself into this mess, it's because he's gotten too comfortable using pawns to fight his battles for him. If I'm to take him on, I do it my way. Alone. No distractions. No proxies."

And no mate. That was one detail Lukka would particularly enjoy—it made him far weaker, susceptible to the crushing doubt plaguing him for five damn years.

"No offense, but it sounds like you have a death wish," Micha pointed out.

"Maybe I do," Bill admitted. Regardless, in addition to the doubt, for the first time in five years, he felt some cruel, twisted semblance of peace having settled on a course of action.

He was done running.

But Black Mountain wasn't the only responsibility he'd abandoned. Sooner or later, he'd need to make up with Loren on *her* terms.

Though, he wouldn't be surprised if she never forgave him.

25

"You look like you're going to puke," Naomi snarled.

Loren had to agree. In the rearview mirror, she looked sweaty. She was wearing yet another of Naomi's old outfits—a pink sweatsuit that highlighted the alarming pallor of her skin. Her heart raced, her entire body jittery. Nausea wasn't the feeling churning her insides, though. Just confusion.

So much she felt she might explode from it.

McGoven had lied to her.

Hidden her memories.

Made her his mate…

And then pushed her away, dismissing everything she'd ever felt toward him.

It was such a strange, intimate concept that her mind couldn't fully process it. More puzzling was that he'd avoided telling her outright what he'd done all this time. A part of her wanted to seethe. Hate him. And why not? He made her feel so damn guilty for something that, for all intents and purposes, was *his* fault.

As she examined her emotions more closely, overall, she just felt… Lost. Buried beneath the recent trauma was a slew of emotions that remained intact. Her admiration toward him —and more. Her longing for his nearness, his reassurance, his touch…

While a mating bond explained her relationship with McGoven in many ways, in others, it fell short. Mainly his insistence that none of her attraction to him had been real. None of it.

That was what he wanted her to think, anyway. As she began to inspect the part of her mind that—ironically—he had helped open up, she wasn't so sure.

If her feelings had been artificial, then…why did they linger? She could still feel that crippling mixture of longing and desperation and need. A gasp ripped from her throat, and she had to bite down on her lower lip to silence it.

Overall, his loss hit her harder than she would have thought. Harder than the death of her father and the despair that had followed. All of it felt so real again, as if she were reliving every tortured minute.

Strangely enough, like always, even the memory of him could distract from the horror. She could smell him. Feel him. Recall his soothing presence, as reassuring as the very first day she woke up in his protection.

But the horror of her recent past wasn't all she had to contend with. McGoven had been right—that figurative box in her mind was now unlocked, allowing old, forgotten memories to seep out when she least expected them. One unfurled in startling clarity, and she sucked in a breath, transported from Naomi's convertible to a small, warm room bathed in sunlight.

It had been one of those lazy weekends she still cherished. Gentle fingers slipped through her hair, belonging to the beautiful woman nestled beside her. Faint remnants of emotion taunted her, just beyond her reach. She couldn't feel them fully—not yet—but she could recognize the sentiment well enough—love. So much so her heart threatened to explode from it.

Then guilt followed as she returned to the present. While he might have taken the bad memories away, McGoven had intentionally given her back a childhood she never realized she'd forgotten.

But he wasn't there to watch her relive it. If anything, he seemed determined to wipe her away for good. His excuse for returning to Black Mountain was supposedly to challenge Lukka, but she knew the truth. He wanted to get rid of her again. Run away. Hide.

Ironically, he'd swapped her for the pack, using her as a way to punish himself for some unspoken crime. That was it. She wasn't a burden to him as much as she was a tool.

A way for Bill McGoven to deny himself any ounce of pleasure or happiness.

He'd rather suffer.

Realizing the extent of his self-hate stung more than the fact that he'd penetrated her mind without permission.

If his motives had been selfish, she could understand that.

Not this.

"I swear to God if you puke on my leather seats… Here—" Naomi struck a button to lower the window on Loren's end. "Just stick your head out or something."

Loren was more than happy to oblige. The fresh air did some good, though mainly the beauty of the landscape whizzing by distracted her from her thoughts long enough to get her bearings.

This place was beautiful—she could admit that much. Rugged and wild, though they had to be hours away from Black Mountain. Still, the truck ahead of them pulled off the road, turning down a winding dirt path where a set of rickety signs led to various public campsites.

"Please don't tell me he plans on us staying out here," Naomi muttered under her breath.

As she turned her gaze to the windshield, Loren suspected that was exactly what he had in mind. This time of year, there was no one else in view, and they had their pick of the lot. Even so, she wasn't at all surprised by their final destination—the most remote area bordering a wild section of forest.

When the truck finally parked and Naomi pulled in after it, Loren stiffened as a wave of dread washed over her. So much lurked between her and McGoven that it almost seemed impossible they could coexist without addressing it.

And they couldn't. He wasn't in charge anymore, and she was done letting him dictate what she thought and felt.

It was her turn to decide what she wanted for herself.

And yet, when he stepped from the truck, head held high, he radiated confidence that rendered her silent. Once again, she'd underestimated his knack for suppressing emotion. It was easy for him to put personal matters aside in the face of the unofficial role he'd taken on as Alpha.

In fact, he excelled at it. Clothed in a black shirt, windbreaker, and jeans, he seemed every bit as breathtaking as he did while in wolf form.

"This location isn't ideal, but it's better than waiting at the farm to be slaughtered," he explained once she and Naomi exited the pink convertible.

They were on the outskirts of a small clearing speckled with wild grasses and a circle of beaten earth perfect for a campfire.

"We can stay here for the night and get the lay of the land before pushing further north," McGoven explained. "For now, we'll get some supplies and set up camp. Oh," he added. "If you were worried about the horses… I arranged for one of the local farmers to check in on them while we're gone—" He frowned at the word choice, even as it left his mouth. As if to betray him, his eyes darted in her direction, though she couldn't name the emotion flitting through them. "They'll be safe."

Loren released a breath she hadn't even been aware of holding. That last piece of information meant little to Micha and Naomi. It had been for her benefit alone.

More confused than ever, she watched him take off into the forest, presumably to scout on foot. Just like that, her hurt and anger diminished in the face of one grim realization. He had been right after all. The mating bond had been merely for her protection.

But, in that case, why did a part of her yearn for him now more than ever?

Maybe it was the same broken, lycan instincts to blame for her delayed ability to shift, and her knack for blending in with prey animals? Bill must have been an example of what a true lycan was capable of—someone able to shut off all emotion in the blink of an eye.

And pretend they never existed.

For three lycans—and Loren, who wasn't willing to classify herself in the same category—their camp turned out surprisingly...normal. Despite the earlier chaos, McGoven had come prepared. He withdrew a series of equipment from his truck, resulting in two tents, cooking supplies, and basic camping materials.

Already, he was in the process of building a small fire, utilizing dried logs he'd taken from the back bed of his truck. Loren could only watch, in awe.

He worked deftly. As his stern fingers glowed in the light of newborn flames, she nearly choked. Once, those very hands had explored her body with a precision that stole the air from her lungs whenever she dared to recall it.

Her salvation from the memories came, ironically, in the form of Naomi, who stepped forward, placing her hands on her slender hips.

"Do you camp a lot in your free time or something?" the blond asked, her tone devoid of some of its usual snark. She fidgeted awkwardly as he fed the embers with crumpled paper.

"No. This stuff is mostly old equipment that belonged to the man who owned the farm before me," McGoven said without looking up. "He loved the outdoors but wasn't keen on fleas and preferred to stay in human form."

"Weird," Micha said, eyeing one of the packaged tents skeptically. "It's gonna be hard to maintain a perimeter out here, though. I'm not familiar with this area, either. We could be stepping on the toes of a lone rogue or something."

McGoven shook his head. "I doubt it. This is municipal property, and most rogues wouldn't stray this close to such a heavily patrolled area. Luckily, with the storms passing through, the park rangers won't risk driving on these roads, and we shouldn't draw notice out this far from pack territory. I suspect we have a few hours at least before they notice we've moved. I aim to take advantage of that." The wicked gleam in his eye was enough to snap even Loren from her daze.

"How?" she demanded.

He frowned as if he'd forgotten her presence entirely. An awkward silence fell afterward, and only the crackle of the fire filled it.

Embarrassment prickled her cheeks. She hadn't spoken to him directly since what happened in the woods. It seemed he wasn't willing to bridge the gap looming between them, either. He just picked up a wayward stick and continued to stoke the fire.

"Ah, why don't you and I set this up, Naomi?" Micha grabbed one of the tents and set off with the grudging blond on his heels.

Bill watched them go, his jaw tight. Finally, he inclined his head in Loren's direction, though he kept his gaze fixed on the fire at their feet. "I have some business to attend to," he said cryptically. From his expression, she could tell he intended to say nothing more. Then he sighed again. "Part of it has to do with finding who your real father is."

"Why does it matter?" she asked. Her niggling paranoia supplied a few possibilities. So that he could have someone new to foist her onto? Someone else who could consider her a burden?

He furrowed his brows, mulling over his reply. "Because it matters. To me, anyway. You should know who your family is. And I want to know who tried to silence you and why."

"You knew him," she pointed out. It felt so surreal to finally put a face to the figure who stalked her nightmares for so long. A phantom more terrifying than even Fred Connors. "The man who took my memories."

His entire body went rigid, but the strangest thing was... She felt nothing—from him, anyway. She couldn't sense that invisible tendril of emotion that had allowed her to read him so easily before. Without it, they were back at square one—he was a stranger she had no idea how to predict.

Going off established precedent, she waited for him to close up again. To push her away. Instead, he met her gaze head-on, and she wasn't prepared for the intensity in his expression.

Gone was that perpetual doubt. Replacing it was a fierce determination. She couldn't suppress the shiver that wracked her spine at the sight. It was the expression he'd worn the day she goaded him into chasing her through the woods.

Right before he kissed her like mad.

"Tell me," she whispered. "Please—"

"His name was Lukas Grehmaine," he said in a low voice. "He was the previous Alpha of Black Mountain pack and a man I looked up to. I only ever knew him to be fair and honest. Though, hell… Maybe I never really knew him."

That bothered him—that he might have been fooled by someone he trusted. More than in an obvious way.

"I need to know why, Loren," he said so softly she found herself inching closer just to hear him above the crackling flames.

"I want to know why he would do something so fucking… Despicable." He stabbed his stick at the base of the fire, sending burning embers into the air.

"I want to know, too," she admitted, surprising herself. "Tell me about him. You shouldn't keep me in the dark."

"You're right." He lowered his head in a rare display of concession. "Even before we recovered your memories, I received intel that led to Black Mountain. Remember what I said about your mother? There was a small band of Scolera in this area roughly twenty years ago. One of them might have been her. She could have met your father then."

His openness emboldened her to ask, "Why do you think he did it? Suppressed my memories?"

"I don't know, but I think I have an idea of who might. They wanted to meet somewhere not far from here. I was planning on going alone. It would be safer for you to stay here with Micha and Naomi." She sensed that was his way of trying to convince her against the course of action she impulsively preferred.

"Or," she said carefully. "You can take me with you and let me find out the truth for myself. I'm not a child, and I'm not your responsibility, either."

"You have no idea—" He broke off sharply, only to sigh. "I want you to understand something. We don't need to talk about it now, but later. Still, you should know that the… Whatever linked us before, it's gone. You severed it."

His confirmation merely served to reinforce what she could already feel. The mating bond was gone. Shouldn't he have been celebrating? Dancing with joy?

Instead, he looked…exhausted.

"How?" she asked, grappling with the idea of it. She couldn't consciously remember choosing to break anything, bond or otherwise. She'd been too overwhelmed, as if every single emotion one person could feel had threatened to explode from her all at once. "I didn't mean to—"

"I don't know," he admitted, though he genuinely seemed as puzzled as she felt.

"You must be relieved," she said thickly. "I mean—"

"You want to come? Fine." He stood, wiping his hands on his jeans. "Be ready at sundown. We'll take my truck. But…"

His inflection dipped to a dangerous octave.

"I need your trust. If I say run, you run. Understood?"

He didn't give her the chance to argue. Already he was storming across the camp, his posture unreadable. Watching him go, Loren had no idea what to think.

Or how to feel knowing that his duty to her had come to an end.

And he didn't seem to care either way.

26

To say this situation was out of his element would have been an understatement.

Mating a stranger was one thing. Interacting with said stranger after said bond had been unceremoniously broken? Bill figured he should have been glad they were both in human form, at least. It made this confrontation marginally less awkward.

But no less tense.

"I'm not sure when we'll be back," he explained to Micha and Naomi once night fell. "Guard the camp. Call me if you sense so much as a leaf out of place."

"Will do," Micha said. "Take care, you two."

Bill took the request to heart. He couldn't even look at Loren as she entered his truck and settled beside him. Her scent flooded the narrow space, prompting him to lower the windows to counteract it. Blast the heat. Hold his breath.

It was either that or surrender to his body's primal reaction to her nearness.

Damn. He naïvely thought her aroma would cease to hold any appeal to him. Obviously, the mating bond had fueled his attraction. He should react no differently to her than he did to someone like Sonia.

Five seconds into the drive shot that theory to hell.

Her scent was driving him fucking insane. He could barely keep his eyes on the road, his thoughts on Lukka and the eventual challenge—or the fact that he was minutes from entering the territory of a rival pack that had made it very clear they wanted him dead.

Ironically enough, if whoever sent the information had planned to set him up, they picked one hell of a spot in which to do so. As it turned out, Wolfie's was a hole-in-the-wall just off the main highway. A swath of forest surrounded it, threatening to swallow it whole. Coincidentally, the dense underbrush made for the perfect cover for any lycan lurking in the shadows.

Under different circumstances, Bill might have liked the place. The location happened to be a quieter part of Elkton where everyone reacted to outsiders suspiciously and smoked indoors, ignoring the local ordinances. As it was— considering his tenuous relationship to the pack just an hour away—he regretted showing up the second he walked through the door with Loren at his side.

Should a fight break out, there wasn't a realistic way to minimize any collateral damage. The building was small and square, with a brick façade and few windows. Cigarette smoke flooded the interior, obscuring the wood-paneled walls and stained flooring. Despite it being just after nightfall, only a handful of patrons were inside.

Even so, Bill realized instantly that he had made one glaring misstep. He had spent too many days isolated, forgetting until now how a young woman with unbrushed hair wearing ill-fitting clothing might draw unwanted notice while in public. To her credit, she kept her head held high, her eyes observant.

And his gut tightened with every glance of her he stole while pretending to scan their surroundings.

"We should have a seat and wait," he suggested, warily eyeing the main bar where a man with a graying ponytail watched them while wiping down the counter. Had he come alone, he might have risked ordering a drink just to blend in. Instead, he picked the most inconspicuous seating arrangement and prayed their contact showed up soon.

Loren followed him to a booth and didn't speak. At first. He watched her eyes flick nervously around the barroom before darting toward his face.

Like a coward, he immediately eyed the battered surface of the wooden table rather than meet her gaze.

"Keep your guard up," he murmured. "I can't guarantee that this isn't an ambush."

In fact, this probably *was* an ambush. Why in the hell had he risked her life by bringing her here? As she quietly cleared her throat, some of his doubt eased up. She wasn't afraid.

She was determined.

"I want to be here."

He nodded, choking back a rebuttal. "How are you feeling? After everything… Breaking the bond can be a traumatizing experience, let alone reliving all those memories."

"I feel better," she insisted.

Skeptical, Bill snuck a glance at her face, surprised to find the statement seemed genuine enough. Her eyes were clear, her posture tense, but not unusually so. The only anomaly was that her cheeks were faintly pink.

He winced. If anyone should be embarrassed, it was him.

"I should have warned you of the risks," he rasped. "I'm sorry."

"Tell me more about him. The man I saw."

He groaned internally, conflicted between two brutal realizations. One, he had no right to deny her anything after what he'd done. Still, the second complication was…

He wasn't ready to talk about this. Though, considering he wasn't the one who'd submitted to having his mind torn open, he figured his emotions didn't matter one damn bit.

"He was the Alpha before Lukka." He swallowed hard, gathering the nerve to look up. When he finally probed those hazel eyes, he didn't find the anger in them he would have expected. Just a raw, naked need for answers.

"He was a good man. Strict but fair. I… I don't know why he would have done something like that to you. I truly don't."

"I believe you," she said, but Bill felt as though she'd stabbed him.

"I don't deserve your trust," he admitted. "Not after what I've done."

Rather than argue, Loren seemed to be in agreement. Her eyes were wide with alarm, and Bill feared he would never gain even a semblance of her respect again. Without thinking through the consequences, he reached for her hand.

"I'm so sorry—"

"I told you to come alone." A shadow appeared at his shoulder, and Bill realized he'd miscalculated the reason for Loren's unease.

Fuck. He fought to contain his hostility as a tall man stood from the booth beside theirs. He recognized him instantly as the Eislander spokesman—at a glance, at least, he seemed to have come alone.

While not cloaked in deer piss, his scent had been intentionally masked with cologne. As a glaring reminder of the human backdrop to this meeting, he'd opted for another inconspicuous sweater and a pair of jeans. Given how suddenly, every patron seemed to be averting their eyes from their table, Bill suspected the outfit was overkill.

"You compelled them to ignore us," he pointed out as the man pulled up a chair to sit at the mouth of their booth.

"And if I have?" the bastard countered. His eyes flickered from Bill to Loren. She stiffened beneath the scrutiny, her expression unreadable.

Bill couldn't silence a growl. Every nerve in his body lurched, ready to rush to her aid should the need arise. "I suggest you start talking."

"Unlike you, a reckless disregard for others isn't my style," the man continued. "I've taken every precaution necessary. But you haven't. Again, I remind you that I told you to come alone."

Bill couldn't muster up a shred of guilt. "Well—"

"If this is about me, I deserve to hear it."

Loren's voice rang out with a strength he'd rarely heard from her. Compared to the frail woman he'd rescued less than two weeks ago, drastic wasn't dramatic enough of a word to describe the change.

Apparently, he wasn't the only one impressed. The Eislander bastard couldn't seem to keep his eyes off her face.

"Well, we're all here now," Bill said coldly, palming the table inches from the man's position. Predictably, he pulled back, an eyebrow raised. "You might as well reveal whatever it is you dragged me all the way out here for, Eislander."

The man chuckled. "Out of respect for my Alpha, I must refuse that title. You can call me Eric, instead. As for what I am about to say… Well, to even suggest, is paramount to treason," he warned. "You really want to involve her in this?"

Bill hissed at his tone—but the bastard had a point, for a variety of reasons. One of which, Loren seemed willing to address, herself.

"I can decide what I want to do." Her voice was soft, devoid of the anger he would have expected. Curiosity was enough to make him face her directly, and he gritted his teeth at what he found in her expression.

Nothing like fear. Just a steely calm that made him regret ever underestimating her in the first place.

"She's right," he agreed. "She should hear this. So, what exactly do you have?"

The man, Eric, narrowed his gaze and scanned the nearly-empty room twice before speaking. "Did you follow up on the information I sent you?"

Bill could sense Loren's shock, but he didn't address it. That was one of the many conversations they would need to have later.

"I did," he said evasively. "Is this the part where you reveal it was all a trap to lure me here so you could execute me for a murder I didn't commit?"

"And if this were a trap, I think it would be easier than I would have thought to take you down. You think I can't sense the change in you? You're weaker," Eric declared. His upper lip curled back from his teeth, and he nodded dismissively. "You've broken the bond. I thought you might have been more shrewd than noble, rogue."

"And if I have?" Bill countered. "Shouldn't you be relieved?"

The man laughed harshly. "Then you're more foolish than I would have thought. Your Alpha is not known for his brute strength, but I'm sure he would prefer you weaker and unmated. A smart man would have waited until after he dealt with him before crippling himself."

Bill seethed at the insinuation. The worst part? He was right.

Not that any Eislander deserved to have any say in what he did or didn't do.

"Why does it matter to you whether I take on Lukka or not?"

"That's the thing..." The man leaned forward, bracing his hands against the table. "I've come across information that has led me to believe you might not have been responsible for Jamal's death. Which means that someone else is. Someone who might have a vested interest in shifting the blame."

Bill raised an eyebrow. "That sounds like a big fucking change of heart."

"Well, it's one that only I seem willing to accept," Eric said, frowning. "Loreck isn't a fool, but he's suspicious of anything dealing with your Alpha, even a rogue. He will require hard evidence to change his mind. Nothing less."

"He might have good reason to be suspicious," Bill said. "According to your intel, Loren's mother was a Scolera, and someone conspired to erase Loren's memory and compel her to suppress her lycan side. Do you have any idea why they might go through the trouble?"

The man went quiet for a long while. Finally, he cocked his head, but Bill couldn't tell what he was thinking. "Do you know how insane that sounds?"

Bill nodded. "Nowhere near as insane as the culprit's identity, but that is a detail I won't reveal until you come clean. No more fucking games. You suspect who Loren's father is, don't you? Who?"

From the corner of his eye, he saw her sit forward. Even without the mating bond tethering them, he could sense her interest. A tendril of protectiveness took root within him, spurring him onward to get her answers.

By any means necessary.

"I suggest you start talking, *Eric*."

"Now, it's my turn to play coy," the man replied. "First, I need to confirm your suspicions."

Bill didn't like the sound of that. "How?"

"I can't stay away from the pack for long, but I'll direct you to an address not far from here. Go. Meet with the person waiting there, and they will be able to confirm without a doubt if she truly is a Scolera."

"Why not bring them with you during your last little visit?" Bill demanded. "Or here now?"

He looked around, spotting no one out of place.

"They're a recluse," Eric said, his brow furrowed. "Paranoid. The fact that they're willing to meet you at all is due to no small effort on my part. Go there. Confirm it. Then we talk."

"No." Bill slammed his hands onto the table. As a testament to the Eislander's skill with compulsion, none of the nearby diners so much as flinched. "We start now. Why dredge up relics from the past in the first place? I want answers."

"You mentioned it yourself," the man replied cagily. "Twenty years ago, a spate of attacks forced the Eislander and Black Mountain lycans to work together. You might have been young, but I'm sure you can remember the time?"

"I do," Bill admitted. Though his recollections were hazy at best. He mainly remembered how tense Lukas had been during those volatile few weeks. Like the world weighed on his shoulders. "Tell me more."

"There was a rogue wolf, terrorizing nearby mortal towns. Their carnage brought unwanted interest to our region, and was directly responsible for multiple deaths and a slew of unintentionally made lycans."

"Like Fred Connors," Bill suspected. "May the bastard rot in hell."

"Yes," Eric said. "Our packs joined forces with the goal of tracking the rogue down."

"Why?" Bill felt his eyes narrow. Now that he thought about it critically, it sounded like overkill. "*Two* Alphas couldn't track one rogue wolf on their own?"

"Not in this instance." The man sat back, crossing his arms. "The problem was *this* rogue was a Scolera. Part of a wayward band roaming the East coast."

Now, things were beginning to fall into place. A band of Scolera with a member that coincidentally had the same name as Loren's mother. Two Alphas, tracking a dangerous rogue from the same clan.

"Go on," Bill spat. "This is getting interesting."

"Do you see now? Once that detail was made clear, it suddenly became apparent why the mad wolf was so hard to track and able to cause so much damage in the meantime. That breed is known for their cunning and stealth."

"Even while leaving a trail of bodies in their wake?" Bill countered.

Eric's lip twitched into the shadow of a smile. "Yes. Even then. You yourself have already been fooled by their tricks. They are notorious for masking their scents and blending in with their surroundings. Some call them 'ghosts,' a rather cliché nickname."

"I'm guessing they taught you a thing or two," Bill suspected. This man had managed to fool his senses not once, but twice. For that matter, so had Loren. If a bloodthirsty rogue was just as adept—or better—who knew what damage they could cause?

"The only way the wolf was found in the end," Eric went on, "was due to a tentative alliance between Loreck Eislander, your old Alpha Lukas, and the remaining members of the rogue's cell. It was a tricky endeavor, mind you. By that point, there were rumors of hunters in the area. We had to work quickly to contain the fallout."

None of his tale seemed like a lie. Bill decided to press for more.

"So, what happened?"

"This is a tale best left until you've proven her—" Eric jerked his chin toward Loren, "to be relevant. Until then, I'm not saying another damn thing. I've piqued your interest. Now go."

He withdrew a slip of paper from his pocket and placed it on the table. Then, he stood and headed for the door.

Rather than challenge him, Bill watched him go. The man had some damn nerve treating him like an errand boy—not that he was in any position to argue. "How do we contact you again?" he called out, snatching the folded note. All it contained was an address to a location north of Elkton.

"You won't," the man said without looking back. "If what you said is the truth, I will reach out to you first."

With that, he exited the bar. Even if he wanted to follow, Bill suspected that he wouldn't be able to. Scolera tricks or not, the man was good.

27

_L_oren sighed while gazing from the passenger window of the truck. McGoven must have broken something in her brain while retrieving her memories. She felt… Different. Her usual urge to cower and hide had been replaced by something else. Insanity? A need to speak up unprompted. Talk back. Even now, she longed to question McGoven more thoroughly, especially when it seemed like he wouldn't speak at all.

Once again, he had played coy, obscured information, and taken charge of her life—even though most of this new information pertained to her. Her mother. _Her_ past.

She didn't even know what to think. After years of obscurity, her mother's memory was coming into clearer focus, robbing her of the tragic mystic Loren had always thought of her with. Now, Eveline Connors was more of an enigma—a lycan with a tormented past of her own.

Loren craved to know more. About Eveline. About who her father might be. About everything.

Confounding her irritation, McGoven remained stubbornly silent on the drive to the meeting place, his attention focused solely on the road. Barely a few hours since her blowup in the woods, and things between them felt so stilted, and yet so…

Unbalanced. It was hard to process her thoughts. Confusion, she would understand. After everything they'd been through, no one could expect her to completely reconcile her feelings toward him so quickly.

The guilt, however… It didn't seem fair that she was the one left stewing in that particular emotion. Especially when he seemed so unaffected by the million unspoken issues hanging overhead.

What better time than now to address them?

She cleared her throat. "You didn't tell me that he was the one who told you about my mother."

"I didn't," he acknowledged tersely. "I'm sorry. I shouldn't have kept that from you. I just…"

"Wanted to protect me," she finished, parroting his trademark line. Though, had that always been the full truth? If not, it no longer mattered. He'd said so himself. "You don't have to anymore. I can take care of myself."

"You're angry about more than that," McGoven suspected, easily seeing to the heart of her emotions. Apparently, he didn't need a mating bond to read her like a book. "You have every right to be. Don't hold back now. Let's address it all."

"Fine." She turned to him while he kept his gaze on the road.

A tendril of moonlight illuminated his features, highlighting just how stern the set of his mouth was. Her belly flipped in foreboding, but she took a breath and blurted the paramount realization weighing on her mind.

"You didn't tell me the truth. That you… About what you did. Why?"

He seemed to wince, though it could have been a trick of the light. Otherwise, his body remained tense, angled over the steering wheel. "I didn't think you would be able to understand."

The answer wasn't quite what she expected.

"I'm eighteen. I understand what mating is—"

"Not like that. I meant…it was too much to lay on you so soon after your father's death. You didn't deserve that kind of a burden." His voice hoarsened, and her heart lurched.

"It wasn't your job to protect me."

But he had anyway. The memories were so real now, clear, and distinct. Perusing them was terrifying, but she had no choice—though one image, in particular, made her palms slick with icy sweat.

"I'm the one who killed him. Fred Connors. You kept that from me?"

"Yes," he admitted, gripping the steering wheel tightly. "And more. Whatever might…upset you. I only ever intended it as a temporary measure. The mating bond allows that level of control between mates. Even mentally."

"But then you wanted to send me away after…"

"I didn't want the bond, Loren."

She swallowed at the unexpected pain slicing through her chest. Regardless, deep down, a part of her appreciated the honesty.

"I didn't," he went on. "I've spent years on my own for a reason. I never wanted you…anyone to get too close. Believe me, it wasn't a personal decision. I thought it would be best for everyone involved in the end."

"Why?"

"Because the last person who trusted me in that way wound up dead." His voice broke openly. He didn't even try to disguise his pain for once, and it bled into every single word. "I couldn't save her, and as a result of that, I realized that I didn't deserve to lead anyone. It might sound childish to you, but to us… Loyalty is everything. So is trust. To make a long story short, I took it hard."

"What happened?" He had avoided this very topic from the start, but she couldn't let guilt get in the way of her own curiosity. Not anymore. "Tell me. Please."

"Lukas, our previous Alpha, had died," he said softly. "It was unexpected. A heart attack. While we are lupine at heart, we are still human to our core. In his absence, I was poised to take over."

His voice fell into a tentative rhythm she didn't recognize. A halting, slower cadence that wormed beneath her defenses. This was the real Bill McGoven—a man who internalized everything.

But, for once, he willingly shared a fraction of himself with her.

"My focus was on securing the perimeter and guarding against any threats during the transition," he went on. "It's rare, but succession is a prime time for any outside enemies to mount an attack. I was more worried about the Eislanders, but I was caught off guard when Lukka approached me and warned of potential hunters spotted in the area."

Loren recognized the term. "Micha told me about them."

Even the Eislander, Eric, had mentioned that the threat of hunters was the driving force behind an unsteady alliance between the two packs.

"They're dangerous," he said. "But rare. I scouted the area myself and found nothing. If we were to take him at his word, that would have meant pushing back the ceremony by a few days. I didn't see the need. Stability seemed more important, but that night... They attacked the perimeter. We lost three packmates that day."

His grim tone alluded to a far more personal loss. One Loren hesitated to even mention. Still, there was no avoiding it.

"Your wife?"

He nodded. "I would give anything to do that day differently. Anything. Her death was my fault. I had been so focused on what I thought an Alpha *should* be that I didn't heed the real threat. I failed her. I failed myself."

"That's why you've been punishing yourself."

He barked a cold laugh. "You sound like Sonia. To hear her tell it, the past five years have been nothing more than an expert exercise in masochism."

"You're worried about her," Loren pointed out.

"She's like a sister to me. If Lukka hurt her—" he broke off, but she could easily fill in the blanks. "The sooner I can face him, the sooner I can end this."

"Tell me about it. The challenge."

He sighed. "There are old laws that govern it. What it boils down to is I face Lukka one on one, and issue the challenge in person. He shouldn't be able to refuse. After that, he has a full day to prepare, and then we fight in the center of the territory for the entire pack to witness."

"That sounds…simple," she said, preferring that word choice over *barbaric.*

"It's how things are done," he replied. "There are other formalities. Usually, the challenger offers up a witness who stays under the control of the opposing Alpha until the challenge is over. It's a way to ensure that both parties have something on the line. Tradition dictates that no harm comes to the witness, but I don't trust Lukka farther than I can throw him. Certainly not enough to offer up a sacrifice."

It sounded way more intense than he'd led her to believe. Yet, there was something he wasn't saying. "What happens if you lose?"

He adjusted his grip on the wheel, eyeing the road with renewed interest. When seconds passed in silence, she was sure he wouldn't answer. "If I lose… Lukka won't have to fear a challenge from me ever again."

"Why?" she prodded, though a part of her warned that she already knew the answer.

"Get ready." Suddenly, he inclined his head. "Looks like this is it."

Loren followed the line of his gaze despite the abrupt change in subject. "It" turned out to be a rundown road leading to a dwelling that resembled a shack more than anything else. Fred Connors' home looked regal in comparison. Weeds strangled most of the front lawn, nearly overrunning a decrepit porch covered with stacks of firewood.

"It doesn't look like anyone is here," Bill said. "Or we've stepped into a fucking trap. Either way, there's no point in running."

"So, what do we do?"

He sighed and cut off the truck. "We wait. And we listen."

"And talk?" When he didn't refuse, she soldiered on. This moment felt too precious to waste. For once, he spoke freely, and she was desperate enough to take advantage. "I want to know more about… About the bond."

He inclined his head her way. "Like what?"

"Was any of it real? My… It felt real—"

"It wasn't." He sighed, leaning back against the headrest. His eyes glowed in the darkness, reflecting the moon's light like mirrors. "I felt it too, but that is the way the bond works. The connection feeds off itself, strengthening the attraction between the two mates, exaggerating whatever concern might already exist. To put it bluntly, it wasn't real. None of it. Just instinct."

Loren tried to think objectively. His explanation sounded logical enough, but she knew what primal instinct felt like —mostly fear. She'd grown up in an environment that left little room for tender emotions. What happened between them had been…

Different.

"It was more than that," she whispered. The most horrifying part? She could still feel something tangled and painful lurking in her chest that belonged solely to him. It throbbed the more she focused on it, triggering snatches of memory.

But they weren't hers.

It was as if a part of her had stolen something from him. Recollections. Snippets… Of her? All of the observations had been from a distance, long before their first official interaction. They were more like hazy images. The many days she spent in the woods behind her father's house. Her smell.

The unexpectedly intimate nature of those insights made her pulse skip.

Were they real?

Yes, a part of her insisted. *They always were.*

"I could feel you," she said, struggling to put the concept into words. From his harsh intake of air, she knew he understood exactly what she meant. "Your emotions. Sometimes what you were thinking. Was that part of it, too?"

"Yes. And I could feel… You."

The tension in his voice made her heart race. She swallowed, her throat so tight it hurt to breathe. "Why did you do it? Why? If you didn't want me, then…"

"Because I couldn't bear to watch you suffer. I couldn't—but don't believe that makes me a hero." He shook his head, as self-deprecating as ever. "I was selfish. The motives for forcing a mating bond aren't always entirely noble."

She shuddered at the prospect. "How do you mean?"

"There are other benefits. I'm sure you can think of a few on your own." He inclined his head, meeting her stare. "Remember how I tracked you while you were with Kyle?"

She nodded.

"Our senses are heightened while mated. Expanded. One of the reasons Lukka was so opposed to what I did is that it could be seen as a direct challenge. A mated rogue is more dangerous than a lone wolf, so to speak."

"So why didn't you want one? A mate," she clarified.

He stared off into the distance as if stunned by the question. Perhaps, he hadn't really delved into the reasoning himself.

"You know about… That I lost someone close to me once," he finally said. "I think a part of me was unwilling to go through that pain again, but…"

He trailed off without stating the obvious.

Because, despite that supposed fear, in the end, that very thing had happened. Loss. Pain.

"Hurting you was the last thing in the world I wanted. I need you to understand that. Loren—" He reached out. She could see the regret dawn over his face the second his hand brushed hers—but it was too late. Their fingers entwined, and he didn't pull away.

Like always, his heat seeped through her skin, igniting a million conflicting sensations. Deep inside, she could feel that twisted mass of emotion unravel a little. One sentiment broke free, clearer than ever.

"It was real for me," she said. Hearing it out loud, didn't inspire the shame she would have thought. It felt more important to acknowledge those feelings. "I know myself."

"You don't know what love is," he replied, wrenching his hand away. "Don't think for a second that you felt it for me. You should move on. After this is over… I'll challenge Lukka," he reiterated. "Then decide from there."

"No." Loren blurted in a rush. "I know myself. I know what I felt—what I feel. I still do. I still—"

"Loren, please." She'd never heard his voice so guttural, on the verge of a growl. That alone made her bite her tongue.

"Let's stay focused on what matters," he insisted. "Please."

"The challenge," she croaked, submitting to the change in subject. "You plan to face Lukka…"

But then what? Would he leave as he suggested and expect her to join a pack of strangers? The idea wasn't anywhere near as appealing as he seemed to think it was.

"Can you fight him?" she asked finally. "Without the strength of the mating bond."

"I'll have to." His curtness warned her to let the subject drop.

But she couldn't. "Eric said it made you weaker. How? Just tell me that much."

"It was a dramatic choice of words," he said dryly. "The mating bond can help with doubt. Uncertainty. You felt for yourself, how I was able to help you?"

It was still hard for her to understand. Her gaps in memory. Her lack of fear and agony over the death of Fred Connors.

That was all because of him.

"You took it away," she said softly. "But after… You didn't feel anything for me at all?"

He *had*. The personal, foreign thoughts of her—long before they ever even met—proved it. His interest in her hadn't always been based on a noble, selfless need to help.

The very first day he ever caught her scent, he'd wanted to…

"Loren." The pain in his voice was palpable, contradicting her building hope. "Please don't do this. I trust you, and that's all that should matter. I trusted you enough to bring you here despite the risk. I'd lay down my life for you if I had to."

He meant it. Every word.

But even that promise wasn't enough to assuage the sting of what he didn't say.

I'd die for you—but I can't ever love you.

I won't.

Two hours into their wait, Bill left the truck and motioned for her to do the same. He withdrew a phone from his pocket and held a short, concise conversation with whoever answered on the other end.

"Naomi and Micha are okay," he said afterward, pocketing the device. "As for why we're here… I think we should scout around and then leave. This could have been a trick, but I'd rather not stick around to find out. Come on."

It was so dark she couldn't see much beyond the road, though Bill seemed to have no trouble with his footing. He moved assuredly, slowing only when she hesitated.

"It's too dark," she said, more aware of her limitations than ever. She might have been able to shift, but she couldn't control it. That part of her brain seemed sealed off, unable to be accessed.

"Close your eyes," he said. "Do you remember the feeling you felt when you shifted? Try to tap into that again. Not the anger, of course. Just that instinct."

"I don't understand." In some ways, she scarcely believed that she'd shifted at all. That creature hadn't felt entirely like her, but some primal extension. An animalistic impulse lurked within, whispering to her from the back of her mind.

At the moment, said voice was entirely silent.

"Trust me," Bill insisted. "Close your eyes."

She didn't understand why until she obeyed. It was as if a curtain had been withdrawn from a part of her mind, allowing in a million different stimuli she hadn't been aware of. Chirping insects. Rustling leaves. The hiss of the wind.

All of it felt magnified tenfold.

"Listen to the sound of my voice and follow it," Bill said next, sensing the second she relaxed. "This way."

She took a step and balked. "It's too dark—"

"Trust me," he insisted. "I won't lead you astray. Keep your eyes closed, and let me guide you. You'll get your bearings soon enough. Remember what I said about trusting yourself over all else? Let your instinct take over, just like before. Come on."

The confidence in his tone reassured her enough to push her unease aside.

With every passing second, her heartbeat threatened to overwhelm any noise he made, but it wasn't long before she realized… He was right. It was as if a disused muscle within her body was being stretched and tested. With every inch gained, a part of her awakened.

She could *see*, though her eyes were still closed. It was a newfound sense gathered from everything in the atmosphere down to the direction of the wind on her skin.

No wonder he could predict the weather so easily. This was…

Incredible.

"Good," Bill praised. "You're getting the hang of it. Now open your eyes."

When she did, the darkness was no less impenetrable. She could barely make out much of substance... At first. A glowing pair of gray eyes drew her notice, and the second she focused on them, the rest of the world sharpened in clarity.

"Wow," she breathed. "This is..."

"There is so much more for you to learn," he said with a hint of gloating in his voice. "So much more. When I..."

He trailed off, and she could sense his mood darken. He was speaking of the future—but one glaring reality stood in the way—whatever happened between him and Lukka was the deciding factor.

"Do you really want to do this? Challenge him?" Loren asked.

"I don't have a choice." He shrugged, eyeing the sky. "If he hurt Sonia... This has been a long time coming."

"And if you win?" Loren countered. "Can you really go back and leave New Walsh behind?"

He sighed wistfully, his eyes silver in the moonlight. "I think a part of me never truly left. But to answer your question, no. I wouldn't return without any regrets. There are a few things I wish I could have done differently, starting with you."

She sucked in a breath as he spun to face her, grabbing her hand. He always managed to feel scorching hot but comforting at the same time. The man was a walking contradiction.

Even now, the heat in his gaze took her breath away, but his voice was as stern and level as always. "I'm sorry for what I did. I had no right to insert myself into your life like that. To take control without your knowledge or consent—"

"Why did you then?" she asked.

"I could say that it was only out of a sense of duty. To protect you… But that would be a lie." He reached out, smoothing a strand of wayward hair behind her ear. Absently, as if he wasn't even aware of doing it. "The truth is, I wanted a connection to someone who seemed as lost as I felt. I think I believed that helping you would distract me from my own doubts. For that, I am sorry."

"But you would have broken the bond anyway?"

He hesitated. Then he sighed. "I… Wait—" Suddenly, he pulled her closer, bringing his mouth near her ear. She held her breath, panicked—until his voice returned to that gruff, cautious tone. "We're being watched. Follow my lead."

Alarm stiffened Loren's spine. She strained her ears, attempting to pick up on any odd sound. Nothing stuck out to her, but Bill had already released her, picking his way through the uneven landscape.

"Come out," he said, raising his voice to carry. "We don't want to harm you. Merely to talk."

As the wind picked up, Loren wondered if he had overreacted. The landscape seemed as empty and deserted as before. There was no one there.

At least…no one in plain sight. A flicker of movement drew her attention to a mass of gnarled trees just paces from their position.

"She can stay," a harsh voice replied from the shadows. "But *you* leave, Black Mountain wolf. Your kind aren't welcome here."

28

Bill hissed through clenched teeth. Rarely had he felt this level of hostility directed his way. Kyle's hatred came close, but the nuances were different in this instance. This shadowy figure didn't just despise him. They were terrified.

Luckily, most—if not all—of their loathing seemed directed his way alone. Instinctively, he took a step back from Loren, drawing the stranger's attention to himself.

Damn the Eislanders and their tricks. What the hell had Eric led them to?

"Show yourself," he called. "I won't harm you—"

"Leave!" The voice came from north of their position, though he couldn't make out anything apart from a few swaying branches. Hell, he couldn't even smell anything out of the ordinary. Just wind, dirt, and Loren.

"I can't leave the area without knowing she'll be safe," he replied while keeping Loren within his view.

"Well then, leave now. I won't speak in the presence of your ilk."

Another cluster of branches swayed, and he homed in on a mass of trees yards away. Oddly enough, he couldn't catch a lycan's scent. Just fresh air. Straining his ears for any sound, he attempted to take a different tack.

"Who are you? Why did Eric from the Eislander pack send us here?"

"Eric?" the figure scoffed. Judging from their tone, he suspected they were a woman. "A pompous git. Ignored me for years, only to come crawling back when his precious pack is at risk. He gave no concern for us. Damn them all."

A flicker of suspicion as to the figure's identity flitted across his mind. They couldn't be…

"Who are you?" he tried again. "Are you alone?"

He sure hoped so—one shadowy figure was enough to contend with, though he couldn't sense anyone else. Eric wasn't the only one to employ tricks when it came to obscuring their presence. At least this figure wasn't into utilizing deer piss.

They were simply…invisible, blending into the landscape in a way he couldn't have replicated, with or without the aid of tricks.

"Someone who knows all about the cunning, twisted ways of your kind," they snarled.

"You are Scolera, aren't you?" Bill suspected out loud. A part of him doubted that. Why would a lone member of that clan remain out here, so far removed from their ancestral lands? Though hell, he was an expert on living apart from society.

Who was he to judge?

"You are from Black Mountain," the figure replied, skirting any confirmation of their own origins. "The fact that you would even dare to bring her here is merely an example of your hubris."

"Her?" He eyed Loren again, prepared to confront any threat that might come her way. "What do you mean?"

"You robbed her of her birthright, and then you parade her before me. Sickening."

"Birthright?" Loren spoke up before he could, and Bill smothered the urge to silence her. This was her heritage at stake. She had every right to steer the conversation.

Even if it killed him to watch her inch closer to the unknown by taking a single step forward.

"Her, I will speak to," the figure declared. "Only her."

Bill wavered between logic and a desperate need for answers. In the end, Loren made the decision herself.

She took another step, and—even though it took every ounce of control he possessed—he stood back, watching helplessly as the distance between them lengthened. A few paces. A few yards. Eventually, she paused right before the largest tree in the clearing—a rotting oak.

"Talk to her," he demanded, fisting his hands helplessly at his sides. "But if you so much as flinch in her direction, you won't get the chance to harm her."

"I remember you," the stranger said softly, uncowed by his threat. While they remained hidden in the shadows, their higher cadence confirmed his suspicion once and for all— they were a woman. "Such a sweet little pup. Such a shame what they did to you. A shame..."

Loren cleared her throat before responding. "What who did to me?"

"*Them*. They culled you from your family. All because of him."

Loren's voice barely reached him, distorted as the wind picked up. "Who?"

It was a second before the woman's reply reached him, a snarled hiss. "Lukas Grehmaine."

Bill gritted his teeth. This wasn't quite how he expected his old mentor's name to come up again. "What do you mean? Why would he want to hide a young girl?"

"Why else?" the figure replied, still lurking out of view. "Power. I warned her what would happen." A low wail pierced the quiet. "I did. But she never listened."

Loren took another step. "Who?"

"Eveline." Suddenly, a figure appeared from behind the oak. They were small and slight, with matted brown hair that obscured their delicate shape. Though barely larger than Loren, Bill could sense they were far older. Early forties, perhaps?

"Eveline?" Loren's voice broke. "What happened to her?"

The figure crouched as if desperate to hide within the scraggly underbrush. "She let herself be part of the trap, only it ensnared her in the end. She trusted them. They lied—"

"How?" Bill's voice mingled with Loren's as they voiced the same question at once.

Another wordless howl echoed in response. "We were outcasts, left behind by our own and driven further east," the figure recounted. "We wanted to join one of the local packs, but both were hostile because of our ways. They blamed us for the local human killings, but we knew who the true culprit was."

"Then what happened?"

"She got too close to the pack leader. I warned her to stay away, but she trusted he would protect her. He didn't. The other one made sure of that. He drove her away, but she didn't go far. When she knew her child was of age, she tried to bring the girl to her home pack. Then she wound up dead. You all will suffer the consequences of the same naivety. I've heard the rumors out here, boy. You think you can win on fair footing? Think twice. He'll rip your throat out while she watches, and you won't ever see the blow coming. I won't die like they did. I won't be a part of this anymore. Now go!"

The figure scurried behind the oak, but Bill sensed even if they tried to follow, they wouldn't find her again.

"Wait!" Loren started forward anyway. "Please. Just—"

"Let's go." Bill approached her. When he grabbed her forearm, she didn't resist, allowing him to guide her back. "I think we've overstayed our welcome."

Besides, they'd gotten more than enough answers. At least one mystery was solved. Loren's mother truly had been a Scolera—one who interacted with both Loreck Eislander and Lukas.

Fuck, what a mess.

"But I don't understand..." Her mouth fell into an anguished frown that tugged at his heart.

"I think I do," he said grimly. He didn't like this suspicion one damn bit, but it was the only one that made sense. "I think Lukas thought he was protecting his bloodline the only way he knew how. By denying his rival of an heir. You."

ill drove them back toward the campsite, but he barely touched the speed limit. Urgency didn't seem to matter for the time being. Loren needed to digest what she'd learned. Even he didn't know how to process the slew of information. Instead of Fred Connors or some low-level wolf, Loreck Eislander might have been her father.

Talk about a plot twist.

That wasn't even the most stunning bit of information revealed. Not only had the Alpha of a rival pack taken pains to obscure her true identity—he'd left her under human jurisdiction to be abused. Neglected. The various implications churned his stomach, and he could barely keep his focus on the road. Though, his feelings didn't matter. Only Loren's did.

Without the mating bond, observing her was his only method of gauging her emotions—and it was proving more difficult than he would have thought. Her face was angled from his, her gaze on the window.

The building tension was too much, even for him. "Talk to me," he rasped.

Suddenly, she sat forward.

"Pull over."

Bill didn't question, parking immediately on a sliver of pavement that bordered a remote stretch of forest. The second he killed the engine, she exited the truck, and he followed, keeping his distance. For a few seconds, she just paced. He could hear her taking greedy, deep pulls of fresh air, and a part of him winced in sympathy. He ached to touch her. Provide comfort in a way he had no right to.

In the end, he settled on words of encouragement. "It's a lot to take in. Your real father… You deserve to meet him. He deserves to know who you are—"

"I don't care about that." She turned to face him, and he recoiled at the expression he saw straining those delicate features. Rage. "You could die tomorrow. You've been dancing around the issue, but that's what's at stake, isn't it? You could *die*."

For a long while, he said nothing. "There is a possibility. But what I do shouldn't matter to you. Your family and your life? That is what you should focus on."

Her eyes narrowed to slits. "And if you do die during the challenge?"

He answered her honestly. "It's a risk I'm willing to take."

He made it sound so trivial. As if death meant nothing to him, when the mere thought of it… Seemed to tear at something inside of her. Maybe it was the aftereffects of the mating bond? Or perhaps he just didn't know her as well as he seemed to think.

"Let me help you," she blurted in a rush. "I can do what you did for me. You said it was fear that stood in your way last time. I can take away your doubt. I *want* to. I know you think I should hate what you did for me… But I don't."

Good, because he hated himself enough for them both. Though, should he? Wincing, he thought back to the person she'd been the first time they met in person—a fearful creature living under a mantra of hiding in the face of danger. In her own way, she'd broken free of that shell and was able to face her life without flinching. That mattered more than any show of force, or protection he could have offered.

More than a bond.

"You helped me," she reiterated. "Let me help you. If you can look at this without the pain clouding your judgment, that could be all the difference."

"No." He shook his head. "I won't ask you to do that for me—"

"You aren't asking." She whipped around to face him. "I know you want to push me away, but I'm not a child. I want to help you because I care for you. I do… I always did.”

A part of him lurched, aching to believe her, though he knew better. She cared for him. From the day he saved her from school bullies and gave her a spare bit of food out of kindness.

And he had always cared for her…

“Let me,” she insisted. “*Please*. Let me do this.”

“No.” He moved away from her, turning his focus to the sky. “Let me be the noble one for once.”

“I don’t want noble. I just want… I want you.”

His heart throbbed, even as the logical part of his brain listed a million reasons why she was misguided. He settled for voicing just one. “You don’t know what you want.”

“Stop telling me that! Stop talking at all.” Her eyes flashed, and he stiffened in alarm. Uh-oh. Loren Connors alone wasn’t speaking to him now. These words came from a part of her she couldn’t control—not anymore. “It’s my turn to be in charge.”

He saw her lunge, but surprisingly, he wasn’t fast enough to dodge the attack. Her hands collided with his chest, pushing him back a step. He couldn’t silence the growl that broke loose.

“Loren, don’t—”

"I don't want to be a burden to you. I want to be your equal. So let me set a rule for once. If I can't shift here and now, then you go into battle alone."

A lethal curiosity kept him from refusing outright. Damn her. Even now, he couldn't back down from a blatant challenge. "And if you can?"

He wouldn't humor her. No way in hell. Still…

A part of him craved to hear her answer.

She went silent for a heartbeat. Then she squared her chin, her gaze alight with the confidence of a new lycan. "Then I run, and you catch me."

He fought to smother a groan. *Fuck.* This was going too far. A good man would end it. Not ask, "And then what?"

"If you can't, then I win."

She licked her lips, and his abdomen pulsed. Bill, the man, immediately took a backseat to the wolf within him. She wanted to play?

Then, just this once, he'd humor her request.

"Is that your final offer?" he asked in a voice he didn't recognize.

Her nod just spurred on the dangerous impulse building within him.

Finally, he took a step and jerked his chin toward the wilderness surrounding them. "Then start running."

$\mathcal{S}$he knew she'd made a mistake the second the boast left her mouth. Still, she couldn't take it back.

And he didn't want her to. His eyes flashed dangerously—some primal part of him couldn't resist such a direct challenge.

Good.

He took a step and immediately backed away several more. "No." His tone lacked that unsteady rasp it had seconds earlier. "This isn't—"

Loren didn't think. Her hair flew out behind her as she pushed past him and lunged. Whatever he'd done back at her old house…

Maybe it was desperation—or a fluke—but she could access that shadowy part of herself again. Shifting this time was almost as easy as breathing, though not painless. Every muscle throbbed, suddenly hot, reminiscent of the shock of diving into water from a height.

She hit the ground unsteadily, struggling to regain her bearings on four legs instead of two—but that wasn't all she needed to quickly adjust to. A heavy thud echoed from nearby—dried leaves crunching and a low growl—the sound of another figure shifting. Every hair on her body stood on end.

As a man, Bill McGoven was intimidating enough, but in this form… His presence overwhelmed and dominated every nerve in her body. His smell was ten times stronger, slamming into her lungs with the force of a punch. A disarming musk mingled within the usual aroma of pine as if, in lieu of words, his very essence proclaimed his intentions.

Game on.

Run! Pure instinct took over as she sprinted between two trees. Instantly she saw that this area was nothing like the farmland near New Walsh. It was rugged and wild. Her heart pounded as moonlight drenched her from overhead, painting everything in an ethereal glow. Beautiful wasn't a strong enough word to describe it.

Towering evergreens loomed above, and rocky outcrops tore through the landscape, requiring her to adjust on the fly to dodge any obstacles. Micha's training ironically came in handy as she did her best to navigate the brutal terrain.

But she was nowhere near fast enough—McGoven gained on her easily. She could hear his ragged breaths. Smell him even more…

Defeat was inevitable, but she made him work for it, driving as fast as she could through the territory. With every inch gained, her body thrummed with the thrill of the chase.

Until, something in the atmosphere shifted without warning—it was as if an invisible pressure weighed her down, putting greater importance on every step. Every breath. This wasn't a game any longer. This was a test. A primal war.

And she was risking far more than losing an argument.

Increasingly, her pulse surged, goading her on. Faster. *Faster!* Up ahead, a small clearing came into view, but as the wind shifted direction, she inhaled a scent that proclaimed her defeat.

In a burst of fluid muscle, a black wolf flew from the shadows, barreling toward her.

And it was over.

Despair wasn't the emotion that had her roll onto her back the second he came near, however. Neither was fear. Her chest heaved as stray twigs crunched underfoot, and the wind blew a familiar scent directly into her lungs—during the tortured few seconds of his approach, she'd shifted back into human form.

Still a beast, he crouched over her, so massive he blotted out the sky. Viewed in this way, he was terrifying, capable of hurting her so easily if he wanted to. As his jaws parted, ivory teeth bared, that very outcome seemed inevitable.

So why was her skin prickling, her limbs so heavy she couldn't move? The wolf lowered his head, and hot breath fanned her exposed throat in warning. When he finally made contact, however, it was with lips so soft they felt like silk. Too quickly for her to even track the transformation, the body on top of her became all male with human limbs that trapped her beneath him. Gone was any hesitation. His hands palmed her waist, every finger trembling with possession.

With confidence that took her breath away, his lips feathered over her jaw, finding her mouth—but calling the resulting act a kiss would have been an insult. He tasted her, allowing her to become accustomed to the gentle, probing rhythm of his tongue.

And then, his teeth caught her lip without warning. Pain and copper exploded over her tongue, but there was no explaining the rush of desire she felt rip through her next. A craving for something… Anything he could give.

What that was, exactly? He seemed to have some idea.

At the urging of his touch, her entire body came to life— times a million. That aching, desperate warmth wormed beneath her thighs, driving her to clench them together just to ease it.

But he was in between them, far too heavy to dislodge—and she didn't want to. When he settled against her, all thoughts of discomfort left her mind. His touch was the cure. His fingers, his desire…

She exhaled, her eyes wide, as that emotion emanated from him in waves, evident in how he held her. Touched her. Pressed his lips frantically against her jawline. She moaned, tilting her head back to allow him better access.

Suddenly, he froze.

"We can't." With a groan like that of a man being tortured, he pulled back. "No—"

"I want this," she whispered, meeting his horrified stare. "This isn't just your choice to make anymore. I want this. I do."

Even if it didn't seem to make sense that she could feel so strongly for someone after a couple of weeks of knowing them.

Her voice echoed with a conviction she'd never heard before. Neither had he. Without giving him the chance to move, her hand found the planes of his cheek, and she smoothed back wayward strands of black hair until nothing obscured her view of those piercing gray eyes.

"I want you. I do."

To her shock, he didn't waste his breath arguing. Instead, he went limp, and his forehead collided with hers with a sigh of defeat. "You have no idea what you're asking for," he grated. "But I can show you."

Her thoughts quivered as a foreign pressure intruded against her conscience. It was like before, when he recovered her memories—but firmer. Persistent.

A part of her would always fear this level of intimacy—she couldn't help it. Though, for once, she wasn't afraid to go after what she wanted.

And she wanted him, no matter the price.

This was *her* choice.

And he was no match.

31

*B*ill groaned, partly in awe and partly in relief. Would Loren Connors ever cease to surprise him? He doubted that.

He naïvely thought he'd already known her mind inside and out, despite however short-lived their previous bond was. He'd been wrong. Entering her mind now was a stark contrast from the horrific aftermath of Fred Connors' assault. Her fear didn't threaten to drown him this time. Her thoughts enveloped him eagerly, with her body acting as his sole anchor to the rest of the world.

What had been meant as a show of force—to convince her to change her mind—became something else in an instant, more akin to an earnest probing of her thoughts and feelings. Greedily, he took whatever she was willing to let him see.

He couldn't stop. Even if he wanted to, the decision was no longer his—the lycan within him howled with the need to fulfill this one driving instinct.

Dominate.

And she gave herself to him in a way that astounded him. There wasn't an ounce of hesitation. No fear. When their eyes met, he barely recognized the woman gazing back, her eyes blazing with a naked acceptance that blew his mind.

And a challenge.

She shifted her balance, catching him off guard. The next thing he knew, she straddled him fearlessly, her hair streaming down her shoulders. Her eyes latched onto his chest, and he could see the intention in her gaze—feel it.

And yet he didn't even fight as she nuzzled at his throat.

And then bit.

"Fuck." He hissed through his teeth as his eyelids fluttered at the sensation of her biting deep, right through the ragged remains of her initial mark. Within, his wolf howled with acceptance, relishing the wound. Her claim.

And his canines throbbed in their gums as he fisted his fingers through her hair, pulled her close, and did the same. She whimpered as he seized a delicate strip of flesh along her collar bone. The wound bled. She would scar, but they would wear their marks in unison.

As they should.

Even as he finally released her, he remained there, his mouth against her neck, too overwhelmed to face her. Her genuine joy washed over him in an intoxicating rush. There was no comparison to the fragile bond linking them before. This connection was so much richer and deeper. Endless.

Soon, he lost track of what was purely mental and what was physical. He shifted his weight, desperate to get closer to her. As if watching a stranger, he saw his hand plunge between her legs, easing them further apart.

His cock throbbed, aching to fulfill this driving impulse that had been building since he forged the first bond—no, before that. When he caught her scent for the first time. He'd wanted her since then.

And now…

There was no holding back.

His body took over, driving him into her as deep as she could stand it. Not deep enough. Her heat was suffocating, every twitch of muscle gripping him like a fist. The fresh air and the moon above worked to enhance this moment despite the dying doubt at the back of his mind.

With a groan, he let go, sinking into her embrace.

The pleasure was a tidal wave, coming out of nowhere to drown them both.

As they finally resurfaced, the forest around them echoed with life, unconcerned by the act taking place beneath its swaying branches. Boneless, Bill groaned as he settled into the damp earth, pulling her close.

For what felt like an eternity, they lay there, catching their breath.

He recovered first, his gaze on the moon. "I should feel far guiltier than I do. You could still be affected by the previous bond. I… This might not be what you want when you grow into your own."

The strange part was, he didn't feel an ounce of regret. Not even a little.

And she could feel it. Her mixture of shock and awe thrilled him in a way he couldn't deny. This was what she deserved from the very beginning. An open, honest relationship in which she had equal footing.

And an equal say.

Her emotions and thoughts flowed into him easily, and there was no wall shielding his from hers. It was a level of openness he had only shared with one other person—and yet, there was no comparison, either good or bad.

Loren was Loren. Her mind was a new breed of animal, so alien to him and yet inherently unique.

"Maybe you're right," she murmured, resting her head on his chest. He craned his neck to watch her and couldn't resist smoothing his fingers through that thick mane of hair. "But I can think for myself," she added. "This feels…good. Right."

He had to agree. A corner of his lip quirked upward as he felt her contentment. Then a twinge of pain replaced it.

"I can see now," she said, grimacing. "Why you did what you did. If I could take your pain away, I would."

He didn't question her sincerity. Through clenched teeth, he replied, "I know. But I need to learn to live with it."

"But not punish yourself." She lifted her head, meeting his gaze head-on. "If I wanted to, how would I?"

He sighed, torn between his pride and… Was this relief? A part of him thrilled at her desire to help him. Craved it.

"You would reach out to me mentally and form a wall," he said. "More like…swallow the feelings you can sense bother me and draw them within yourself. But I don't want—"

He was too late. A grunt escaped him—he could feel her, creeping through their connection tentatively, eager to put his instruction into practice.

And yet, she seemed determined to distract him, continuing their conversation out loud, "So, what now? Will you still issue your challenge?"

"I could, but…"

Just like that, reality threatened to descend on their tiny sliver of peace.

"You're worried about something."

He couldn't hide the truth any longer, even if he wanted to. "Sonia called me. She thinks it's too dangerous. That Lukka will arrange an ambush the second I even think about approaching the boundary. She was supposed to feel out support for me among the others, but now… I have no way of knowing what the hell is going on. The smart thing to do might be to turn back. Forget the pack and take my chances by leaving without a formal release."

Even as the words left his mouth, he knew he could never bring himself to actually follow through.

Loren shifted, sitting upright, her gaze pensive. "That man we met with, he was from the other pack? The Eislanders. What if they helped you?"

He scoffed. "As if they would. You heard him. Loreck still doesn't buy my innocence, and there isn't enough time to convince him."

"What if you *could* get their help? And make sure that Lukka had no choice but to respect your challenge."

He raised an eyebrow. "How?"

"If you think I am…" She seemed unwilling to voice more, not that he could blame her. He couldn't imagine the upheaval she'd experienced over the past few weeks. First the mess with Fred Connors and now this—not only was she a full-blooded lycan, but the daughter of an Alpha.

"I believe that you *are* Loreck's daughter," he said, dropping that bomb for her. "Whether he knows about you or not is another matter."

"We could go to him," she continued. "Get him to back the challenge on your behalf."

"No." Bill couldn't disguise his frustration. "That won't work. If Lukka doesn't show his face, I can't honorably issue the challenge in the first place. Besides, if I show up on their doorstep with the Eislanders in tow, I might as well declare war. All of Black Mountain will react as if it's an invasion."

"Not if you *can* issue the challenge," Loren countered. "I could go to the pack, demand to see Lukka. If he came out to meet me himself..."

"You would do that?" He craned his neck, alarmed to find there wasn't an ounce of fear in her gaze. It was long past the point where her bravery should have surprised him.

Still, the sheer strength of her resolve took his breath away. Enough that he felt the need to humor her, despite the obvious risk.

"I would never let you. But yes. I could corner him then and there and issue the challenge in plain view." He chuckled coldly at the mental image. It was a plan so sneaky Kyle couldn't have come up with one better. "He'd have no choice but to adhere to the old laws. There would be too many eyes watching."

"Then I could find Sonia," Loren went on. "And help her gather support—"

"No." He slid his hand up her back, noting how her pulse surged beneath her skin. Physically, she was so delicate, but her eyes blazed in a way that conveyed anything but weakness. "Besides, they would never buy it. Lukka will make sure that I'm killed before I can even get within shouting distance. And let you go in there alone? Hell no."

"They won't expect any trouble from me," she pointed out.

He wasn't so sure. "They'd hurt you just to get to me."

"Not if they thought the bond was still broken."

Bill couldn't help himself—he played out the scenario in his mind. Forget Kyle. Lukka himself wouldn't see such an underhanded trick coming, not from him. It was a tempting prospect. Still, he sighed as logic prevailed. "No."

"I'm not asking for permission."

He recognized that hard tone in her voice. One suspicion was confirmed—any rebellious instinct in Loren Connors was entirely her own.

"Please… Look at me." He cupped the side of her face and silenced a groan. "I can't let you be hurt."

Even as he spoke, he sensed that her determination didn't waver. Not a damn bit. Chin in the air, she fixed him with a probing stare he recognized. A challenge was coming, and he stiffened in anticipation.

"Then fight for me," she said. "Because I can't let you keep holding yourself back just because of me."

Before he could argue against even entertaining her scheme, her conscience mingled with his, allowing him to see her thought process in detail. If she really were Loreck

Eislander's daughter, and he shared even an ounce of her intellect, no wonder Lukas had been so threatened by him.

Few could match their level of cunning.

"It could work," he admitted grudgingly. "But it's risky. Reckless. It—"

"It has to work," Loren said over him. "At least let me try."

After everything she'd been through, her confidence took his breath away—as did one emotion he could feel resonating through her, entirely her own.

Trust.

The moon shone brightly by the time they returned to camp. After Bill stealthily grabbed fresh clothing for them both, they found Micha and Naomi waiting by the fire. One look, and Micha blushed, averting his gaze. Apparently, their changed relationship was glaringly obvious, even to him.

"It looks like you guys worked out your differences," he said. If Bill wasn't mistaken, he caught a hint of sadness in his voice. A thought that he promptly quashed.

Now wasn't the time for jealousy.

"It's time to make our move," he said. "But I realized that I can't go barging in alone. If this is going to work, I'll need backup, and... Help."

"You know I'm in." Micha sat forward and propped his chin on his fist. "So, what's the plan?"

"Well, it isn't *my* plan." Bill stood aside, letting Loren take his place. "It's hers."

She handled the spotlight well, her head high. Bill couldn't deny his admiration, even though a part of him railed against putting her in danger even for a second.

"It's risky," Loren said. "And dangerous, but if we all play our part, it could work."

Micha and Naomi shared a look.

"I'm in," the former declared.

The blond had her lips pursed but nodded in the end.

"That settles it," Bill said warily. "Now, we put the pieces into action."

Win or lose, there was no turning back now.

He was ready to fight for his home.

And let the cards fall where they may.

$\mathcal{T}$he sun had barely finished its descent toward the horizon as Loren left the campsite alone and hit the open forest.

She ran blindly. Not long into the sprint, her lungs heaved, her pulse surging through her eardrums. In contrast, the world around her became a muted, blurred backdrop. She didn't even see a figure lunge from the shadows until it was too late.

Wham! Strong arms caught her by the shoulders, holding her close to a body that seemed cut from stone. His touch was all wrong—too firm. Not McGoven. The scent flooding her lungs cemented that fear. This man was a stranger.

"Let go of me!" Panicked, she swung her arms, kicking her legs. Only when she paused to suck in air, did she hear the person holding her shout.

"It's okay! It's alright," they insisted. "Who are you?"

Heart pounding, she whirled around to face a tall man with dark hair. He watched her warily, flicking over her filthy, tangled hair before settling over her mud-splattered jeans and sweater. She couldn't discern what impression—if any —she made.

"Do you know where you are?" He inclined his head, calling attention to the two men behind him watching from a slight distance.

The landscape surrounding them was rugged, unfamiliar terrain—nothing like the gentle, rolling hills of New Walsh. It was frigid. Every intake of air stabbed through her chest with a mixture of foreign smells.

"Black Mountain," she said. "I'm here to see Lukka."

The man frowned, and she couldn't tell what he thought. As his eyes flickered toward the woods behind her, she felt a tendril of alarm gnaw at her confidence. He was suspicious. "Where is your pack? What are—"

"I came here for a reason," she said over him. "Bring Lukka to me. Please. I'll only speak to him. He should know who I am."

"The Alpha?" the man replied, frowning. "Who are you? I can't just—"

"Tell him that Loren Connors is here to beg for his acceptance," she said. "Please."

His eyes widened, but she couldn't tell if he recognized the name or not. From the corner of her eye, she saw that more men appeared, lurking in the shadows, watching. Luckily, confusion seemed more prevalent than hostility.

The one nearest her, cocked his head, speaking to someone behind him. "Send word to the main house," he said. "Let's see what they decide."

"They" being Lukka? For a heartbeat, she longed to have Bill's guidance—or at least his ability to explain what might be happening. Just as quickly, she smothered the weakness and just watched.

And waited.

Minutes seemed to crawl past as she and the men surrounding her remained at a quiet impasse.

Finally, two men parted, and one figure appeared between them, his hair golden, his eyes a haunting blue.

"I'm here." His voice rang out with unmistakable authority. Tall and thin, he appeared to be the total opposite of Bill McGoven. "And you must be Loren Connors."

She didn't know what to do. Bow? Instead, she nodded, clearing her throat. "Are you Lukka?"

"This is a long way from McGoven's territory," he replied, his voice dangerously soft.

Loren licked her lips. "He brought me in a truck. When he wasn't looking. I... I just needed to get away," she said weakly. "I just ran."

"Where?" Something flickered across those blue eyes Loren couldn't name. Fear? Either way, he inclined his head toward the woods, and two of his men stood at attention. "Which direction?"

Loren could only shrug. "I'm not sure."

"Well, you're safe now," the blond man said, sounding as noble as if he were her twisted knight in designer armor.

"But where is he?" Another figure stepped from the woods, his sharp brown eyes unsettlingly familiar. Kyle. "Where is William McGoven?"

Somewhere close by. Loren could feel him, railing against the thought of her being even near this man.

The trap had been baited.

Now it needed to be sprung.

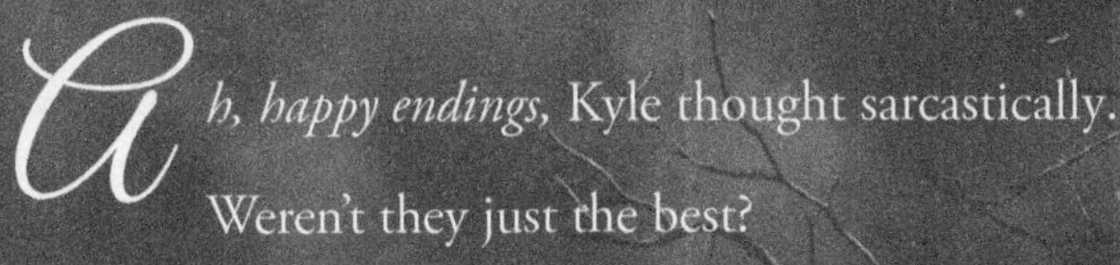

33

Ah, happy endings, Kyle thought sarcastically.

Weren't they just the best?

He, for one, sure as hell felt all warm and fuzzy inside as he watched Lukka assure the Connors girl that everything would be "A-OK." She was safe now, and the big bad monsters were at bay.

Such the hero, that one.

It didn't matter that the girl looked traumatized and filthy. Or that she had come out of fucking nowhere—without her supposed captor in tow. Kyle figured he was the only one to second-guess this thrilling rescue.

Good ol' Lukka only cared that his entourage was there to witness every single action he made. With every halfhearted insistence of safety, the Alpha was all but screaming, "Look at me!" "I'm being an Alpha!" "I totally care."

Though Kyle figured that, for once, he and McGoven were of the same frame of mind—the rogue had been right to be skeptical. Any concern Lukka showed the Connors girl was purely for show. The comforting words sounded hollow. His "reassuring" touch was more restraining than anything else.

"Where is the rogue?" he asked again.

Loren Connors blinked, turning toward a section of the woods.

Lukka stiffened, his nostrils flaring. "Fan out," he told his men—those who had been patrolling this boundary of the territory. "He's close. I can smell the bastard."

Showtime, Kyle thought coldly. After all, this was the main event he had been itching to see.

Not the rescue of some damsel in distress, but *this*—the big bad Bill McGoven about to be verbally spanked—all before being put down for the crime of being an "incorrigible rogue." He had some damn nerve venturing this close to their doorstep. At least there was no need to travel to that shithole human town. Kyle just wished they had brought cake and ice cream to celebrate this occasion.

At the girl's indication, Lukka started forward. "Stay back," he told them—not that Kyle listened.

Eyes narrowed, he brushed past Loren Connors and headed along a break in the tree cover. Sure enough, none other than McGoven himself was in the process of boldly advancing. Even now, he sported that infamous, stony expression, as cocky as ever.

Lukka seethed. "You have some damn nerve showing up here." He raised his voice so that it would carry to the crowd that had more than likely gathered, watching the chaos from the shadows. "You've broken a lot of rules, William McGoven. You took a mate without consent and trespassed on another Alpha's territory. You've committed murder—"

Kyle really had to hold in a snicker at this point—as if that pansy-assed bastard would ever *murder* someone without the instinctive urge of the mating bond. Only a real man, and a true lycan at that, could do what was needed to be done for the greater good and all that shit.

Kyle was pretty insistent that McGoven's eventual death would be for the good of *everyone*. He couldn't even bring himself to shed a tear at the fact that—technically speaking —the rogue had done nothing wrong.

It was all in the details anyway, like that random bastard he'd killed on Eislander territory.

Somebody had to do the dirty work.

"For all of these crimes," Lukka went on, in a tone that practically dripped satisfaction. "You will receive death. Do you understand?"

For someone who was facing the end of his road, McGoven looked pretty damn smug.

"You came yourself. It took you long enough…" His voice was soft, not out of fear—McGoven just didn't think Lukka was worth the effort. Of shouting. Of any anger at all. "You really didn't think I would make this easy, did you? You want me? Then face me. I challenge you here and now, before these witnesses. For the position of Alpha."

Kyle didn't believe his ears at first.

Not until he saw Lukka's reaction. He sputtered. "You can't—"

"I am," Bill said over him. "Tomorrow night. In the heart of the territory before the pack. We settle this the way it's been done for generations. One on one combat for the right to lead."

"And I'm supposed to be at the beck and call of a disgraced rogue?"

"If you want confirmation that I will return on good faith, you have the one person who will assure I will. I also want assurances that Sonia Carlisle is alive."

Kyle couldn't remain silent any longer. "You dare to make demands of us?"

"This isn't a demand. This is a promise." He nodded toward Loren, raising his voice for her benefit alone. "She will serve as my witness. I fight for her, and for the good of the pack."

Were they on that shithole farm, Kyle knew that Lukka would dispatch the bastard with little forethought. But here…

There were too many witnesses. Too many mouths to silence.

And that seemed to be exactly what the bastard McGoven wanted.

Kyle might have been impressed somewhere beneath the hate. Then he came to his senses—McGoven would never sink to such tricks.

He might break a nail or something.

Regardless of his intent, this little stunt would work in McGoven's favor. Word most likely was already traveling back to the heart of the territory. Any way they sliced it— there was no way in hell Lukka could avoid it now.

"And if anything happens to her between now and tomorrow," McGoven added. "I will kill you."

"Take her through the main entrance," Lukka snarled. "I'll join you later."

Kyle approached the girl, biting his tongue. He suspected Lukka would run for cover and plot a way out of this.

No way in hell would the bastard submit to a fair challenge, not that Kyle blamed him.

William McGoven didn't deserve an ounce of honor. He never had.

$\mathcal{L}$oren didn't know whether to celebrate or panic. Their plan had worked well enough to lure Lukka out into the open and convince him to accept the challenge. But now what?

As the adrenaline wore off, doubt crept in.

There was no going back. For McGoven's sake, she needed to ensure that nothing went wrong between now and tomorrow night.

A feat she was starting to realize was a very tall ask.

While she pushed for this plan, she wasn't foolish enough to suspect she would be safe behind the pack's boundaries. Not for a second. Even the overall landscape seemed to drive in the danger she was in. Gone was that rugged beauty that had captivated her earlier. This time of the day, very little light pierced the cover of trees overhead, rendering the landscape immeasurably more hostile.

She couldn't see much. Her only sense of reference was that they were on a road that winded through a thicker, inhospitable section of forest. Kyle stood ahead of her while another man took up the rear, radiating caution with every step.

The scene flashed her back to the night somewhere near these very woods, where the man guiding her now had left her alone to die.

"You're no longer needed," Kyle said abruptly, addressing the other man accompanying them. "Get back to your post."

The man acquiesced with a grunt, and Loren felt the hairs on the back of her neck stand on end as he retreated.

Was history about to repeat itself?

As they rounded a bend in the road, a massive wooden fence came into view, distracting her from her fear. Now she saw why Bill had been so worried about drawing Lukka into the open. This barrier was formidable, almost as tall as the nearby trees. Like some winding part of the landscape, it wove into the forest, blending in seamlessly with the shadows.

Just as daunting, was the metal gate presumably serving as the entrance to the territory beyond. Nailed to its front was a faded sign, barely visible through the dark, that read, "Black Mountain National Reserve."

That façade might have been easy to believe—especially to the average passerby—but two men stood on either side of the road, broadcasting alertness well beyond that of a typical park ranger. Tall, they cast long, lean shadows over the earth, bright eyes glowing.

"What's going on?" one of them demanded. "Where is Lukka?"

"Open the gate," Kyle commanded, avoiding the question. "Then go watch the border. Anyone approaches who isn't one of us, you attack. No questions asked."

Loren wondered if that were usual procedure before a challenge, though she tried not to let any doubt dissuade her.

"Yes, sir." The man and his partner rushed to open the gate, grunting with the effort it took to move the heavy sheets of metal. Once finished, they cleared the road, allowing unfettered access to the land beyond.

"Welcome to Black Mountain," Kyle said dryly.

As she peered over his shoulder, Loren was surprised to find only a gravel road stretching onward through a seemingly endless swath of trees. Already rushing to meet them, though, was a familiar figure whose appearance made her sigh in relief.

"Loren!" Sonia ran to them, panting with the effort. Her dark hair streamed behind her, her chest heaving as if she ran all this way for who knew how long. "What are you doing here?"

"Being rescued," Kyle snapped. "What a lucky coincidence that you show up for the welcome party. I'm taking her to the main house. This doesn't concern you, Carlisle—"

"Where is Bill? Is he—" Sonia seemed to stop herself from voicing the worst-case scenario. Her eyes couldn't disguise her fear, however, and they darted nervously to the yawning landscape beyond the still open gate. "Where is Lukka? What's going on?"

"You're impeding official business," Kyle replied. "Though I'm sure you and McGoven planned this down to the last detail. Ignorance doesn't suit you. Now move."

"No." Sonia placed a hand protectively on Loren's shoulder before Kyle could reach for her first. Thin and lithe, she easily slipped between them, a surprising match for the larger man's bulk. "No matter what's going on, there is no need to rile the entire pack and create a ruckus by parading a newcomer through the heart of the territory during supper. She can stay with me until Lukka can come for her himself. If he has a problem with it, he can tell me so in person."

Kyle raised a reddish eyebrow, and Loren was sure he'd refuse. Instead, he nodded, displaying his hands in a gesture of surrender. "Fine. Have it your way. Just to be on the safe side, I'll keep watch to make sure no one enters or leaves your cabin. Sleep tight. Tomorrow, we will make sure she's protected during the challenge."

"Challenge?" Sonia's eyes widened, and she swayed as if struck. "You mean… Bill?"

Kyle laughed, pushing past her. "I suggest you stay in tonight, Sonia. Because if you or your guest leave, I'll be watching. No need to cast doubt on tomorrow's proceedings, right?"

Without addressing him, Sonia took Loren by the arm. Behind them, the doors to the gate rattled as the two men rushed to close them again.

"Come on. There's no use worrying out here," Sonia whispered above the clamor. "We should head to my cabin. There, we can talk, and you can tell me exactly what the hell is going on."

Loren relented with a nod, allowing the older woman to guide her down the gravel road. The two men remained on the other side of the gate, and no one else was in view. Even so, she could sense countless pairs of eyes watching their every step.

If she'd been overly optimistic before, this moment reinforced that now was not the time to celebrate—and seeing this plan through would be nowhere near an easy feat to pull off.

She could only hope that Bill had evaded any tricks Lukka threw his way.

They would need all of his strength, and then some.

35

*L*etting her go was pure hell. Bill dug his heels into the earth to keep from following—right away, at least. Fear wasn't what held him back—not even respect for the old laws that supposedly dictated Lukka couldn't hurt her. It was respect for Loren alone that tempered him. After all, this was *her* plan.

He was merely along for the ride.

Though while he owed her his trust, he didn't dare underestimate Kyle or Lukka one damn bit. They wouldn't take this challenge lying down. As far as allies went, though, he didn't have many options—which was where phase two of Loren's plan came into play.

Providing he could enact it in time.

The obstacles were already mounting. If he knew Lukka, the bastard would have sent scouts on his trail—and he wouldn't put it past the Alpha to have him killed before the time came. Stripping his clothing, he shifted and took off in a full sprint that few short of the strongest scouts could match.

Fear pulsed through him anyway as Loren's fate weighed heavily on his mind, but the last thing he expected to feel, seeped into his veins in a slow but steady trickle—excitement? Joy, even? It had been so long since the last time he'd traversed these forests. Predictably, the earth hadn't changed much since then, but in a natural, gradual way. It was much like visiting an old friend who had matured in his absence. By the time he reached the very edge of the boundary, his heart swelled with painful nostalgia.

So much for honoring his role as a rogue. Fear was the real reason that kept him away. Fear of what might happen when he smelled the mountain air and neared his ancestral home again.

Being here, so close to the land he'd grown up on, he couldn't remember his reasons for leaving in the first place. For a second, he longed to breach the border, punishment be damned.

He was relieved when a figure finally broke the underbrush nearby, displaying familiar youthful energy. Micha. With one look, Bill drew his focus back to the task at hand, though it was harder than he would have thought to shift direction away from Black Mountain. Albeit, toward a far more dangerous strip of territory.

Even Micha's presence didn't lessen the insanity of what he planned.

If the Eislanders weren't already paying attention to their neighbor's borders, Bill would give them a good reason to. Together, he and Micha covered miles in minutes. As he neared the ragged plains the Eislanders called home, he boldly skirted their outer limits, putting every sentry on red alert.

Good.

He could only hope the provocation paid off as he finally stopped, just beyond the reach of both territories. Micha lurked nearby, acting as his lookout.

Though, an Eislander response was exactly what they wanted—needed.

Seconds ruthlessly ticked by. Minutes. As time stretched on, he strained his ears for any sign of trouble. True to her word, Loren kept a wall between them—but he could sense her beyond it as if peering through a sheet of frosted glass.

She had to be deep inside the territory by now. Would she be at Sonia's? Or would that bastard, Lukka, put her somewhere else?

A part of him bristled at waiting. He didn't trust Lukka further than he could throw him. Besides, he still knew all the old exits...the secret ways in. All he had to do was sneak in, seek out her scent, find her.

Forget his role in her plan. It was taking too damn long.

A rustle of motion was the only warning that someone approached, and he snapped into a fighting stance. They weren't a sentry. The intruder hadn't bothered to disguise their scent, and he recognized it easily. Within seconds, he was back in human form, lurching to his feet.

"Took you long enough," he rasped at the tree line.

"Well, you certainly have more balls than I gave you credit for." The Eislander, Eric, stepped from the shadows, his eyes glowing in the darkness. He had exchanged the nondescript clothing for a black tracksuit that seemed to suit him far better. At least this way, he resembled what he truly was—a dangerous threat, at home in the shadows.

"That was some stunt you just pulled," he said softly, jerking his chin in the general direction of Black Mountain.

"So, you've heard." Bill raised an eyebrow, though he didn't know whether to be impressed or alarmed that the Eislanders were so well versed in their neighbor's political drama.

"I've heard that you signed yourself up for what some might call a suicide mission." Eric inclined his head, and Bill couldn't tell what he thought. Not even a hint. "After what I'm sure you learned last night, I can't say I'm surprised by the route you've taken. But why come here now?" His tone dropped an octave. "Is this your way of declaring war on not just your own pack, but the Eislanders as well?"

"No." Bill forced some semblance of respect into his voice. "That was my way of getting your attention. You sent us to that Scolera for proof? Well, you got it, and if you intend to make amends to Loren for your Alpha leaving her in obscurity for eighteen fucking years, I have a few ideas of where to start."

"Oh?" The man scoffed. "And where do we come in? You think we would intervene in an official challenge? I hate to hide behind tradition in this instance, but some laws cannot be undone. Not even by you."

"Lukka isn't reckless enough to circumvent an honest challenge if it's made in view of the others," Bill pointed out. That was their hope, anyway. "He had no choice but to accept. That doesn't mean he has to oblige by it. In fact, I don't expect him to."

"So why come here? Without your mate, I see. I hope she's somewhere safe if you took on your Alpha directly."

Now came the tricky part.

"She's in Black Mountain as my witness," Bill said.

Eric chuckled, shaking his head in disbelief. "So, she's as good as dead, then. Have you lost your mind?"

"No," Bill countered, though a part of him hissed that same insult. "I trust that she can handle herself. But she has faith that your pack might owe her some shred of loyalty. What else can you do? Hide in your territory hoping that Lukka doesn't turn on you next?"

The man went silent just as the wind picked up, bringing a newer scent along with it. Bill tensed, picking up Micha's alarm. They had company.

"No," Eric finally said. He stepped forward, raising his voice to address whoever might be lurking behind him. "*We* don't plan on waiting at all."

Bill didn't even have time to react as the second intruder made himself known. They took their time approaching, partially hidden behind the trees.

This is it, he thought grimly. So much for Loren's plan—apparently, the Eislanders didn't want to cooperate. Oh well. He wouldn't go down without a fight.

Growling low in his throat, he crouched, intending to invoke the shift, while he observed his opponent from a distance. Their eyes were the first thing he saw clearly.

But their *hazel* hue caught his attention.

Abruptly, he stood upright and lowered his head with the minimal amount of respect he could muster. "Loreck Eislander."

Stepping into full view, the man didn't return the gesture, and Bill feared that Lukka was the least of his problems. He was dressed in a similar ensemble as his beta, his dark hair unbound, his steps firm with unmistakable strength.

"So, you are William McGoven," the Alpha said, his voice a guttural baritone. "Give me one reason why I shouldn't kill you."

It was a good thing, then, that Bill could think of several. Regardless, in the end, he decided to state just one.

"I am the mate of your heir. The daughter you abandoned."

$\mathcal{S}$onia lived among a lonely stretch of trees, along what appeared to be the edge of the territory. Her small cabin looked peaceful, nestled in a pool of growing moonlight. For all intents and purposes, it resembled McGoven's farm haven in New Walsh, isolated from any prominent structures.

"Let's get inside," Sonia suggested, unlocking the front door. "It looks like we have company."

Loren looked over her shoulder. Kyle had kept his word, it seemed. Farther down the road, three men remained at a distance, just watching.

Waiting.

As she followed Sonia inside, she was surprised to find that the interior was much smaller than even Fred Connors' house—though way more lived in, with delicate homey touches. With every new observation, it was harder to contain her surprise. Bill told her once that the pack territory was deceptively normal. He hadn't been lying. All in all, the cabin contained the same amenities any house in New Walsh might have. The only noticeable difference was that everything was made of wood, from the furniture to the floor.

Sonia flitted about the small living room and made a show of closing every window and drawing the curtains closed. Only then did she face Loren with a heavy sigh.

"What are you doing here, really? Goodness, we're just lucky I had the window open and caught your scent in time to intervene." Her voice sounded hoarse. "Is Bill... Is he?"

"He's okay," Loren said tactfully. "He's issued a challenge scheduled to take place tomorrow night. I am his...witness."

The term still felt strange on her tongue, but Sonia reacted to it instantly.

"You? Tomorrow?" She exhaled and sank onto a couch with a wooden frame. "My God. He's really going through with it." Her tone was a restrained mixture of hope and fear— but Loren didn't miss the way those blue eyes warily took her in. "I was praying he would go through with it. But still... Lukka won't take this lying down. I'm surprised Bill even let you go. He must be furious."

Loren bit her lip, unsure of how much to reveal. In the end, she settled on a vague explanation. "I ran from him. But he was worried about you. He was afraid Lukka might have hurt you."

Sonia scoffed. "I'd like to see him try. Though he has had my every move watched. I'm sure if you look carefully, you'll note a handful of his men lurking beyond the tree line."

She approached the nearest window and withdrew a sliver of the curtain. The road was now clear, and nothing of substance stood out from the swaths of emerald forest. Not at first. As if on cue, however, a man appeared in a gap between two trees without bothering to hide.

"You see? Though, if you're here… Bill is serious." Sonia's eyes widened, and she raked a trembling hand through her hair. "Well, then it looks like I can't let you out of my sight. Come on. I'll get you something clean to wear at least—" She darted down a hallway and reappeared with a pile of folded clothes. "Get dressed. Then I'll fix you something to eat, and we can try to figure out how the hell to get out of this mess."

"That's the thing," Loren said cautiously. "We already have a plan. Mine."

"Oh?" Sonia raised an eyebrow, but it wasn't obvious if she were skeptical or intrigued. "Well then, we definitely need to talk. The bathroom is down the hall. Take your time."

Loren followed her directions and entered the modest room. With trembling fingers, she gripped the edge of the sink, and for a second—just one—she let the mounting doubts creep in.

She was too weak. Without Bill, what could she do?

Even as she indulged the fear, she remembered his strength. His heat. His body against hers…

The weight of what happened between them felt more than any trivial biological term some might call it by. More than a kiss. More than sex.

He had entrusted himself to her, and she couldn't lose sight of that now. With a heavy sigh, she looked up, finally facing the mirror, and did a double take.

The girl staring back at her wasn't the beaten, broken Loren Connors she was used to seeing every day. She didn't even recognize herself. Her bruises were gone, the scratches faded. She had no idea why, until she remembered that McGoven and Micha had seemed to heal after they shifted.

On second glance, this new Loren wasn't completely flawless. The old scars were still there, telling a silent tale of too many beatings to count, and a hint of fear still haunted those hazel eyes. Still, it was easier than she would have thought to shrug off the unease and get dressed in Sonia's borrowed clothing.

As she reentered the hall, Sonia's voice rang out.

"Loren? I'm in the kitchen."

The cabin seemed to be one long level, with large windows looking out into a landscape that appeared bluish in the twilight glow. The kitchen looked clean, though lived in. Magnets covered the fridge, and appliances cluttered the counters.

Sonia watched her from over the rim of a steaming mug of coffee she held in her hands. Meat seemed to be frying behind her in a pan on the stove, but it sizzled unattended. For once, even cooking wasn't enough to soothe Sonia's emotions.

"What a mess." With a sigh, the woman set her mug down and crossed her arms. "I'm sure you and Bill have a plan of action, but I need to know. Ignore those spying bastards outside. It's just you and me here. What is his end game?"

Loren drew in a steadying breath. "He's challenging Lukka for the pack, but he's worried that he won't face him on an even playing field. So, he made sure to issue the challenge in front of witnesses."

Sonia's eyes widened. "And he used you as the bait to lure Lukka out into the open. Fuck!" With a sound of exasperation, she stood and marched from one end of the kitchen to the other. "I've been out of the loop. Lukka's kept me on a leash—I think he knows where my true loyalties lie. I've barely been able to take a walk without them watching me, but I know there is support out there for Bill. But if we're to capitalize on it, we need to move. Fast. There are people I need to talk to, but doing so now would be too suspicious."

Loren paced as well, picking up on her nervous energy. "How can I help?"

"You can't. No…" Sonia chewed on her lower lip. "He'd kill me if I even thought about letting you anywhere near a treason plot—"

"I'm here," Loren said bluntly. "It's a bit too late for that. Let me do something."

Something other than sitting in a cage like a damsel in distress awaiting her rescue.

"Fine." Sonia braced her hands against the nearest counter, her head bowed, knuckles white. "There is one thing you can do—stay safe," she said quietly. "Lukka or Kyle will come for you. I know it. If the challenge is tomorrow, they might try to lure you to the main house before then. In usual circumstances, that wouldn't be unheard of. As a witness, your duty is to serve as a neutral party. But where Kyle is involved, I wouldn't let my guard down for a second."

"What happened between him and Bill? It seems... personal," Loren said, though she suspected that was an understatement.

Sonia's sigh cemented that belief. "It's complicated. I'm sure Bill has told you about Emma?"

Loren nodded, though she couldn't suppress a painful mixture of guilt and envy. It felt wrong to be jealous of someone who was gone. Even a little.

"She was Kyle's twin," Sonia said. "I don't think he ever forgave Bill for what happened to her. It's a petty feud, but grief can make people do twisted things..."

Genuine pain echoed in her voice. Suddenly, she shook her head and stepped back from the counter. "It doesn't matter now. All that does is keeping you safe. God, I don't even know what to—"

"I can go with them." Loren's voice sounded so rough to her own ears that she swallowed as Sonia whirled to face her. "With their focus on me, they won't be watching you."

"And if they hurt you?" Sonia countered. "I can't promise you that they won't. In fact… It might be their plan. Goodness, Bill should have never let you come here—"

"I can handle myself," Loren said with a confidence she didn't feel. "You do what you need to do. Let me distract them."

Sonia didn't agree to the plan outright.

But she didn't challenge it, either.

37

Kyle was celebrating. Sure, he was alone, no decorations in sight. Even so, this was an occasion requiring commemoration. For that very reason, he'd taken up on the first floor of the main house, his feet propped against a desk in the study while he sipped liquor directly from the bottle.

Hurray.

It was important to cherish every victory, however short-lived and half-assed it might have been, right? And the fact of the matter was that they had *beaten* Bill McGoven.

By nightfall tomorrow, once and for all, the bastard would be put out of his misery in front of the entire pack. Though, why Lukka had chosen to waste said time on pretending to heed the rules of an official challenge?

Well…

Kyle tried not to include *brooding* in his celebratory plans.

After all, he wasn't an Alpha. Scheming and evil planning weren't his forte—his job was to put those plans into action, no questions asked.

"I hope you're enjoying yourself."

Kyle winced as his entire body prickled with the awareness of his Alpha. He looked up to find the man in question watching him from across the room. With a sigh, he wiped his lips with the back of his hand but wasn't inclined to stand to attention like a good little soldier.

Yet.

"Hphm." Lukka glanced around, blue eyes deceptively bright, demeanor relaxed—though Kyle wasn't fooled. "And here I was thinking that you would be upset. After all, McGoven issued a direct challenge, despite your clever little murder scheme. He wouldn't do so if he didn't have the Eislanders on his side already."

Mentally, Kyle rolled his eyes, preparing for some lecture on "loose ends" and shit. As if he didn't already know that. He hadn't been unable to sleep at night thinking of that bastard roaming free.

But hey, he was trying to "look on the bright side" and "be optimistic."

Which scenario would be more satisfying?

Tearing apart McGoven himself or watching the man be ripped to shreds by the very people he had once been hand-picked to lead?

Maybe if he drank enough, the latter option might sound more appealing…

"I'm sure you have nothing to fear," he grumbled, fighting to keep his tone under control. A flash of warning shot through his chest anyway. To distract from it, he snatched a bottle at random from the desk, tore off the cap, and downed it in three vicious gulps.

The low percentage of alcohol didn't affect him like heavy booze would. Maybe it had something to do with his metabolism that basically rendered the liquid into water before it ever had a chance to work its magic on his system?

Hmm, he thought, dropping the bottle to roll across the floor. *Lycan physiology…*

"I want him dead, Kyle." Lukka's tone bordered on the edge of a growl even while he maintained that nicey-nice posture. Anyone who walked in on them now might have thought that they were in the middle of a conversation about *sparkles* or something equally as asinine.

Not revenge, or subterfuge and…well, murder.

McGoven's would just be the beginning.

Kyle snatched another bottle from the desk, though this time, he cradled it in his palm, feeling the firm contours. *Easy,* he thought, frowning. It would have been damn easy to turn the delicate glass into glitter with the right amount of pressure, at the right spot, at the right time.

That was how most things in the world worked—so easily susceptible to damage by those who knew how to inflict it.

"Fuck a direct challenge. You force him to trespass. He will come after *her*," Kyle said. "Either that or you let this charade go on so he can unman you in front of the entire pack. Before you panic and sick your minions on him, of course. Because that's what you're planning, isn't it?"

That stupid idea alone deserved another drink.

"Remember who you're speaking to, subordinate."

Alarm raced up and down his spine in response to the anger he could sense in the Alpha's tone—*dangerous ground.*

"I say we just kill her," Kyle grumbled, skirting an apology. "Frame it as the Eislanders. Use her body to goad McGoven into making a misstep. You kill two birds with one stone."

Mate or not, the murder would whip McGoven into a frenzy—making him about ten times the threat he already was—but the thought of seeing the bastard in that kind of pain was too tempting to resist. As far as Kyle was concerned, sticking Loren Connors' head on a pike was a damn good plan of action.

Of course, it wouldn't be so easy. Still, he couldn't risk adding, "But you'll adhere to the old laws…right?"

Lukka shrugged. "Of course. I am bound to them. But you? I'm letting you off your leash."

Kyle blinked. "Huh?"

"Provoke him," Lukka snarled, turning around to face the doorway. "By any means necessary."

As Lukka left the room, Kyle finally lunged from his chair and snatched the very last bottle from the desk, wrenching off the cap with his teeth.

Suddenly, it had turned into a *real* celebration after all.

38

*L*oren felt like a medieval prisoner, right before the executioner came calling. Anxiously, she hovered near the living room window, peering through the curtains at the empty road winding through the trees.

As the darkness grew, so did the tension weighing down the atmosphere.

Behind her, Sonia puttered in the kitchen. Every now and again Loren heard the thud of the cupboards being opened and shut, but neither party spoke a single word. She tried not to relive what the woman had said to her—keyword being *tried*. Every time she shut her eyes, she'd see *his* face, engrained right there behind her eyelids.

Had she done the right thing by pushing him to this point?

Or had she only offered herself up on a silver platter and heralded McGoven's doom?

The sound of a knock on the door snapped her from the thought. From the window, she could see nothing out of the ordinary. Still, another stern knock rattled the door and Sonia rushed to answer it.

From behind her, Loren couldn't see who waited on the other end, but Sonia stiffened, her entire body rigid.

"I thought he would come for her himself?" she croaked. "That's what the tradition—"

"He was…" an oily voice replied, and Loren had no trouble at all conjuring a pair of soulless brown eyes to go along with it. "But, lo' and behold, he decided to send me instead. Alpha business. You know the drill, eh Carlisle?"

Sonia didn't answer, but when she stood back, finally revealing the man standing in the doorway, Loren wasn't surprised.

Kyle's blood-red hair clashed with an ebony sky and enhanced by the darkness, his eyes glowed, as sharp as a hawk's. When he smiled, it was a cruel expression—all teeth, zero warmth.

"Loren Connors. Do I have permission to escort the female from your premises, Carlisle?" he asked Sonia. Something in his tone reminded Loren of a cat, impatiently toying with a mouse.

"I…" Sonia glanced over her shoulder, biting her lower lip —the only hint of unease. "He didn't send word that *you* were coming."

"Didn't he?" Kyle raised an eyebrow. "I didn't know that the Alpha had to answer to a subordinate, silly me. According to the laws of the challenge, she must be prepared to oversee tomorrow's ceremony, no matter who comes for her. Or do you object?"

He smiled, but a fool could tell that he wasn't joking. All his weight was balanced on the tips of his toes as if he would have liked nothing more than to barge into the cabin—whether Sonia "allowed" him to, or not.

"Lukka's the only one who has any 'business' with her," Sonia snapped. "I know tradition was never your forte, but I'm sure you know that much."

"Well, Lukka wanted me to take her…sightseeing, first," Kyle said, eyes glowing. "It's time this pup learns her place, in the pack, of course. When the challenge is over, Lukka wants her to get a feel for her 'new home.'"

Sonia didn't respond to the concealed threat, though her face visibly paled. With her body angled toward the door, she blocked Kyle out *physically*, but Loren sensed that—even in her own home—she couldn't deny him for long. Authority was ingrained in the way he held himself, chin in the air.

Maybe not an Alpha, Loren thought, but he definitely wasn't someone to be ignored.

"Fine." Sonia shoved the door open wider. "But remember the code, Kyle. She's an innocent—a witness, nothing more. It won't do good for anyone to proclaim an early victory."

"Have faith, Carlisle." Kyle's mirthless grin widened. "I'm sure our Alpha will prevail, especially against a rogue. Now —" He cut those gleaming eyes to Loren and jerked his head. *Come.* "It's time for you to see the big, bad world of pack life for yourself."

No longer was he smiling. His expression had fallen flat, mouth in a cold, hard line.

And, as she stepped out onto the porch, Loren couldn't help feeling that she had jumped right from the proverbial frying pan...

And into an inferno.

As if reading her mind, Kyle chuckled and he headed down the front path, leaving her to follow—but his final words reached her in an ominous murmur.

"Carlisle turned into a bit of a hermit when her father died. As a witness to an official challenge, you belong in the heart of the pack. Right where Lukka can keep an eye on you."

Loren didn't say a word as she followed him down the trail leading from the cabin. Instead, she tried her hardest to take in every little detail of her surroundings—every potential route of escape.

Initially, she tried utilizing the tricks Bill taught her while meeting with the strange woman in the woods. Breathe. Close her eyes. Trust in her instinct.

But her instinct went to war with a growing sense of foreboding.

Run, a part of her whispered. After living around dangerous men for more than half her life, she liked to think that she was an expert at picking them out of a crowd—and Kyle displayed all the wrong signs.

How did that old saying go? *If it walked like a duck and quacked like a duck…*

Using that logic, Kyle's aggressive stance and Sonia's reaction to him all but proclaimed, *quack!*

You're being paranoid, she tried to tell herself—but the thought didn't make it any less apparent that she was alone with him in the middle of nowhere.

Massive trees loomed overhead, and a carpeting of thick foliage swallowed everything else. Endless green and a colorless sky were all she could see, stretching in every direction. Sonia's house must have had its own generator because there wasn't as much as a telephone pole around— nor any trace of modern technology. Nothing but the long road ahead that seemed to stretch on for miles.

Storm clouds gathered on the horizon, a darker shade of ebony against a slightly lighter sky. It was cold enough that snow was just as likely to fall from them as rain—not that Kyle seemed concerned by the threat of either. He wasn't even wearing a jacket, but a T-shirt that showed off thick, solid muscle and, when they reached the point where Sonia's thin, gravel road fed into a larger one, his strides took on a slow, almost leisurely pace.

"It's one of the largest territories for miles," he announced in a husky purr while eyeing every tall pine they passed. "Plenty of rogues would kill to get their hands on it."

His boasting tone made that almost sound like a *good* thing—as if the threat of conflict was somehow more important than the land itself. But there was that word again. One that seemed to have been tossed around almost as frequently as "Alpha" and "mate."

"What makes someone a rogue?" Loren didn't know what in the hell possessed her to speak up. Her voice was soft, rising barely above a whisper.

Good, a part of her murmured. *Be meek. Let him think you're not a threat.*

"Rogues turn their backs on the pack way of life," Kyle said without turning around. "They live in *exile*—what? McGoven didn't tell you all about his sordid little past?"

When she didn't answer, he whirled to face her and flashed a chilling smile that made the tiny hairs at the nape of her neck stand on end. "Then, by all means, allow *me* to do the honors."

He paused in what Loren cynically figured was his way of adding a dramatic effect. Only a second later did his lips part to add, "Believe it or not, the dear and honorable Bill McGoven *killed* someone."

Ice washed over Loren as though a bucket of freezing water had been dumped on her head. She faltered, nearly tripping over her own feet, but Kyle continued, unconcerned.

"Not *literally*, of course," he said, sounding disappointed about that fact. "But in our world, there's no such thing as an 'accident.' There is only failure—and when it came to protecting his own mate, McGoven *failed*. You didn't think you were his first attempt at a mated life, did you?" He chuckled, shaking his head. "No. *Her* name was Emma."

His voice was strained as if he were speaking through gritted teeth, and Loren didn't miss the flash of pain that shot through his eyes.

"She was beautiful. Of course, a boy scout like McGoven was drawn to her. But in the end, he killed her—I don't give a damn what anyone else says. He let her *die*."

Die! The word hit the air like a blow just as several snowflakes began to drift down, glinting silver in the darkness.

"Your hero has more skeletons in his closet than you give him credit for," Kyle added in a tone darker than the clouds up above. "Come on."

He kept walking, leaving her no choice but to follow or be stranded.

She was so wrapped up in her own thoughts that she couldn't name the point when the road ended, and civilization began. At least, as much "civilization" that one could find on a mountain in the middle of the wilderness.

Objectively, it looked like a logger's camp, illuminated by a few streetlights and external lamps. The buildings were mostly made of wood, with a few simple ones made of aluminum siding scattered here and there. The structures were spread like a children's toy set, haphazardly with no rhyme or reason—almost as if a new home or building sprung up whenever and wherever it was convenient.

The ones that weren't close to the road were all connected by a slender maze of paths that twisted as intricately as a spider's web. In the center, overlooking it all, was a grand building on a hill. It too, was made of wood, but nearly every inch of it sported elegant carvings. Four stories high, it dwarfed all other nearby buildings.

"The pack house," Kyle explained, as they passed. "I bet you've never seen anything like that, before?"

Despite the taunt at her expense, Loren had to shake her head. Even the courthouse—New Walsh's tallest building—didn't look half as grand. From this distance, she could make out snarling faces carved into the two, massive wooden columns that supported the roof on either end—howling wolves.

"Come on."

She struggled to keep up as Kyle led her right through the makeshift town. They didn't run into very many people, but the few they did see were dressed in warm jackets and hats against the cold. None of them spoke, choosing to eye them warily instead.

Despite the scrutiny, she didn't feel relieved when the road curved and the watchful eyes faded from view.

No witnesses, a part of her whispered.

Kyle hadn't been exaggerating when he claimed the territory was massive. The distance from Sonia's alone had to have been more than several miles. Yet, no matter where she looked, there seemed to be *more* stretching on in every direction—more forest. More trees. More impassive sky. More emptiness.

Despite the beauty of the landscape, she felt increasingly uneasy as Kyle led her deeper into the forest, and the warm glow of the town center faded. Soon, they left the road altogether and had to pick their way through the underbrush bit by bit in total darkness.

Something's wrong. The warning prickled down the back of her spine like an itch she couldn't scratch. Insistent.

When they finally reached a wide, open clearing, the sense of unease only grew, and Loren forced herself to speak up. "Where are we?"

Kyle didn't answer.

He kept moving forward until his boots seemed to toe an invisible line, just near the edge of the field. There, he finally stopped and scanned the horizon, as if hunting for someone who might have been lurking out of sight.

"I bet you're out there," Loren thought she heard him growl into the wind. "Watching. Well, watch *this* McGoven, and know that you've failed, once again."

Without warning, he turned to face her, and Loren knew his expression all too well.

"I suggest you run," he told her, sounding miles away, even as he advanced, step by menacing step. "That will make this all the sweeter."

"What are you talking about?" Loren wasn't even sure how she was able to talk—let alone breathe—fear seized her lungs, squeezing the air from them. That tired, old mantra ran through her mind on replay—*run, run, run!*

"Oh, I think you know what," Kyle murmured. "I think you know *exactly* what."

He kept coming, even as she staggered back just as quickly. Only too late did she realize, as her back hit the bark of a tree, that she was blocked in.

"Well?" he wondered, still creeping closer, as a predator would on a bleeding, hapless doe. "Aren't you going to kiss your new mate?"

RUN.

Loren lunged. Her boots skidded, sending mud flying in every direction as she tried to dart past Kyle for the woods behind him. He caught her before she could even go a step. Harsh hands snagged her hair, yanking her backward and down onto the ground.

Dazed, she struck a patch of damp, icy grass just as a heavy boot slammed into the small of her back.

"Scream," Kyle suggested from above her, as casually as if this were nothing more than a game. Loren gasped, choking on the damp earth, as he knelt down, pressing his knee against her spine. "Go on. Maybe he'll even hear you if he hasn't already turned tail and run like the coward he is. Hell, maybe…" The knee dug in, twisting as it did so. "Maybe he'll come running to the rescue, big, strong Bill McGoven? I'll even give him a head start."

Wham! A sudden kick to her side forced her onto her back. Dazed, Loren blinked up at the sky as Kyle moved to stand over her.

"Why don't you and I talk for a while?" he proposed, still speaking with that eerie sense of calm. "I wouldn't want to rush him—he must be pretty busy, being a hero and saving damsels in distress, and all. So, let's have a little chat. Don't look so terrified," the man admonished. He chuckled when she shied back, instinctively pressing her body into the earth.

"When you're mated to me, I'll make sure that you won't remember a single thing. You'll be the same, stupid little pup you were with McGoven—and seeing you like that will *break* him," a smug chuckle revealed just what he thought of that prospect. "He'll probably even surrender himself like a good little hero, though I hope he fights. That bastard's death by my hand has been long overdue. After all…he did kill my sister."

His expression clouded over, as if he were seeing years into the past. Seeing another face where hers was. "I knew he wanted her. Everyone knew. He was Mr. Golden boy and

Emma… She was perfect. Good. Kind. All the shit someone like him couldn't wait to prey on—" He laughed coldly, clenching his hands into fists. "I should have seen that. Fuck! I should have known. But I was fooled like the rest of them. I… I was happy for her. I thought that if anyone could protect her, it would have been him. But I was wrong," he went on in a deadly soft whisper, crouching over her. "He failed her. So, I think it's only fair that I take someone from *him*. And when McGoven's dead, Lukka can have you—"

Dead. The word snapped something inside of Loren, and it was like a dam breaking apart.

"No!"

Kyle scoffed at the sound, apparently pleased that she was finally playing along in his sick game—at least until she sharply drew up her knee, ramming him right between the legs. He rolled off her with a groan, and she shot to her feet, instinctively balancing her weight on the tips of her toes. McGoven's voice echoed through her mind. *Don't think. Don't hesitate. React!* Real or imagined? It didn't matter. Lunging into action, she took off across the clearing.

"Bitch!" She could hear Kyle behind her, staggering to his feet.

Don't look back, that dark, shadowy voice in her mind, warned—this time not McGoven's, but her own. *Focus! Run! Run, run, run…*

It took him longer to catch up to her this time. She had nearly made it over the boundary of the field when a hand snagged her collar, and she went flying.

"You'll pay for that," Kyle swore as she landed hard on her knees. Using his hand on her jacket for leverage, he began to purposefully tug until the seams tore beneath the strain. *Rrrrrip!*

No, no, no, no! Panic welled before Loren could help it. Memories jarred through her thoughts like blows, threatening to drown her in fear. Fred Connors' harsh hands on her bare skin. Older, darker memories she could never relive without screaming.

No, no, no…

With a grunt, Kyle knocked her legs out from under her, and she went down hard, coughing on mud and snow. One final yank, and he succeeded in tearing the jacket from her shoulders. She could feel his fingers tugging at her thermal next.

Hide, that old, familiar part of her whispered. *Curl up. Disappear. This isn't happening…*

A tendril of recognition shocked her—it was the same voice that had lulled her the night she killed Fred Connors. That same desperate urge to just give up. *Give in.* Kyle was too big—too strong. There was no way in hell that she could fight him…

Bill had been right all along. She'd confused his strength for her own. Alone, without his presence, she couldn't drown out the doubt.

She was too weak. Useless.

Give in.

"I wonder what McGoven will think when he sees you with me?" She heard Kyle remark. His hands had left her shirt and had begun to work on her pants instead, thick fingers attempting to slide beneath her waist in search of the zipper. "I can just picture the look on his face."

Loren could, too—silver eyes burning with rage, perhaps glaring from the body of a black wolf. He'd hate himself for ever letting her do this in the first place. For trusting that she could handle herself.

Just like that, the suffocating fear went away. Suddenly everything was lethally sharp and as crystal clear as the thick snowflakes that had begun to fall. McGoven would come— a part of her just knew he would. The same way she knew without a doubt that he would protect her. Defend. Fight. Die...

If she were to prove herself, it had to be now.

Kyle never expected her to move so fast, which was probably the only reason she managed to catch him off guard as she reached out behind her, nails drawn, and swiped blindly at his arm. The moment she felt the give of flesh beneath her fingertips, she dug in, raking down until she felt the warmth of blood.

"Fuck!" Kyle drew back with a hiss of pain, and Loren lurched to her feet—but for the first time, her only impulse wasn't to run.

Instead, she turned, facing Kyle as he crouched, snarling at the sight of his arm. The deep ruts left by her nails bled freely, leaving a metallic scent in the air, but fear didn't deter her from taking a step toward him. And then another. The wind tore at her hair, whipping it out behind her as she lifted her foot, swaying with the effort, and delivered a strong enough kick that he fell back.

He stared up at her, dazed as she balanced the sole of her boot on the center of his chest and crouched down, much like he had. After a second, he started to struggle, cursing as he attempted to shrug her off. "What the hell—"

Loren didn't have to raise a single finger to stop him. All she did was stare into those eyes and finally release the anger she supposed had been building within her all this time. Building during those dark years living with Uncle Bart, and the months living with Fred Connors… It flared, like a smoldering inferno, blazing white-hot.

Like a puppet with its strings cut, Kyle fell back. His head hit the ground with barely a *thump!* Before he could regroup, Loren allowed herself to utter only one, single word that flew from her tongue as easily as if she'd been born to say it.

"Submit."

It wasn't like the previous instance in the woods.

This time, uttering the word was merely a formality. A part of her surged, just as violently as his previous assault. Instead of hurting him physically, this penetration went deeper.

Into his mind? Thoughts flooded her conscious, but they weren't her own—or even like McGoven's. They were prickly, wrought with so much rage and hatred nausea churned her stomach as they unfolded.

So much anger.

So much loathing.

But beneath it all was a pain that took her breath away. She winced at the force of it, feeling tears prickle her eyes.

"N-No," she heard Kyle rasp, though his voice seemed to come from miles away. "No."

He tried to resist—she could feel it—much in the same way she fought against McGoven's commands what felt like a lifetime ago. But as she stared into his horrified gaze, Loren realized that the fight was over before it even began.

"You don't hate Bill," she croaked, feeling a mixture of shame and disgust wash over her in response. "You hate *him*."

An image came to mind, growing in clarity—blue eyes, blond hair, mocking smile. She wondered if Kyle was even aware of the subconscious truth nestled within his own mind.

"You always knew," she went on, as the color drained from the face of the man before her. He looked hollow. Broken.

"You just couldn't face it," she said. "You know what he did. You don't hate Bill for Emma's death. You… You hate him for—"

"Stop!" Kyle threw her off, scrambling to his knees. "Just stop!" His throat corded with the force of the shout, but he didn't make a move toward her.

"No." As she found her balance, Loren shook her head. "It's the truth. You hate Bill for leaving," she continued, swaying with the effort it took to remain standing. Somehow, she did, though Kyle slumped, his face downcast, body trembling. "For leaving him alive. The man truly responsible for your sister's death."

He said nothing, but he didn't need to. A connection still lingered between them, weaker than what existed between her and Bill. It wasn't powerful enough for her to touch his emotions, or sense them clearly.

Though, she knew that she'd spoken the truth. And he knew it, too.

"If you still want to honor Emma, you know how you can," she told him. "Because he expects you to help him, doesn't he? Lukka?"

It was getting harder to grasp his thoughts clearly. She could only glean fragments of their plan—though it seemed as twisted as any Bill might have feared.

Kyle flinched and lifted his head. His eyes blazed, but with a different, colder intensity.

"Even if I don't, someone else will," he rasped.

"Not if you beat them to it," Loren countered. "And if you truly want to honor your sister's memory, you won't have a choice."

Of all the places he might find himself on the road to redemption within the pack, little did Bill think he'd wind up here—in a circular room in the heart of a building far less ornate than any found in Black Mountain. Still, his entire body prickled with awareness and a grudging sort of respect only an Alpha could inspire.

One with several decades to his tenure, at least.

Why he'd followed the Eislanders into their territory, he had no idea. Either way, it was too late for doubt.

Here he stood, facing down Loreck Eislander himself.

"You heard me," he began, his voice hoarse. "If you doubt anything that I've said, then let me know now so I won't waste my time asking for your help."

He took a step, fully prepared to leave. The funny thing was…

Loreck didn't look doubtful, smug, or even enraged by the convoluted tale involving him, a rival, and a daughter he'd never met. Instead, the man frowned, his gaze fixated somewhere in the distance where no one else could follow.

The other man, Eric, cleared his throat, stepping forward from the corner he'd stood in before now. For once, his probing stare lacked the hostility Bill had become accustomed to. He merely seemed curious.

Though if that was a good development or not remained to be seen.

"What exactly do you want us to do?" he demanded. "Send our men to the border? That could trigger an outright war, and I'm sure your Alpha would love to use a distraction from your challenge."

"He would," Bill admitted. "But I don't need an army. I just need protection. Yours—" he addressed Loreck, who finally inclined his head to face him. "I'm sure Lukka has a trick up his sleeve. Be there as a witness. Make sure this unfolds fairly."

The man's expression was unreadable, and Bill felt a pinch of recognition in his gut. If he still didn't believe in a connection between this figure and Loren, one similarity put all doubt to bed—their eyes. They shared the same piercing intensity, boring into him before he could even think to guard against the intrusion.

Where Loren gazed at him with only that haunting earnest hope, this man harbored anything but.

"And why should I?" he countered, raising his chin. "You forget rogue—if what you claim is true, I should have every right to go for your throat."

For mating his daughter, of course.

Bill gritted his teeth, uncomfortable with the thought. Rather than cower, he raised his head, holding the leader's stare.

"I thought I was protecting her," he explained. "But, as it turns out, she's more than capable of protecting herself."

He explained the events leading up to Fred Connors' death and selected snippets of what happened after—some things, however, such as his genuine attraction, he held back.

Still, by the end of his tale, Loreck looked conflicted between disbelief and confusion.

"So, you think your Alpha framed you in order to have me intervene?"

Bill nodded. "I didn't kill anyone from your pack. Just the outsiders who threatened Loren."

"It's true," Eric said softly. "Jamal was killed, but I have reason to believe he was ambushed by someone else. While the bodies of the men he claimed to have fought weren't found initially, my contacts in Elkton alerted me of several mutilated bodies found in the next town over."

"Which brings us back to Lukka," Bill said, empowered by the revelations. "He needs to be stopped."

Loreck grunted. "You really believe your Alpha would listen to me?" His voice boomed throughout the room, sending a shiver down Bill's spine that he couldn't deny. "If so, you've been gone far too long."

"I don't trust Lukka to play fair," Bill countered. "But if he knows that at least part of his ruse has been uncovered, it might drive him into a corner."

"And what do you intend to do when he does retreat to said corner?" Loreck stood from behind a massive desk and began to pace. At least four men in addition to Eric were in attendance, watching silently. Their lack of reaction didn't put Bill at ease.

Not at all.

As Loreck neared his position, the older man fixed him with a cold stare that penetrated down to his core. "Will you fall back like you did before and fail to uphold the duty placed before you?"

Bill winced. Maybe he deserved that. "What about you?" he tossed back. "Did you really not know? About her? Your own blood?"

Any anger he still harbored toward the man sputtered and died in the face of his answering frown. As if snuffed out, the fire left the man's gaze, rendering him hollow.

"I won't pretend that I understand why your Alpha would do such a thing."

"But..." Eric stepped forward, his head lowered in respect. "I'm beginning to have an idea as to *how* he did it."

"How?" Bill exhaled, caught off guard by the sheer panic that welled in his chest. Even now, some small, childish part of him might have held hope that he'd gotten everything wrong. Lukas wasn't behind this—someone else had been the true culprit all along.

As Eric met his gaze, however, he surrendered to the inevitable. "Tell me," he rasped.

The man looked to his Alpha, who nodded in approval. They must have discussed this information before deciding to share it with him.

"The hermit you met with is a lycan by the name of Eilene Branshaw, sister to Eveline," Eric explained. "They, along with a brother, formed a band of rogue Scolera who ventured east, eager to seek refuge with one of the established packs in the area."

"I think I can guess where this is heading," Bill said gruffly. Loren, it seemed, wouldn't be entirely spared of violent family members. "The brother was the dangerous rogue who wrought havoc."

"Yes," Loreck said, taking over the tale. "He cut off contact with his sisters and began to feed on humans. Casualties mounted, and we had no choice but to form an alliance with anyone able to track him down. While few in number, and disorganized, Scolera wolves can be formidable and stealthy opponents."

"So, you had to form an alliance with Lukas Grehmaine," Bill supplied. "I know that part. What happened between you and Eveline?"

Loreck had a mastery of his expressions that Bill had encountered in few men. Regardless, even he couldn't disguise his reaction to that name—he winced, and his eyes took on a faraway gleam.

"Yes. I knew her," he said tersely. "She wanted admission into a pack. I thought she had decided to join mine… Then she vanished, and I always thought she'd returned west." His jaw tightened, his eyes narrowed. "I never thought…"

"There is something else," Eric said, steering the reins of the conversation. "Something that was never made public knowledge about the demise of the lone rogue." He looked to Loreck, again seeking permission to continue.

The Alpha, however, said nothing. Eric sighed and soldiered on anyway.

"With the help of the two sisters, we were able to devise traps, and learn the ways of Scolera hunting methods. But it wasn't enough. If we went that route, it would have taken weeks, if not months, to corner the rogue."

"All of that for one wolf?" Bill questioned, his skepticism apparent.

Eric scoffed. "More than once, I've been able to catch you off guard by utilizing only a fraction of what I learned from the Scolera. Imagine that skill, but mastered by someone much faster, and afflicted with an insatiable taste for human blood."

"I see your point," Bill admitted, wincing. He hated to acknowledge just how easily Eric had been able to infiltrate his own territory. Such a wolf would be a danger not just to humans, but to any nearby lycans foolish enough to stop him. "So, how did you track the wolf?"

Loreck inclined his head, his eyes ablaze as he and Eric shared a look.

"Don't be shy now," Bill snapped. "Let me guess—by using your deer urine trick?"

"No," Loreck said. "By using hunters."

"You… What?" It sounded insane. Desperate. "No. There is no way that Lukas would have—"

"Who do you think put us in contact with them?" Loreck snarled. "Lukas was a man who valued survival of his pack and his bloodline above all else. Even if that meant making an alliance with a lone hunter. It didn't matter to him either way."

Bill couldn't process it. This was a trick. A way to undermine his resolve by attacking one of the few bastions of his past he still held dear.

"No," he insisted, shaking his head. "I don't believe that. Not for a second."

"Then don't," Loreck said, lifting his shoulder in a dismissive shrug. "And let your mate and everyone else you pretend to give a damn about die. The time for wallowing in uncertainty is over. State now exactly what you expect from me. I won't have my people go to war with yours."

"I'm not asking you to," Bill replied. "I'm asking for—"

A wave of emotion barreled into him with the force of a punch, nearly taking him off his feet. He staggered and braced his hands against a nearby wall just to stay standing. Something was wrong. He could feel it. An ache tore through his chest, and only one thing could be the source of it—Loren had dropped her wall.

She was in danger.

"I need to go."

He tore from the room, exiting the building. In the darkness, few landmarks caught his eye, not that he needed any guidance to find his way. He merely fixated in the direction of Black Mountain and took off, shifting in seconds. Minutes later, he cleared the border, and he didn't even see his pursuer until they collided with him, knocking him off his feet.

"What are you doing?" Micha's bones audibly popped with the force of his change. He still sprouted a pelt of brown fur even as he lurched upright on human legs. "Are you crazy? What about waiting until tomorrow? If you go in there now, he'll have you ripped apart."

Bill growled. Whatever fear he'd felt had already vanished. He expanded his consciousness, seeking out Loren's, but ran into a wall. Her mind was closed off and out of reach.

Damn it! Logic warned him that giving Lukka any excuse to question the validity of his challenge would backfire.

When he felt another foreboding tug at his gut, it was already too late.

He took off, sensing Micha on his heels and Naomi right behind him. They weren't his only company—he picked up the approach of at least two others racing from the direction of the Eislander territory.

But diplomacy would have to wait.

Barging onto Black Mountain in a blind rage would do no good in the end. But neither had trusting in honor for the past five years.

The time for restraint was over.

It was time to play dirty.

oren wasn't sure how she found her way back to the center of the pack territory alone. Her chest heaved, her skin slicked with sweat as her eyes adjusted to the tendrils of moonlight filtering through the trees. Despite the time of night, the winding streets snaking through the sparse buildings weren't deserted.

People streamed from various directions, all of them staring.

At her.

The fact that she was a stranger seemed to be a moot point. Her hair was a mess, her steps disjointed. Sonia's borrowed clothing was caked in mud and rumpled, but she didn't give a damn as to how she might look.

Tension laced the air, prickling beneath her skin. Something was wrong.

Though she didn't have to look far to find the source of the unease. She barely managed to crest the hill overlooking the heart of the territory's center when she noticed a black streak cutting across the landscape. Mid-lunge, the creature shifted, transforming into a man, bathed in shadow and silver.

Her heart throbbed with recognition. Bill.

But, for once, she wasn't his focus.

"Lukka!" he bellowed, his voice easily riding the wind. With a start, Loren recognized that he was advancing on the large ornate building Kyle had pointed out to her. Ablaze in the orange glow of lamplight, it resembled a wooden palace.

And Bill was an errant warrior ready to burn it to the ground. Watching him, her hold on their bond snapped. A wave of emotion flooded into her—his fear, his relief as he sensed her nearby. His grudging realization as to who might have caused her terror.

And his resolve to punish those responsible.

"Show yourself," he bellowed, eyes affixed to the towering structure before him. "Lukka!"

The growing crowd gathered, flooding the narrow streets, but he seemed unaffected, his head held high. Despite his nakedness, he radiated confidence that took her breath away. Unlike any man she'd ever met, he embodied the term Alpha exactly as Micha had described it.

A true leader.

Her heart throbbed as she navigated the crowd, rushing toward him. She was barely paces away when he whirled in her direction. Their eyes met, and Loren could feel the relief that washed over him—but the sight of the two men accompanying him made her stop short.

They came from the same direction he had, but were in human form, their steps slow and cautious. They weren't here to hurt Bill, it seemed. But for what purpose? Her nostrils flared as the wind blew their scents in her direction. One she recognized instantly—the man who intruded onto Bill's property uninvited. But the other?

She didn't know him. Yet… The way he moved sparked an overwhelming sense of déjà vu that rooted her to the spot. A sudden recognition came to mind. Was he Loreck Eislander?

Any emotion she might have felt at the prospect was quickly replaced by loathing, only it wasn't her own.

"You dare to trespass onto our property?" Lukka's voice was a gnarled hiss as he descended the steps of the main house. He still wore the same clothing from earlier, his eyes an icy blue. Streaming behind him were at least four men, their postures tense—but Kyle, predictably, wasn't among them.

"This is treason," the Alpha went on. "This is—"

"I tried to do this nobly by the rules," Bill said over him in a rich baritone that put the leader's to shame. "That's what your father would have wanted, or so I used to believe." He raised his voice to carry through the assembled crowd. Loren swallowed hard at the sight of him, boldly facing the obstacle in his path. But she could still sense his pain.

His ever-lingering doubts.

"I admired Lukas more than anyone," he confessed. "I always believed him to be just and fair—but, as it turns out, you two were more alike than I could ever imagine. You always resented me because of the threat I presented to you, but the truth is, Lukas had little faith in your ability to lead before he ever chose me as his successor."

Lukka visibly flinched, and a murmur went through the crowd, growing in intensity. Loren couldn't sense which side the general sentiment was on. Just an increasing feeling of alarm.

And fear—especially as the two Eislanders drew near. Several men broke off from the crowd to stand menacingly in their path. None came to blows.

Yet.

"Like you, Lukas was willing to sacrifice anyone who might stand in his way for power," Bill continued, and Loren swiveled her head back to him. "Even an innocent. Your father decided to sabotage the heir of a rival leader, but you?"

He glowered at Lukka, his voice thick with disgust.

"You allow your own righthand man to attack a witness, merely to deter me."

Loren shivered at the rage she could hear in his voice as well as feel. It blew her mind that he had so easily discerned the truth merely from her haphazard thoughts.

Though, she could feel a mixture of emotions from him in return that her brain rushed to unravel. Anger, yes, but something else, mingled beneath. Determination?

"No more," Bill declared out loud, drawing her attention back to the present. "We fight here, and we fight now. I challenge you for the position of Alpha."

A shock went through every witness, rippling deeper than Loren figured was apparent to the naked eye. This was more than a simple statement.

It was a direct challenge to the way of life of every person living in this territory.

While she couldn't decipher much from the deafening din of voices, with every growing murmur, Lukka seemed to shrink. "Fine," he said. "You want to be released? I release you. You are no longer a rogue tied to the territory, free to resume your exile—"

"No." Bill shook his head, seeming more regal than his disgraced status would imply. Bathed in the glow of the full moon, only one word came to Loren's mind, worthy of describing him.

Lycan.

"My exile is over," he bellowed. "I am here to challenge you for the position of Alpha. Should I win, you step down."

Lukka's voice was a harsh shadow in comparison. "And if you lose?"

Bill met his gaze without flinching, forcing the other man to voice the outcome for him.

"If you lose, you die."

41

*L*ukka advanced on Bill's position as the crowd closed in, forming a circle around the pair. Loren noted women, men, and children among the watchers, their faces sporting varying degrees of fear and…

Excitement.

Tall and wiry, Lukka still managed to cut a striking figure as he stripped his shirt and faced Bill, his head lowered with determination.

Then, with seemingly no word spoken between them, both men shifted. A black wolf took the place of McGoven, growling low. Across from him was a leaner, more gracile creature with a golden pelt that blazed like sunlight.

From Bill's scattered recollections, Loren had no idea what to expect when it came to how a challenge might unfold. She sensed, however, that this one lacked any of the usual ceremony. All the better—the only thing that truly mattered was action over all else.

The first thing that struck her was the smell—musk tainted the air. Human sweat and a primal, animalistic undercurrent that made her nostrils itch. Then a growl drew her notice to the darker of the two wolves.

In a beautiful, chilling display, the creature threw back its head and howled.

The bloodcurdling lament echoed on the wind, and the sound seemed to trigger an avalanche of actions taking place simultaneously. The first was a swarm of people who seemed to come from nowhere, swelling the crowd three times its original size until Loren found herself fighting toward the center.

Someone larger muscled past her, knocking her off balance —only a stern grip on her arm saved her from falling.

"Careful!" That voice made her look up. Sure enough, a familiar figure appeared by her side seconds later as if drawn from thin air, his green eyes more serious than she'd ever seen them. Micha.

"Stay close," he warned, shouting to be heard over another howl—this one was shriller, as if answering the call of the black wolf. Lukka? As Loren struggled to keep up with the scene unfolding, she heard Micha mutter, "Get ready. This could get messy."

She hated to agree. With only a jacket slung over his waist, she suspected he'd shifted to arrive here in time. Not far behind him was a grim, fully clothed, Naomi followed by a panting Sonia who appeared in the distance, racing their way. Given that she wore only a thin sweater, Loren guessed she had been the source of Micha's makeshift ensemble.

How had they managed to get past the barriers?

Now wasn't the time to parse through the logistics. In the center of the chaos, the two beasts finally faced each other from either end of their makeshift ring. Displaying restless energy, they began to circle each other, fangs bared.

At a glance, the apparent mismatch of the two was painfully obvious. Lukka's form was smaller and compact, composed of solid muscle that rippled beneath a golden pelt. Visually, he seemed no match for McGoven's larger mass.

Without even an officiate or referee to signal the start of the combat, both wolves lunged.

Loren winced as they collided, her heart in her throat. It wasn't a fight as much as it was a beautiful dance of violence and muscle. Their bodies rippled in a grisly unison, as they grappled for control.

Loren bit her lip, wincing as McGoven growled, thrown back as Lukka collided with him. She had imagined what this moment would be like. None of her worst fears had come close. It was bloody. Almost instantly, scarlet speckled the road at their feet, and it became clear that, despite the size difference, both lycans seemed equally matched. Where McGoven was strong and domineering, Lukka was wiry and fast.

Lightning quick, his jaws latched over McGoven's side, and a howl ripped from him. Then, just as quickly, the black wolf turned the tables, putting the other on retreat. Snarling, he caught Lukka's leg between his jaws, biting so hard the latter yelped and threw him off.

But it wasn't over.

Suddenly, Lukka took off with McGoven nipping at his heels, disappearing beneath the trees.

"This is wrong," Sonia said fearfully. "This must be done in view of everyone. Lukka knows that. What the hell is he doing?"

Loren knew exactly the reason for the trick.

Ironically, she might have had her own plan in action—though it entirely depended on the one person other than Lukka who wanted Bill dead.

She could only pray that she'd reached him.

And that, beneath the hate, the love for his sister would prevail.

$\mathcal{B}$ill ran blindly, despite every ounce of common sense he possessed warning him to go back. Pride wasn't the sole reason why he continued to give chase. Cynicism played a part—to back down now would be to admit defeat. Lukka would spin any ounce of hesitation to his benefit. Whether he liked it or not, he had no choice but to follow.

But he wasn't stupid.

This was a trap.

And, surprisingly, he suspected it wasn't the first time Lukka had employed such tricks against him. From the second he'd first learned that Lukas might have contacted a hunter, he hadn't been able to put it out of his mind. The man he knew and respected would have never stooped so low.

But his son would have. For five years, he never doubted the circumstances around Emma's death. Not once. But now?

The pieces were beginning to fall into place, and he didn't like the picture they formed. Not one damn bit. Even the prospect that Lukka might have played a role in Emma's death made his blood boil.

And his heart constrict with guilt. How damn ironic. He'd left the pack out of shame, convinced that a true Alpha should have been able to lead without any regrets.

But as he gained on the creature bounding ahead of him, Bill felt none of the awe he'd always harbored for that sacred role. None of the respect a leader should command. He just felt hate.

From the direction of the compound, he could sense Loren's presence—her alarm, her fear, her aching need to help. But he didn't want her to take these emotions away.

He needed to feel them.

He needed to fight with every ounce of rage in his body. So, as Lukka slowed, still in lycan form, Bill skidded to a halt and shifted first, rising to his feet.

It was a risk. Lukka would be inherently faster, but he didn't care. He needed to hear the truth for himself, straight from the bastard's mouth.

"Did you do it?" he demanded. His voice echoed, betraying just how far on the outskirts of the territory Lukka had led him—Bill knew from memory that a steep cliff wasn't far away. Few from the compound would hear anything said from this distance.

The perfect spot for an ambush. Still, he pushed any concern from his mind, focusing only on Lukka.

"Did you call the hunters to our territory that day? I never even considered it. That was a step too far, even for you! But as I say it out loud…"

It sounded a lot more plausible than a random attack. A grunt of astonishment escaped him. How could he have been so damn naïve?

"You son of a bitch—"

Lukka growled, his eyes wild. Bill expected him to lunge then and there.

Instead, he shifted, his face contorted with rage. "You're insane," he hissed, rising to his feet. "And you accuse me of treachery, but what about yourself? You think I can't tell?" Suddenly, he cut his gaze beyond Bill's line of sight. "You're mated. This is no fair fight, and since you've forsaken the rules, so can I. Kyle!"

His gaze was fixed somewhere over Bill's shoulder, but he didn't even care enough to switch targets. *Mated.* The way he'd said that word made something click. It was as if a light switch had been flicked. Suddenly, he could see clearly into everything building to this moment. Everything.

"Was that why?" he croaked. "Why you wanted Emma dead? Because I would be less of a threat to you? You were so damn worried about facing me on an even footing that you killed her?"

It sounded so damn pathetic. So deranged.

And yet…

"Kyle!" Lukka's face reddened, the veins in his throat distended with exertion. "Help me, you son of a bitch!"

Bill scoffed, prepared for any assault that may approach from behind. Instead…nothing. If Lukka were bluffing, or if he truly expected his second-in-command to come to his aid, no one did.

The air was thin, devoid of any other scents. They were alone, far from the crowd a typical challenge should command.

Somehow, this felt more fitting.

Lukka didn't deserve a public death. Just this. Silence and darkness.

"We end this now." With a sigh, Bill faced his opponent and purged everything from his mind but the need to fight. To protect his mate at all costs.

In the end, he felt only a small shred of mercy before he lunged, shifting in mid-air while Lukka scrambled to do the same. Teeth parted, Bill put all doubts from his mind.

And he allowed instinct to take over completely before tearing into his prey.

It was strange. As he made his way through the trees in human form, his main concern was a growing list of all the rules he'd already broken.

All the traditions he'd desecrated.

How many things he would have to rebuild should he decide to truly take on the position of Alpha.

Triumph wasn't the feeling flooding his veins as he finally reached the outskirts of the main compound.

Just sheer exhaustion.

And relief, as Loren's mind melded with his once again.

43

The second Bill came into view, bloodied and naked, Loren ran to him. Before she could say a word, he caught her waist, holding her close. Pressed against him, she could sense just how exhausted he was. He favored his left side, and blood dripped freely down his arm.

Even so, the absence of Lukka betrayed who'd won their battle.

But the victor didn't look triumphant, in the slightest. For a moment, Loren rested her head against his shoulder, sensing the intensity of emotions that washed through him. Relief. Regret. Pain. She wished she could take them all away, every last agony. As if aware of the thought, he gently withdrew from her and moved to stand alone, drawing the focus of those nearby.

Already, most of the crowd had migrated toward them, their expressions wary in the moonlight.

Bill faced them all, seemingly to acknowledge every last

person. Finally, he inclined his head, and spoke in a voice Loren could only remember him utilizing once before.

The day he wistfully reflected on what pack life meant to him.

"It isn't with arrogance that I accept the mantle of leading this pack," he said, letting his voice carry on the wind, "but humility. I once left these lands, believing it was for the greater good. But now, I see the folly and the sheer cowardice in that belief. I can't expect your loyalty after such a betrayal, but I am here, offering myself to all of you. An Alpha is not a ruthless leader, but a protector. A provider. I will do my best to understand the needs of Black Mountain and respond accordingly."

He looked beyond the growing circle of people to the few who lingered on the outskirts. Sonia. Micha and Naomi. Even the two men from the Eislander pack who lurked far beyond the rest.

"If you will have me. I will lead."

Utter silence fell, and Loren tensed. Could the pack still be loyal to Lukka?

The fear barely took root before several among the crowd sank into a crouch. Slowly, others followed in a silent display that said more than any verbal words of loyalty.

The display wasn't just for show. She could feel it— unwavering fealty being offered by everyone from the men down to the children.

Another pang of regret ripped through her, unlike anything she'd ever felt. Despite Bill's repeated insistence that she join a pack, it wasn't until that very moment that she understood exactly what she'd been missing.

This.

Luckily, there was plenty of hope she could experience it, still.

And that was only due to the man whose gaze locked with hers.

44

*I*t was far easier than he would have thought— reintegrating into pack life despite years on the outside. Even the role of an Alpha felt as natural in some ways as breathing.

Which terrified the hell out of him.

There were, of course, old wounds that would be difficult to heal—the rift Lukka had forged between their pack and the Eislanders being one of them. For the time being, he would allow Loren to helm that front, letting her dictate how and when to initiate contact with Loreck.

Another bit of unfinished business was more internal, lingering in the memories he resisted even now. After five years, he could finally face the pain of Emma's death. She was still gone, but now he had grim closure that allowed him to recall those recollections of her without guilt.

Dwelling wasn't his aim—he only needed that last goodbye.

It was funny how the place looked the same as it had all those years ago—a meadow, just outside the reach of both the Eislander and Black Mountain territories, where he had spent pretty much his whole childhood. Back in those days, he'd come out here, into the fields, alone. Sometimes with Sonia. And then with her…

Before everything changed.

The tiny, simple grave, marked only by a round headstone, looked just the same. Worse even, it still *smelled* the same. Like the salty scent of the tears, he had shed for the first time in this very spot.

It was pathetic. But…if he tried hard enough, he could still smell her. That crisp, light scent of honey and rose—so different from Loren's.

Heart heavy, Bill sank down on the wet earth inches from the tombstone.

"Hey, Em," he called gruffly, reaching out to trail the worn name carved into the stone. "I… I'm sorry."

The pain didn't suddenly go away. He would always carry it.

But now, he could finally stop punishing himself for moving on. Emma was his past.

But the present?

It might hold just as much happiness for him.

No longer did he need to feel guilty. Just hopeful.

45

*J*ust a few days ago, killing Fred Connors had been the most traumatic experience of her life —in many ways, it still was. Loren knew she would have to deal with the long-term aftermath of that trauma later.

This moment, however, was a close second, though in a very different way.

Meeting Fred Connors had been a stilted, unpleasant experience wrought with disappointment. She could still remember the resigned way she'd accepted his cruelty without question. Already accustomed to violence, she had considered dodging blows a normal part of everyday life.

Loreck Eislander, however, didn't face her with a sneer or a brandished fist. He waited with his arms by his sides, on the other end of a small clearing on the outskirts of Black Mountain territory, far from any prying eyes.

Save for one—she could sense Bill nearby, lurking just out of sight—but she didn't feel the need to rely on him. Yet.

This moment felt too fragile. Too…delicate to risk even the presence of a third party.

As the minutes ticked by, Loren had no idea what to do or say. All she seemed capable of was staring at the man before her. Physically, Loreck looked so much older than Fred Connors. His brown hair was speckled with gray, his hazel eyes shrouded in wrinkles. Even so, he carried himself with confidence much like Bill's.

As if nothing in the world could defeat him.

Until they made eye contact. He swayed, his jaw tight, but Loren trembled with a similar unsteadiness. Bill had told her once that her father would recognize her on sight.

She didn't understand what he meant until she saw Loreck sigh, as though an invisible weight had been lifted off his shoulders.

"You look like her," he rasped, taking an unsteady step only to hesitate. One of his hands threatened to bridge the gap between them, his fingers trembling in the air.

Loren froze as tears prickled behind her eyes. Only recently had she been able to recall her mother more clearly, her round face, and gentle smile…

Whether they looked alike or not, she couldn't be sure, but Loreck seemed pained by the realization.

"I...." He shook his head as if fighting to find the right words. "He told me, but a part of me still doubted... I didn't know. I didn't know."

Her brain struggled to process his words. Was he relieved that it might have been true? Disappointed? Before she could fully comprehend, he moved.

And she followed. There wasn't any conscious thought to approach. Much like her interactions with Bill, instinct took over, and she had no choice but to give in.

She was in his arms without warning. An old, instinctive fear rose up before a sudden calm replaced it.

He won't hurt us, that inner voice murmured. *Family.* It was a new concept to her, but that primal instinct within her seemed to know exactly what it was supposed to feel like.

Not resigned terror, but a tentative sense of welcome.

Warily, she relented to the stiff embrace, settling against the unfamiliar contours of his larger, harder body.

"I didn't know," he said against her scalp. "But I'm here now... For what it's worth, I'm here."

She wasn't sure what to think of the offer. There would be time to mull over the details later. Either way, for the first time, fear wasn't the overriding emotion she felt toward the idea of having a father in her life again.

Just a strange sense of relief.

Maybe hope, too.

"How do you feel?" Bill asked as she rejoined him once Loreck retreated. Together, they lingered on the edge of the main compound, just as dawn was beginning to light the sky. In the short time since the challenge, he'd managed to change and shower away the dirt and grime, but one look at his face revealed the drastic shift in status he was struggling to adjust to.

Loren watched him through her lashes, struck by what a difference a few hours could make. Gone was the perpetual frown. His lips were in a softer line, not quite a smile. But close enough.

"I feel… Afraid," she admitted finally. Looking past him, she eyed a sliver of sky visible behind the canopy of branches overhead. "This is a lot to get used to."

An understatement if there ever were one. A part of her quivered at the many changes that were destined to come—forming a relationship with her newfound father being on that list.

"I know." Bill sighed and offered his hand, gripping hers gently. "I think we should get started with the introductions and go from there. Later, we can move onto the trickier subjects."

Like Kyle, and his eventual punishment for treason, should he return. Hours after Lukka's defeat, and no one had seen him anywhere within the territory. Loren felt a pinch of guilt that she might have been responsible for his escape.

Another dilemma to add to the growing pile.

For the time being, she pushed the stress aside, to focus on one of the few bright spots to look forward to.

"You plan on introducing me to everyone?" She wasn't sure if the sound trickling from her throat was a laugh or a groan.

Bill seemed to assume it was the former. "One step at a time," he said, guiding her to face him. "I think introductions would be a good place to start before we move onto diplomacy, at least."

There was so much requiring his input or judgment. Helming the pack and assessing the damage Lukka had done for one, let alone what would happen with Micha, or Naomi. Then there was the issue of where she truly belonged—on Black Mountain with Bill?

Or with Loreck Eislander…

Loren knew she would have dwelt on the milieu of problems for hours if it weren't for the strength seeping into her from an outside source.

It reassured her enough to push the worries aside for now.

Whatever awaited them, they would face it together.

As one. Eyeing the man across from her, she could think of several far worse positions to be in.

"I think I could use more lessons on the mating bond in the meantime," she suggested, feeling her cheeks ignite. Still, she felt a stubborn sense of pride as she met Bill's gaze and saw him swallow.

"That can be arranged…" He moved closer and released her hand in favor of palming her waist, groaning under his breath at the feel.

She inhaled in anticipation, lowering her gaze to his mouth. Their relationship still felt so strange, navigated on two planes at once—mental and physical. At the same time, nothing had ever seemed more natural. More right…

Until Bill frowned and cut his gaze to something behind her.

"One thing I miss about exile?" he said with a hint of amusement, "Privacy."

Loren whirled around to find what had his attention—namely, who.

Micha stood in between two trees, wearing an ill-fitting oversized shirt he must have borrowed and a pair of sweats. Sporting his sheepish grin, he appeared completely unaffected by any of the upheaval that had just taken place. At least, Loren would have thought so until she met his gaze and noted a hint of seriousness she wasn't used to finding there.

"I don't want to ruin the moment," he said, lowering his head in an unusual display of unease. "I just…"

"What is it?" Bill stood back from Loren and faced him, instantly embodying the leadership role he'd taken on. Even his voice changed, deepening an octave.

Micha shrugged. "Just that I won't stick around long, so there's no need to work me into your grand Alpha plans." He laughed, but Loren felt her eyes widen as the true meaning of his words sunk in.

"You're leaving?" she asked.

"You're more than welcome here," Bill said, inclining his head.

"I know," Micha said with a helpless shrug. "But… I think I need to take off for a while. Think things over."

Bill nodded as if he understood exactly what he meant. "Like returning to your pack?"

"Maybe…" Micha seemed to shrink beneath the question. After how he'd spoken of his old pack, Loren couldn't imagine him ever wanting to return. But when he finally looked up, his green eyes shone fiercely with determination. "I'm ready to think about it," he said.

"Good." Bill approached him, and for the first time, Loren realized that—despite the differences in their physical builds—they carried themselves the same way, heads held high, radiating steely confidence.

"If you ever need my help, you have it," Bill said. "In any way. I mean it."

Micha flashed his trademark smile. "I may have to take you up on that. One day. Don't worry, though. I'll stick around long enough to make sure Blondie doesn't get up to any trouble before you ship her back to high school." He cast a glance over his shoulder, in the direction of the main compound, presumably where Naomi happened to be.

Bill sighed. "She'll have a choice to make as well," he admitted. "So do you." His gaze shifted to Loren, and she held her breath, relishing his unusual brand of scrutiny.

In so many ways, helping him retake the pack had been just the beginning.

So much more lay ahead, but for once…

She wasn't afraid of what might come.

~ Want more from this world? Sign up for Lana's Mailing list to receive the latest updates on upcoming projects! ~

A WORD FROM THE AUTHOR

Hey there!

Thank you so much for reading! If you enjoyed the story, please leave a review and recommend the book to any friend you think would love this twisted world. You'd have my eternal gratitude. Even a short sentence goes a long way!

Then, come join the rest of us dark romance lovers in my Facebook Group where you can get snippets, sneak peeks of upcoming books and even help vote on aspects of future novels.

Come to the dark side:
https://www.facebook.com/groups/lanasbeautifulmonsters/

WANT MORE STUFF TO READ?
Join my newsletter and get a **free book**! Plus, you get to stay updated with any new releases, random giveaways and exclusive sneak peeks!
https://www.lanaskybooks.com/newsletter

Other Novels: https://lanaskybooks.com/

ABOUT THE AUTHOR

Lana Sky is a reclusive writer in the United States who spends most of her time daydreaming about complex male characters and parenting her Cockapoo Joey. She writes dark, twisted romance across several genres. Her titles include everything from mafia romance to vampires.

facebook.com/AuthorLanaSky

twitter.com/lanasky101

amazon.com/author/lanasky

pinterest.com/lanasky101

goodreads.com/lanasky

instagram.com/lanasky101

bookbub.com/authors/lana-sky

tiktok.com/@author_lana_sky

www.ingramcontent.com/pod-product-compliance
Lightning Source LLC
Chambersburg PA
CBHW071426190726
48292CB00001B/132